By *Thomas Hoving*
DISCOVERY
MASTERPIECE
TUTANKHAMUN: THE UNTOLD STORY
KING OF THE CONFESSORS
THE CHASE, THE CAPTURE

DISCOVERY
Thomas Hoving

SIMON AND SCHUSTER

NEW YORK   LONDON   TORONTO   SYDNEY   TOKYO

SIMON AND SCHUSTER
Simon & Schuster Building
Rockefeller Center
1230 Avenue of the Americas
New York, New York 10020

SIMON AND SCHUSTER and colophon are
registered trademarks of Simon & Schuster, Inc.

DESIGNED BY BARBARA MARKS
Manufactured in the United States of America

10   9   8   7   6   5   4   3   2   1

Library of Congress Cataloging in Publication data
Hoving, Thomas, date.
    Discovery/Thomas Hoving.
        p.   cm.
    I. Title.
PS3558.08755D5   1989
813'.54—dc20   89-35437
                                                              CIP

ISBN 0-671-68248-2

TO

MY WIFE,

NANCY

DISCOVERY

Thomas Hoving

FOREWORD

The news took days to circle the globe from Naples. Yet as it emerged, it picked up speed. The initial explosion, more a pop than a roar, followed the routine publication of the will of a curious little man, the Count Don Ciccio Nerone, a local landowner and amateur art expert. Though something of a mystery, he hardly seemed the kind of man the entire world would want to read about. Or so the editor of the *Messaggero Antico,* the local newspaper in the little resort and tourist town of Herculaneum, had thought when he learned that he held exclusive rights to publish the Don's secret archaeological chronicles in installments.

The size of the voluminous chronicles annoyed him. He would never be able to attract enough advertising to make up for the publishing costs. He was thoroughly bored by archaeology, as only a native of the region could be. On the verge of rejecting the material without even a glance, the editor suddenly remembered rumors that the Don had been linked to the Mafia and decided to give it a quick read.

Three days later, having grabbed some sleep in snatches, the editor laid the folders down. He had devoured them, and he knew now that he had a fatal obligation to publish the chronicles intact, without a word cut or a sentence edited. The publication of the complete story would lead to the rewriting of history.

He smiled, imagining the fame and honors that would soon be his. This would make him rich, too, he realized. All at once he loved archaeology, at least Don Ciccio's interpretation of it. *His* archaeology wasn't about musty fragments of faded time; it didn't concern itself with scraps of old wall paintings or lifeless antique marble statuary. The Don's "secret archaeological chronicles" moved with life and adventure. This wasn't just one scoop, it was a thousand. The editor grabbed a notepad and jotted some notes about what he had to do to protect his prize. With the help of his lawyer, he would secure the worldwide copyright and, most important, all television and film rights.

The secret chronicles had everything—treasure, competition, and above all, mystery. Don Ciccio's secrets would captivate all of Italy, and his discoveries would amaze everybody on earth. Most intriguing would be the solution to a mystery that had long baffled the world press, the carabinieri, and the FBI

—the unexplained disappearance of two international celebrities. Eleven years before, Andrew Foster, the dashing, globe-trotting president of the Metropolitan Museum of Art in New York, and his wife, Olivia, the museum's glamorous director, who had gained world attention through her international cable television show on art, had vanished during a sabbatical in Italy. The chronicles explained their fate.

The only question was how to let the world know that the chronicles explained the Fosters' disappearance and lots of other even bigger mysteries. How to capture the most publicity? The editor decided on a low-key approach. Yes, this would be the way. The first excerpt would run without fanfare. But gradually the news of the chronicles would spread as the ramifications of the stories became clear.

The uproar would be incredible, perhaps violent. The Catholic Church would be aghast. Could Don Ciccio's story be a lie? Impossible. But still, the editor was skeptical of every source he encountered. He played several random hours of the videotapes that accompanied the chronicles.

"Has to be authentic!" he said to himself again. He sighed as he watched again a radiant Olivia Foster, facing the camera, describing the stunning entrance beside her, a door sheathed in gold, decorated with strange winged sea creatures. The portal was ajar.

Don Ciccio

I am the Count Don Ciccio Nerone. All you need to know about me is this: I'm gifted mentally; I'm striking physically. My face is strong, full of character, yet at the same time it possesses what some would call a feminine delicacy. My hair is uncharacteristically blond for a southern Italian, a family trait. My eyes are cloudy blue, like the depths of glaciers, as my dear late mother used to say to everyone. Tragically, however, I am not as hale as this description might suggest. I am but three feet seven inches tall, a dwarf as noble as any depicted by Diego Velázquez.

Although I can get about on crutches, I prefer to spend much of my time at home in a motorized wheelchair of my own design. And when I want to step out, I proceed on the arm or shoulder of one of my husky majordomos. This ensures that I make a startling entrance at dinner parties, the opera, or the opening of an art exhibition. Curiously, the sight of me has quite an effect on women. Perhaps my presence suggests power.

In the carabinieri it provokes suspicion: they think I'm a don in the Mafia, a disguise I myself created for my personal safety. In Italy terrorists stage a dozen kidnappings each year, but even the Brigate Rosse shy away from those thought to have "family connections." These alleged connections don't seem to bother my friends and acquaintances, who come to me from all over the world. To them I appear a well-off Neapolitan landowner and art collector. They think my wealth comes from an annuity and my adventures as a *marchand amateur.* In fact only an insignificant amount of my riches comes from my land or my art dealings. I have on occasion tinkered in the art market, for the most part selling choice paintings to friends like Andrew and Olivia Foster, less for the money than to strengthen our relationship.

The bulk of my fortune, which accumulates at the rate of a little over five million dollars a week, comes from my skills as a computer trespasser, a "hacker."

I began penetrating other people's data banks before the rest of the world realized such a thing was possible. Before the invention of the now standard "police system" I had worked up a foolproof technique that gave me access to virtually any mainframe or data disk I cared to penetrate. Soon I perfected a technique for programming a pair of mainframes to break down another computer's defenses in the time it takes to snap a light switch. At the same time, I devised sophisticated processes to elude any internal security system.

With a speed that sometimes amazes me, I'm able to break into the best-guarded files of the institutions which provide my financial well-being—the Pentagon, the Politburo, a host of multinational corporations, Wall Street investment houses, and a number of shady enterprises that nourish and feed off the financial networks of the world. And I can do it all from home.

My home, the Nerone Palace, as every Neapolitan knows, dominates the verdant hill just above Capodimonte, reigning supreme over the bay. The view from the site has been praised by poets since Roman times. On one side, Vesuvius beckons. On the other, ancient Herculaneum waits, buried under the Roman hills. My palace was commissioned from Pirro Ligorio, who, working in perfect accord with the architectural tenets of the early sixteenth century, created a structure which appears both lighthearted and monumental. Painted in the original colors of pastel green and rose, the place at first appears to be a series of architectural tricks. Then the grandeur of the place asserts itself. My home is a perfect image of my ancient family—and me: small in scale, handsome, enduring, and full of surprises.

No one would imagine that deep beneath this Renaissance masterpiece lie vast modern spaces, housing my computers and laboratory, the tools of my newest artistic obsession—archaeology. The principal computer room lies at the bottom of a shaft cut one hundred and fifty feet into the tufa that spilled when Vesuvius erupted in the year 79. The same eruption buried Pompeii and the archaeological treasure at Herculaneum which has become my greatest passion.

I almost never visit the underground chambers during the day, a time I reserve for my gardens. Besides, I have computers to oversee my computers, computers that never sleep, that never stop inching through the defenses of someone else's computer, playing ticklish games of trial and error during every minute of every day.

I visit them after dinner. After my last taste of sweet dessert wine, two manservants enter the chamber and lift me into my electric wheelchair, which I maneuver to the far wall, where a magnificent millefleur tapestry hangs. I stop and punch three numbers, changed every day, into the console on the arm. The tapestry sweeps aside to the door of an elevator, which takes me deep underground to a labyrinth of softly lighted corridors, lined with some fairly interesting works of art—ancient marbles and bronzes and a mediocre set of frescoes of the Third Pompeiian style depicting hunting and fishing sagas. They're nice but not distracting. Of course, the antiquities authorities do not know of their existence.

My first stop is the exercise room, where I have a long, sensuous massage. Then two attendants bathe me in an immense Roman porphyry tub. Returning to the chair, I roll several hundred meters to the gleaming door of a huge safe, tap a series of numbers and letters into the console, wait for exactly sixteen or twenty-one or seventeen seconds—the time varies each day—and type another series. The safe swings open to reveal the main computer chamber. On the right side of the long chamber are dozens of computer terminals. There is only one on the left. After activating it, I go back to see what information the "business" terminals have come up with.

Aha! My scheme to sell Lloyd's paid off! My private source had recently indicated that one of the company's principals had been trapped by a licentious creature of legendary greed. My hunch was that sooner or later he would have to increase his normal income. When the scandal boiled out into the press, the stock plummeted. My profits on his sins? Ten million.

Cotton futures collapsed. I knew they had to, thanks to my Egyptian representative. Despite the government's announcement that the last three cotton crops had been disasters, my agent found out from contacts in the central warehouse that the harvests had, in fact been more than adequate. I invested a sizable amount just before futures soared, then turned short moments before the fall, which was triggered by my leaking the news of what was actually a bumper crop to the press. Five million more! A modest take, but a pleasing maneuver.

Politically the world fluctuated. Good news and bad. The Americans had succeeded at manipulating the Mexican elections and the Leftists had won. Having heard the news of the American interest months before, I had cut my investments in the companies owned by the ruling party and had transferred them to businesses controlled clandestinely by the Marxists. I do admire capitalist endeavor no matter what its politics happen to be. No earnings yet, but in time I expect to make as much as fifty million dollars.

Bad news from the White House! My computer link picked up some of the young President's PC doodlings for a forthcoming speech: "I pledge the dawn of a new economic epic [sic], a financial climate without fear in which all our peoples will be insured by government against any kind of monetary loss." He actually plans to say this.

Fool! He could trigger another period of spending and debt. I gave the order to my computers handling my extensive American portfolio to start gently moving the assets elsewhere.

That was enough business. I turned to the delights in my life—art and archaeology.

The galleys of a Sotheby's catalogue announced the forthcoming sale of two majestic black-figured amphorae by the "pig painter." I dashed off a fax to my auction agent, a cleverly detailed story. It was designed to convince the auction house that these pieces had been discovered in an illegal dig (which, of course, they hadn't been). My agent will make arrangements to purchase them for me.

In another sales catalogue I saw a perfect opportunity to play a joke on an old rival who was effectively blocking my buy-out of Australia's largest life insurance company. *Night Cypresses* by Van Gogh was about to be sold in Zurich, and the "low" estimate was seventy-five million dollars. I had learned from the most perceptive connoisseur of the master that the picture was not by Van Gogh but by his pupil, Frank Schouffenecker. My plan was to bid heavily, forcing the price up to at least one hundred million, and then allow my rival to win out in the last bid. After that I'd think of an appropriate way to make the facts about Schouffenecker public. *Caveat emptor!*

Enough of the art market. The end of the evening was always reserved for the computer devoted to archaeology. "What have you discovered today?" I asked the softly humming Amdahl "special," trying to predict what it would tell me.

Damn! Virtually nothing. The screen filled up with the computer's mechanical prose: "Traces of two tenements in the west quarter of the city of Herculaneum. Partial traces (current total = 1,876 in P-category and 869 in PAR-category) of five shops, three wine bars, and eight laboratories. Based on this, the isometric map cannot be effectively enlarged. Will await further information before enhancement."

I went to bed, my mind spinning with the project. I expected some action soon. I had timed the arrival of Andrew and Olivia perfectly.

THEY arrived an hour before lunch the next day, full of themselves and the excitement of New York. The Fosters! They drove up in a yellow Rolls convertible they had bought in Rome, where they had stopped to pick up clothes for their sabbatical. The Fosters didn't like to pack.

Andrew, at forty-one, is the scion of one of America's most illustrious families. His forebears, some say, were the original robber barons. But they started earlier than the nineteenth century. Their wealth, which got a regal boost in the eighteenth century from George I's land grants, increased at a rapid rate along with the tales of their ruthless deals and the women who came as naturally to them as the money. The Fosters were always in on everything. They "owned" the whaling industry when it was still vital and profitable but sold out to invest their gains in a newer brand of oil called petroleum. The stories go on and on.

One of Andrew's forebears anticipated the Civil War and established factories to make uniforms. He cornered the market, North and South. After the conflict, this same Rufus Foster launched an attack on the profiteers who had gotten rich on the sale of munitions and tainted meat. A hero on both sides of the Mason-Dixon line, he tripled the number of his factories, and sold cheap dresses and suits to the vanquished Southerners. In gratitude, he was handed virtually the entire textile industry of the old Confederacy.

Another Foster struck gold in 1849. Another made a fortune by recognizing and quietly financing the young genius Amadeo Peter Giannini, who purchased and reorganized the Bank of America.

A generation later, Andrew Foster was impressed by two young men in his hometown of Rochester, New York, and funded them to start businesses. One was an inventor who started something called the Haloid Company (which later burgeoned into Xerox). The other entrepreneur, a tyro who combined aggressiveness with religious fanaticism, was named Watson. His dream was a firm ambitiously named International Business Machines.

Andrew Foster II, whom I came to know because of his art collection, was bright, erratic, lucky, and oversexed. He married five times and kept, as the story goes, five mistresses. Forced aside in the family business because of his flamboyance, he set himself the task of doubling the family fortune in a way that would drive the lawyers nuts, or so he told me quite often (the Fosters all tell their favorite stories again and again). One night in a Hollywood bistro, Andrew II bumped into a buddy, a popular singer, who rambled on about some odd investment venture. Foster bought in for half at once. That is the way the frozen food business began.

When his father died, Andrew III, the current head of the Foster clan, inherited some three hundred million dollars. A typical Foster, Andrew is bright, highly sophisticated, and driven, yet he sometimes appears exactly the opposite, affecting what some misinterpret as a lackadaisical attitude. He is, I find, a rather puzzling blend of rapscallion and opportunist. When it suits him he is, I am told, an unscrupulous liar. But nobody cares once they see him. Andrew is compact, athletic, and dark-haired, with flashing blue eyes and a smile that suggests he will do anything for pleasure. All this makes him rather dangerous. I like him because I can never predict what he'll do next.

At twenty-nine, he was appointed the director of the National Gallery of Art in Washington, where he spent an active decade, buying everything in sight, planning new buildings and exhibitions, scorning all the old rules that museums hold so sacred. When he retired "out of sheer boredom," his ambition was to be appointed the director of the Metropolitan in New York and "shake the bejesus out of the place." He had powerful allies on the board and seemed to be the certain choice until a young, studious, altogether mousy female Met curator foiled all his plans. Before then, he had hardly known of Olivia Cartright's existence.

Olivia has always been something of an enigma—and sometimes a vexation—even to me, her mentor. Secretive to a fault, Olivia admits only that she was born in Long Beach, California, the only child of a German immigrant. She entered Berkeley at fifteen, graduated third in her class, and at eighteen was, in her words, "not at all immature, either." In graduate school, Olivia specialized in art history, which she had fallen in love with during her undergraduate days. There are always plenty of brilliant graduate students in the art history department at Berkeley, but few have her eye, or, I might add, her luck. Olivia has an uncanny ability always to be there when something big in the art world happens. There are any number of stories about her rare combination of "eye" and fortune. My favorite is the affair of the two Pollaiuolos.

While in graduate school she visited a restorer of furniture and paintings in Oakland, a man the university museum occasionally contracted to do routine work. The fellow casually remarked that he'd been given a "curious" job a few days before, to clean two little wooden panels with scenes of Greek mythology. She didn't portray any surprise when the restorer showed her two panels, measuring only four by six inches, depicting Hercules fighting the Hydra and wrestling with Antaeus. "God," she said later, "I knew instantly who had painted them! Antonio Pollaiuolo! And I suspected they had come from the Uffizi! They had to be the ones stolen at the end of the war; I had heard about them in passing in one of my courses."

Together they called the FBI, which discovered that the "owner" was a German who had served in the Wehrmacht in Italy in the war, and had no clear explanation of how he had entered the United States. He was glad to turn over the paintings in exchange for no further questions about his immigrant status. The gorgeous panels went back to the Uffizi in a blaze of publicity, which Olivia managed to give the impression of avoiding. But she always had a way of knowing whom to talk to to get her name in the best publications.

During her graduate work, Olivia received a fellowship to travel to Rome to research her thesis on the portrayal of religious agony in the art of the baroque period. It was there that I first met her—under agonizing conditions at a restaurant near Regina Coeli prison, a restaurant which specialized in a diminutive variety of game bird which we are no longer allowed to eat. I was with my lawyer, chatting away about finances, when I felt a horrible piercing pain in my throat and upper chest. I tried to cry out, but my companion didn't notice, just kept his face buried in his pasta. As I passed out, my last sensation was of intense anger at the idea of dying in the presence of an incompetent lawyer.

The next thing I remember was the scent of a delicate perfume. I knew I hadn't gone to heaven; the fragrance was too carnal for paradise. For a second I felt faint again, until I saw the face of a young woman very close to mine. She was attractive, though rather unsophisticated-looking. She had administered the Heimlich maneuver. I felt a profound gratitude followed by a rush of sexual attraction. Every time I meet her I have the same feelings. Despite her marriage, I have never given up the idea of Olivia. Perhaps this meeting will be the beginning.

When I came to on the stone floor of the restaurant and gazed into her lovely concerned face, I pledged that for the rest of my life I would do anything she asked. Her reaction was vexing. At first she burst into tears; then she laughed at me. Lying on my back, I lectured her, rudely I'm afraid, that it wasn't up to her to turn aside my vow. It was what I must do, and she must accept. She agreed then, realizing at that moment, I presume, that I was an important and powerful person. She has never regretted that decision. Although she doesn't dwell on it, she's told me more than once that it is I who "made" her. I did—partly. Because of her grades and her perceptive doctoral thesis she alone won her first job at the Met. And on her own she earned her promotion to full curator. But it was I who filched the superb Velázquez, the *Marchesa Odescalchi,* and told her how to acquire it for the Met, and in doing so, she foiled Andrew, then her keenest competitor.

She alone transformed herself into a startlingly attractive woman from the gray curatorial mouse she'd been. Without me she might have married Andrew. Without me she might have become the director of the Metropolitan. She is a natural social climber and manipulator. Her only failing is that once an idea becomes imbedded in her mind, she can never get rid of it. She's also devastatingly persuasive.

It was she who convinced the Metropolitan trustees to elect herself as director and hire Andrew as president of the museum (although I can take a little credit for tipping the scales in her favor). Now the board members adore them both and were so delighted at the construction of the new Decorative Arts Wing the Fosters organized that they presented them with a year's sabbatical. I have to admit to having a hand in that, too. The chairman and I have mutual shipping interests, and so when I happened to mention that I yearned to have Olivia and Andrew visit me for a time, he said he'd fix it.

If anything, the Fosters had both become more attractive in the three years since I'd last seen them. He still had the devilish expression in his eyes, but he was thinner. A slight touch of gray at the temples made him look distinguished, and the sun had crinkled the skin around his eyes a bit, adding to his outdoorsy appearance. Olivia had made herself even more lithe and graceful—I suspect she'd taken ballet lessons for her figure—and she sported a sexy new short blond hairdo.

"Fabulous to be here!" Andrew announced at dinner. "We're slaves to that museum, and it's gotten to be a damn bore. Details—they nickel-and-dime me to death with details. But now I've got a whole damned year. No answering machines. No curators. I've got only one thing to do—visit my house at Morgantina in Sicily. The rest of the time I personally plan to relax."

My guests were filled with art museum gossip and rather heady descriptions of their own accomplishments. Andrew spoke of the changes he had instituted. "I completely reorganized the staff and the board, which got me into a little trouble," he said, "but what the hell, enemies are part of museum work."

Olivia regaled me with a story of how she had unmasked a rather ingenious forgery.

"One morning I entered the building through the parking garage—something I almost never do—and happened to walk through the Greek and Roman galleries. I wasn't really looking at anything, I was rushing, you know, but in the Etruscan gallery, I suddenly looked up. I have no idea why. There in front of my eyes was the world-famous Etruscan *Loving Couple,* you remember, the gorgeous man and his bride—I presume it's his bride; lover, anyway—smiling away for eternity . . ."

I started to smile.

"Sometimes a quick, unexpected look at a work of art reveals more than long, careful study," Olivia continued. "I looked and I laughed. I had to laugh because I recognized in a flash that this venerable piece, published in all the books, this symbol of the ancient world, could not be genuine. I mean, suddenly I saw that the smiles on their faces were too pretty—not that classic 'archaic' smile. And I knew that the fluttery drapery couldn't be authentic. It was weak, meandering."

"Aha! And?"

She shook her head and laughed. "I made a beeline for the office of the curator, the formidable Dr. von Kraus. I told him of my suspicions. That was a mistake. I should have figured out some way for the conceited prig to take credit for the discovery himself. But I didn't think about it, and he blew up. He said some nasty things about my "eye" and intimated that I, as a woman, knew nothing about the art of the ancients. That did it. When I got to my office I ordered the statue removed from view at once and taken to the conservation lab. Von Kraus had a fit. But within two days, we knew that the terra-cotta, supposedly of the sixth century B.C., contained chemicals that could not date earlier than 1900. When von Kraus came to apologize I made him suffer through it."

I could have told her about *The Loving Couple* years ago. I had learned the facts from the grandnephew of the forger. But never mind.

I listened to their description of fund-raisers, galas, and receptions for donors or aspiring ones, the countless museum feuds, the scandals, larcenies, and love affairs of the kind that seem to flourish in the overheated environment of the American art museum. The Fosters were proud of a massive construction program they had put into motion to complete the museum buildings, which had been unfinished for one hundred and fifty years. Their efforts had been achieved through Andrew's "intense, sometimes overbearing sense of organization" (as Olivia rather tartly put it) plus the fortunate discovery of a singular patron, Albert A. Stearns, a new arrival into the upper ranks of the nouveau super-rich. I knew of him. Who in Italy doesn't? When I heard Olivia mention his name I knew suddenly that he, too, might have a place on my archaeological "team."

"I call him Fat Al," Andrew said, "though not exactly to his face, mind you. After Two-Ton Tony Galento, heavyweight boxing champ in the late forties. Remember him? The guy who trained for fights by eating eight plates of *pasta asciutta* a day and avoiding his trainers. Stearns has the same appetites and he's just as scrappy. I first approached him because I noticed in donor files that he had given, totally anonymously, three hundred thousand dollars in response to a hundred-dollar membership request. I thought it was time for a follow-up, so I called him and met him—and boy did he hate my patrician guts. He said he thought Wasps were too snooty to 'hustle.' So I said the Fosters had been hustling since they stepped off the prison ships from England, and he hugged me. I thought he was going to choke me, but from then on we were great pals, and when it came time to start the capital fund drive for the Dec Arts Wing, he rather casually told me that he'd give . . . on one condition. Now, I've been in the fund-raising game a long time, but this was a unique condition. He said he would foot the entire bill himself if Olivia asked him for the money."

"And I asked," Olivia chimed in, "and he gave, to my utter amazement. One hundred and fifteen million dollars! And he forced Andrew to take all the critics' flak for the postmodern design. God, they howled! But Al hinted, not so subtly, that he'd cut the funding if Andrew didn't take the heat for everything."

"Christ, did we catch hell for the wing!" Andrew said. "Listen to this!" He pulled a clipping from his pocket. "It's a review from *Edifice and Architecture,*" he began. " 'This is a dog of a building, a postmodern runt' . . . oh, can this kid ever write. He called our beautiful building, get this, 'a bastard from the darker side of the history of architecture which includes the ziggurats of Babylon, the towers of Trebizond, and the Cloaca Maxima. This is not the mother of the arts, this is a bitch.' Great, eh?"

"You should have seen Al at the opening," Olivia said. "Silver hair perfectly coiffed, white tie and tails from Savile Row, wearing the Medal of Freedom that his crony the outgoing President had given him the day before. But his hands were trembling. He clutched the mike, he was so scared. And after thanking everybody, he said, 'This is a *marvelous* wing. Something to be proud of. This wing carries my name because—' he paused and then pealed out, 'because . . . ah . . . I paid for it!' "

She laughed in a way I had never heard before, a laugh with more than a hint of contempt for Al Stearns. Had Olivia become a bit society-struck? Yes, sadly. Andrew, not knowing what it is like not to have status, is refreshingly unsnobbish.

"Ah, I like the guy," Andrew said. "But I'm really tired of the Met. After five years I think maybe we—I—have done it. Time for a new scene." He hesitated, giving his wife a tentative glance. "Olivia doesn't agree, Don Ciccio."

"I'll say," Olivia shot back. "I can understand Andrew's feeling that, well, being in administration he's seen the merry-go-round spin too many times. But as a curator, I never get bored. There's always something new. I'd go crazy if there were nothing left to look for."

Olivia had given me the opening I needed.

"My dear friends, I have followed your every move in the press. Now let me tell you about what I have quietly been doing. Since we last met I've developed an obsession which has changed my life."

"Something you've added to your art collection?" Andrew asked.

"In a sense, yet something deeper . . . and much more enigmatic."

That caught their attention.

"Believe it or not, I spend most of my time in a lab, deep underground, just beneath where we're sitting, floating in the air, like a trapeze artist . . ."

"I wouldn't have associated you, Don Ciccio, with a circus," Andrew drawled.

"Then don't. But I do spend hours a day floating above an enormous stainless-steel tank of distilled water mixed with a solvent called polyprophylaxine."

"Medical treatment?" Olivia asked.

"You don't get it, Olivia. He's got a stash of old masters floating around in that brew," Andrew said, laughing.

"Yes, very old masters. Ancient ones," I told him. "And I'm just floating and pushing them around, bringing them back to life."

"Do get to the point," Olivia said.

"I shall. I've become an archaeologist since we last met, a postmodern archaeologist. My tools are computers. When I'm not hanging in midair in my trapeze, I'm hunched over a keyboard typing in coordinates, asking questions, waiting for translations from Greek or Latin. By the way, I have unique programs for the translation of the dead languages. My scanners and computers can easily handle an almost infinite variety of ancient scripts."

"*This* is archaeology?" Andrew exclaimed. "What about picks, shovels, trowels, scalpels, delicate brushes?"

"No, no! That's for *field* archaeologists," I answered. "Can you imagine *me* in the field? Scurrying around? Getting my hands dirty? No. I work exclusively in the laboratory."

Andrew raised his eyebrows. "Has this got anything to do with Pompeii?"

"Thank God, no!" I said. "That's a tired old story. My project is a combination of Park Avenue, St. Moritz, Versailles, and Neuschwanstein, the Louvre, and the Kunsthistorisches-museum in Vienna."

"Never one to exaggerate, Don," Andrew laughed, slapping my back and causing one of my bodyguards to tense reflexively.

"Dammit, what is it?" Olivia implored.

"I'm working on something to do with . . . Herculaneum," I answered quietly.

"I had no idea that there was a dig going on at Herculaneum," Andrew said.

"There isn't. But there might be. It depends on you two."

"Us?"

"Why else did you think I had you come here?"

ANDREW

When Don Ciccio came out with that comment about having us come to Naples for a dig at Herculaneum, I believed him and felt like strangling the little sneak. It was obvious that he had somehow arranged our sabbatical; he probably has a few friends on the board. Still, I was excited. Archaeology has always fascinated me. But what else was the bastard up to? Whatever, he already had Olivia hooked. I could see her giving off sparks across the table.

Sitting up in his chair, knowing he held us in the palm of his hand, Don Ciccio started his tale.

"Everybody knows about Pompeii and the eruption of Vesuvius in A.D. 79, which buried it under several meters of hot ash and pumice. Well, who cares? Pompeii is a bore! But not Herculaneum! Now this is a treasure that merits our attention. In ancient times, at the first sign of summer, all the wealthiest citizens of Rome set off for their villas and palaces at Herculaneum. With views of the Bay of Naples, the city must have been spectacular, lavishly decadent, I suppose, with houses owned by the most renowned families of the Empire—consuls, senators, merchants, financiers, and landowners, all jammed together cheek by jowl. In ancient times it was apparently fashionable to live in your neighbor's lap."

The ancient site of Herculaneum was first discovered in the 1730s, Don Ciccio said, some years before Pompeii was found. Few people knew of or cared about the place. It was before the passion for antiquities. In the 1730s and '40s, diggers were after gold. Ancient marbles were melted down for lime. Who knows how many hundreds of fine Roman and Greek statues by the great masters were destroyed in the kilns? No one bothered about Herculaneum, because of the thin crust of lava and mud called tufa, which was nearly impossible to penetrate, and because the family who started the excavations used to kill anybody who got wind of what they were doing.

"The Dorsoduro family—the name literally means 'hardback'—controlled the site and cut a complex network of tunnels into the tufa. Most were at the southwest side of the city, where the lava was thinnest. As one generation after another of Dorsoduros dug away, their techniques became increasingly more sophisticated and their instincts got sharper. I believe they were the first to recognize that antiquities were more valuable as art objects than as lime for cement. I'm convinced that were it not for the efforts of the Dorsoduros, especially the patriarch Enrico, who engineered the operations in the 1770s, and their skills in marketing the paintings, marbles, and bronzes, the Neoclassic movement would never have come about."

The Dorsoduros found some amazing things, Don Ciccio told us, including two chambers of the now-famous Villa of the Papyri and the lavish walled-in estate of the Calpurnia Piso family, of which Caesar's wife was a member. And then they found the most astonishing thing in the history of archaeology. But they didn't know what it was. Now after all this time, Don Ciccio coyly told us, he knows. I was on tenterhooks.

This find, said the Don, involves one of archaeology's great bumblers, a man who fell upon the key to the secrets of Herculaneum accidentally. The man was "General" Hans von Richter, a self-described brigadier of the Imperial House Guards and, he claimed, a member of a family prominent in Viennese society during the late seventeenth and eighteenth centuries. But Richter was neither distinguished nor military. His real name was Florian Graebenhaecker, and his military career consisted of a few years as an ordinary soldier. Apparently his only talent was in coaxing horses to copulate.

Records of the Austro-Hungarian police, sparse as they are, indicate that von Richter/Graebenhaecker was married three times—each time to a woman much younger. Each of his spouses had died of a respiratory disease. The police investigated but found nothing. But still suspicious, they had expelled Graebenhaecker from Austria.

It isn't known how he got to Naples or whom he victimized along the way, but he arrived in 1756 and married the youngest Dorsoduro daughter, Judith, a nineteen-year-old. Her family was impressed by the General's military bearing and the exploits he described. They were even more impressed by his wealth, which was at least equal to the plentiful dowries of his three former brides. In time, the family suggested to Graebenhaecker that he invest some of his money in a hunt for treasure at a place known in antiquity as Herculaneum. The General was captivated. He agreed to pay a thousand gold sovereigns outright and promised to hand over to them a quarter of the value of everything he found. The Dorsoduros would manage the commercial side of the venture.

The Dorsoduros concocted a plan for Graebenhaecker to register an official claim to perform an excavation at the site of old Herculaneum. They guaranteed he'd find an abundance of silver and gold, and they even faked ancient maps which showed subterranean vaults the ancient Romans were supposed to have constructed deep in the bedrock.

"So Graebenhaecker embarked upon what he expected to be an exhilarating adventure in treasure hunting." Don Ciccio chuckled. "He arrived at the site on the first day with a crew of fifteen workers and four mules, which he intended to hook up to a huge wooden screw sheathed in bronze plates. He had decked himself out for the event in a uniform of blue, green, and gold. Hundreds of citizens turned out for the show. Admittedly, Graebenhaecker cut a dashing figure—he was six feet five, and, by standards of current taste, handsome. He commanded his crew with courtly flair."

But the work turned out to be far more arduous than he had expected. The problem was that Herculaneum, unlike Pompeii, had been flooded by warm, watery mud, which after cooling had solidified. This was topped by a layer of lava flow, which had also hardened. The General struggled through fifteen feet of lava before starting to grind through the much softer tufa. Yet, after churning away for weeks, he discovered nothing.

Disheartened and with his funds running low, he was about to quit the field and reconsider his future in Naples, which meant, of course, doing away with his young bride. Then the unexpected happened.

Don Ciccio's voice dropped theatrically. "Late in the afternoon on the thirty-second day of digging, at a depth of twenty-two feet, the scaffolding which supported the immense bronze-and-wood drill shifted. Graebenhaecker slowly sank out of sight. It was like some Neapolitan comic opera. The workers fled, and only the General's furious bellows convinced them to return. To their astonishment, there at the bottom of a hole some ten feet deep stood Graebenhaecker, not a hair disturbed."

The General had broken through the roof of an ancient building buried deep underground but preserved in an air pocket. Convinced that he had discovered the treasure chamber described by his in-laws, he ordered his men to set to work. In a few days and nights they unearthed four rooms, but no treasure. No coffers filled with gold or silver. No frescoes. No sculptures in bronze or marble. Graebenhaecker's diary describes rough-hewn tables and benches and an astonishing feature: every square inch of the walls of the four rooms was filled from the floor to the ceiling—over ten feet in height—with a series of square wooden pigeon holes. There were thousands of them. The place looked like the chart library of a boat.

"Maps?" Olivia asked in amazement.

Don Ciccio just smiled.

"Every one contained the same thing—a tightly wrapped dark brown, dry object that looked like a cigar. Puzzled, the General pulled one from its hole and sniffed it. It didn't smell like tobacco. He tried to light it, but the thing didn't smolder. Then apparently he thought he recognized what he had found and snapped it—it was about eight inches long—in two. He expected to find a bar of gold or silver or pieces of jewelry inside. But no. Only layer after layer of the wrapping. He broke another, then another. Nothing.

"When he finally stopped, he had demolished more than a couple of hundred of the 'useless' objects. Furious, he threw down the cigars and left."

What was the Don up to, I asked myself, and what was the point of the story? I figured the cigars were some kind of writings. When I mentioned this, Don Ciccio smiled again and went on with his tale.

His money almost exhausted, the General's thoughts turned to his bride and his getaway. But the Dorsoduros had other plans. This wasn't Judith's first marriage either. Since no treasure was forthcoming, they decided to settle for the General's money. Judith and her mother slipped into his room just before dawn and chopped off his head. Then, with the father's help, they threw his remains into two leather sacks, carried them to the site of his discovery, and threw them in.

But the General's mysterious objects did not disappear, though no records have survived to identify who actually saved them. "One of the most enlightened souls in the history of archaeology," Don Ciccio said.

Anyway, he went on, all anybody knows is that thousands of the rolled-up objects—5,764 of them—were removed, bundled into batches, chucked into dozens of burlap bags, and taken to a safe place, where they remained for a century and a half.

Then, sometime during the Second World War, a local antiquities dealer by the name of Carlo Bonfante, now dead, heard about them from someone who claimed that his grandfather had saved them for humanity. Bonfante bought them for almost nothing. He also tried to pick the "cigars" apart, believing that they contained baubles of some sort. After several crumbled away, he recognized what they had to be.

"Ancient scrolls," Don Ciccio told us in a dramatic voice.

Just as I had figured!

"To his credit," Don Ciccio said, "Bonfante didn't take them to a museum or university, where they might have languished." Don Ciccio has a low tolerance for scholars.

"Carlo gave them to his nephew Aldo, who, foolishly, tried to soften them in alcohol. Nothing is more damaging to such things than alcohol. But before they fell apart he was able to copy snatches of Latin writing. He took them to another Bonfante who was a Latin teacher and learned that the writings were parts of a pornographic play. Ecstatic, he contacted the one man he knew who might pay handsomely for what he thought was a sizable collection of erotic literature.

"That, of course, was you," I said.

Olivia almost jumped down his throat. "You got us over here for a couple of smutty plays?"

"The scrolls are by no means all pornography," Don Ciccio assured her. "Although I've found a few more prostitutes' plays that could, I suppose, find the right market. The bulk of the material can be equated, I do not exaggerate, to the contents of the library of Alexandria . . . before Caesar burned it!"

"What? Where *is* the stuff? Where is it now?" Olivia demanded.

"The scrolls are in my lab, where my assistants and I are carrying out techniques to unroll and read each one, techniques perfected by Israeli specialists."

"Can we see them?" my wife burst out. She was on her feet.

"Why not?" the Don said cheerily.

Our sojourn in Don Ciccio's lab lasted the entire night. At first we were overwhelmed by the number of scrolls. They were stacked a couple of feet high on long tables. It looked like ten years of work.

There were two groups. One type was thin, tightly wound, made of the finest Egyptian papyrus. These, the Don said, were literary, historical, and philosophical texts. The second ones were thicker and cruder, made of parchment, and filled with what the Don called mundane information—building permits, accounts of street repairs, tax records, zoning regulations, minor judicial activities, and real estate inventories.

Olivia and I were relieved when we were shown how easy it was to soak and unroll the things. The Don explained how the harnesses worked and how easy it was to maneuver from scroll to scroll as they lay soaking on the bottom of the tank. We learned to massage the scrolls themselves, how to turn them until they swelled slightly. We learned to recognize when you had to start unrolling fast. I got it down to one smooth, practiced motion. After a scroll had been stretched out, it had to soak for twenty minutes or so before we could take it to the drying table.

The writing on the scrolls became legible even while they were still submerged, but they were easier to read once they were stretched out to dry. Don Ciccio showed us how he made a photographic record of each scroll and how these were entered into the computer with laser scanners. Then he glanced toward the ceiling.

"Go on," he urged. "Get up there into harness. Both of you!" In minutes we were swinging from spot to spot, hanging above the tanks.

Olivia, my dear overachiever, beat me out. She scrambled quickly into the contraption and within minutes had learned how to position herself anywhere over the huge tank. She reached down and plucked a stretched-out scroll.

"Give it a bit of gentle pressure," Don Ciccio told her. "Does it feel slightly malleable? When you feel the outer shell softening, it's ready. Bring it over here and I'll show you what to do next."

She spread the scroll under the water. It was huge—two feet long and over half a foot wide—and every square inch was filled with a neat, tiny Latin script. We got it out and took a photograph which we placed on the scanner for translation.

Then I threw down my ace. I announced that I could translate the text. Don Ciccio was impressed and, I think, a bit envious. Score one, finally, for the tall guys! I took the gist of it in and burst out laughing. Christ! The script was so perfect that I had assumed it had to be something important. But it was far from the library of Alexandria!

"What, what?" Olivia could hardly contain herself.

"It's about moving," I told them. "As in shipping and moving."

The Don roared as I paraphrased the contents, a protocol for how goods should be delivered to the houses of the wealthy. Nothing was to be carted in the morning or after nine at night. Never during the midday siesta. Everything had to be hauled to outlying depots, where the stuff would be carried in on the backs of slaves. There were harsh penalties for making noise.

We entered the information into the computer, as Don Ciccio went on about how we had to record every scrap, no matter how dull or unimportant it might seem. Those computers were expected to do far more than provide a translation of each scroll.

"Every time I come across a street location, the computer

takes note of it and fits it into a developing isometric plan of the city," he explained.

"What *was* this place that what's-his-name, the General, stumbled on?" Olivia asked.

"What he found was apparently a cache of records of a puzzlingly wide variety. I can only imagine it was some sort of imperial headquarters—possibly the police—with a potpourri of information on various important citizens of Herculaneum."

"God, Don Ciccio, this is one of the most amazing discoveries in history. When are you going to tell the world?" Olivia asked.

"I don't know," he said quietly. "Better to keep it a secret for a while. Take a look over there. That stack of scrolls is the reason for my secrecy. They are thoroughly mundane, but they are the most important, more important than the plays or ancient histories or poems."

"How can they possibly be?" Olivia asked.

"They may become our guides. Bear with me for a few moments. These are all about stones and sand and earthworks." His voice became a whisper. "I never thought I'd be so interested in construction. But one night I was working away, completely absorbed, when I noticed something peculiar in that pile of scrolls." He motioned toward the batch he'd just pointed out to Olivia. "They seemed more tightly rolled, finer in texture. I threw one in the tank, and it began to open up faster than any of the material I had fiddled with before. As the text became clear, I was surprised again. The writing was distinctive—neat, round, and admirably legible. Down the right side of the parchment was a band of purple an eighth of an inch wide. On the top right was a tiny black ink drawing of a marvelous hippocamp, a winged sea creature you sometimes find in ancient decorations. Underneath was a monogram of some sort, but the document was stained, so I couldn't read it."

"What was on it?"

"The description of a stable."

"That's all?" Olivia asked.

"But quite a stable. Room for two dozen horses. A tack room. A garage, you might call it, for a dozen chariots. Storage areas for feed, tools. I know little about ancient Roman stables and I gathered that this one was part of a very rich estate."

"Any idea whose?"

"I started working on that immediately, despite the fact that I'd been hanging in the harness for hours. I tossed four more of these special scrolls in the tank—you can't really handle more at one time. The first one to open was also decorated with a hippocamp, which, it suddenly struck me, was likely to be an armorial device. This scroll appeared to be a building permit for something, I'm not certain what, granted to someone in 'the second year of the administration of Flavius Flacillus,' which I was able to pin down to approximately the year 65. The next one stunned me. A fragment of an architectural drawing, it also bore the hippocamp device. It looked like a ground plan and showed half a dozen chambers next to an exceedingly thick wall of a structure of indeterminate kind."

"What did it show? You're driving me crazy! Was there more?" Olivia was almost shouting. She had practically thrown herself at the Don in her excitement. Her face was aglow as she brushed a lock of hair away from her face with her hand. No one is sexier than Olivia when she's onto something new.

"By this point," the Don started in again, "I forgot about my exhaustion and rashly, knowing I'd be trapped for hours more, threw in four more of the special scrolls. The first one

the computer translated was incredible! First there were someone's initials. Take a look at this enhancement. QMT, isn't it?"

"Clearly," Olivia answered quickly. "Who is he? Any
idea?"

"I believe so. But first let me show you what else I found."

The first scroll, like the others, carried the hippocamp
crest, the purple stripe, and the initials QMT. It said, "Ours is
the proudest house of all, with chambers too numerous to count.
Our gardens, encased in gleaming marble from Thasos, are
legends of beauty. But by far the most exquisite treasures are
the libraries."

At this piont a tear in the manuscript obliterated the rest
of the passage. After it, there were a few more lines. "How
often Phryne has wandered among the works of Myron, Polycletus, Phidias, and Praxiteles! How much she has spoken of
the paintings of Zeuxis and Euripitates. The still lifes are so
vivid that the birds hover around them. The portraits of ancient
heroes . . ."

"It stops there?" I asked. "Do you realize what this means?
This house owned by this QMT has works of art made by some
of the most illustrious Greek artists who ever lived. Phidias?
Praxiteles? Zeuxis? No one since ancient times has seen a painting by Zeuxis! God, and the scroll just stops?"

"Yes, dammit! What's worse," Don Ciccio said grimly, "is
that it is, of course, the description of QMT's incredibly rich
villa. But where is it? And, more important, is there anything
left of its treasures? I think I may have found the answer—in
a series of scrolls about stones and sand. Yes, the most mundane
information may hold the most golden secret."

He told us how he had stretched out the next scroll. And
what he saw he could hardly believe. The same person who had
written so poetically about his "house" was now making copious

notes about sand. Twelve oxcarts of it, "twice sifted and cleaned," delivered to a building project on his property. Scroll after scroll listed facts about sand—two hectares of the stuff, fifty-eight oxcarts sent to the "earthworks on the mountain-side."

Why did they need so much? I wondered. Don Ciccio looked at me as if he knew what I was thinking.

"My head was aching," he continued. "My shoulders burned with pain. I longed to retire. But I had to look at just one more scroll. Its subject was stones—prime river stones, one hundred and fifteen carts of them. The sand and the stones had to have cost a vast sum. I remembered a reference in one of the earlier documents to a bill for 'three talents and two hundred sesterces.' That was a staggering amount of money. In ancient times a 'talent' could purchase something like fifteen hundred head of cattle. One talent was equivalent to a small empire. Whoever this QMT was, he was spending millions of dollars on a building project, the villa of his treasures. It is not an exaggeration to say that this undertaking was equivalent to creating a modern hydroelectric dam. But why?"

Although it was almost dawn, the Don had continued to open and translate scrolls. He had found more descriptions of "earthworks" and three fragments of architectural drawings of what looked like massive concrete dams—always abutting some mysterious edifice.

"I slept for a couple of hours and then I went to my library. I spent the day delving into treatises of Roman domestic architecture and standard histories of Pompeii and Herculaneum, and finally I knew. I'm not sure I have the courage to tell you."

"I've never seen you so indecisive!" Olivia said, "You must tell us!"

"What I think QMT was doing revolves around a minor

incident in Roman history. It took place in A.D. 63 and was localized to the area surrounding Vesuvius. There had been a series of violent tremors and an escape of steam and vapors near Pompeii and Herculaneum. There had been no eruptions, just recurring waves of earthquakes. Since there was no extensive damage, the quakes were soon forgotten and the farmers, land-owners, and noblemen went back to their work or settled down in their lavish summer retreats. But let's say one man didn't forget—QMT. Say he became alarmed. What if QMT was ahead of his time? What if he was convinced that the tremors were forerunners of some devastating event? Suppose he built a massive series of earthworks and dams of concrete to . . ."

"To protect against the disastrous lava flows and mud slides of 79," Olivia whispered.

"Yes, precisely. And what if it worked? Isn't there at least the slim possibility that at Herculaneum, buried under the lava crust, there might be an intact building of some sort—full of these art treasures and precious libraries mentioned by QMT?"

I had the disquieting thought that Don Ciccio knew that the building's existence was more than a "slim" possibility. Olivia's thoughts, however, had turned to QMT.

"You know who he is," she accused Don Ciccio.

"Yes, I do. There's one more scroll I haven't shown you yet."

The thing was fragmentary, like so many of the others, but it was legible:

> Our palace was originally modest, having only twenty
> rooms in all. Then the expansion began in the five
> hundred and sixty-fifth year from the founding of
> Rome, when the seeds of luxury were first sown in
> our nation. In that year Lucius Scipio returned from

a triumphant procession of battles with fourteen hundred pounds of engraved silverware. My ancestor Septimius Tertullian, a general under Scipio, returned with five hundred silver vessels and two hundred gold vases, the product of a new and exceptional technique. Septimius engaged the freedman Flavius Fontanus to design and build our vaulted strongroom with the Corinthian portico, and it remains the architectural spectacle of Magna Graecia. When I was a child I was amused by these thick silver vessels with their depictions of birds and the ages of man. I spent long moments gazing at the hundred-gazelle vase and the autumnal tray with its scenes of the harvesting of wheat and the peasants carousing at midday. I played with the jewelry with the saga of Aryx, the Scythian. Since I was a boy, I have dreamed of the gold vessels, their strange barbaric shapes laden with garlands, cornucopias, and stars.

I could only shake my head.

"Yes, Don Ciccio said, "it's amazing, and there's something even more amazing. Look here in the upper right-hand corner. Perfectly clear, delicately drawn, stunning in its vibrant reds and blues . . . don't you see a name? Quintus Maximianus Tertullian?"

"Yes! Hey, he's mentioned by Pliny!" I shouted in triumph. "Got you there, Olivia."

"I knew—and hesitated, on purpose, for you," my wife quipped.

The Don was impressed. "Good for you!" he said. "Here it is." And he pointed toward a leather-bound modern edition of Pliny the Younger's *Natural History* on the table.

I snatched it and quickly began to paraphrase from the Italian translation what he had written about the Tertullians.

The family was originally Greek, with roots back as early as the fifth century B.C. One of the forebears was recorded as having been a member of the Athenian war council under Pericles. The family's wealth was prodigious. They owned thousands of tracts in the most fertile parts of the Nile Delta, and among their islands they owned Patmos and Samos. By the time the earliest Tertullians had assembled their estates in Magna Graecia in the south of Italy, making Herculaneum their headquarters, they had become so powerful that in the earliest days of the Empire they were the only citizens who could lord it over tyrants and emperors alike. They loaned enormous sums to Octavian, and when he became Caesar Augustus, they shrewdly refused his attempts to repay, and they were rewarded a thousand times over.

Pliny's description of the Tertullians was a formula Roman panegyric no doubt commissioned and paid for, yet there seemed no denying his glowing statement that "the illustrious family never produced a son or daughter who was not gifted or honorable."

The clan had produced talented offspring in an astonishing variety of fields—government, philosophy, rhetoric, jurisprudence, the military, athletics, literature, teaching, aesthetics, and even gardening. The Tertullians appeared to have been art collectors from their earliest days. Pliny reported, in his florid way: "They possess Greek paintings, sculpture in marble and bronze by the likes of Phidias, Polycletus, Scopas, Lysippos. They have amassed the richest collection of jewelry in the world. They have a series of libraries containing the works of philosophers, poets, playwrights, historians, and mathematicians. One whole library has nothing but the works of Aeschylus, Sophocles, and Euripides. Another is reserved for spiritual writings gathered from all over the world."

"The Tertullian libraries," the Don quietly interrupted my reading. "I believe I have encountered examples of things that must have been in them—some miraculous things."

"What could possibly be more intriguing than what you've already found?" Olivia asked.

"This fragment," he said.

... on the fifth day of the march, the weary hoplites crossed the wadi and, once having gained the crest, found themselves looking down upon the ramparts of a fortified village which seemed to them to be bursting with treasure. Runners were sent to the lord Alexander. His spirits would be lifted, for the precious things would still the rebellious troops, who had begun to taunt their fallen leader. Without treasure there is no doubt that Alexander would be in danger of his life....

"Is that what it sounds like?" I asked. "Something about Alexander the Great? His men at the brink of rebellion? That's different."

"It's a fragment," Don Ciccio said calmly, "of an account of Alexander's conquests written by his arms bearer. It seems to be a copy of the one in the library. But, wait, listen. There are more reasons than that for the rewriting of history."

The Don described the scrolls that must have been hand-copied from books in the Tertullian libraries. It appeared that the family had allowed the city library to reproduce them. There was a tract by the ancient physician Dionysus of Halicar-

nassus in which it was actually written in precise and unambig-
uous terms that dreams were *not* sent by gods or demons, but
were phenomena owed to the personality of the individual.
Next, the Don read us some blank verse composed by Sappho,
whom the world knows as a Greek poetess, none of whose
works, so praised in antiquity, have ever been found. And here
we were listening as the Don read a fragment of her blank
verse:

> *breasts like fresh grapes, nipples succulent with her*
> *honey. With my tongue, I entered her shell-pink ears*
> *and sweet nostrils and mouth and was awakened once*
> *more to her pleasure. Then, hard as a gladiator, I*
> *remained there nestled, sheathed, through the night.*

"That's a male! Sappho wasn't!" Olivia exclaimed.

"There is much to rethink," Don Ciccio said with a laugh.
"I've also found snatches of the historians Thucydides, Sueto-
nius, Strabo, and Cicero," he said. "All vary markedly from the
versions on the shelves of my classics library. All. One of the
most astonishing items is a denunciation of Julius Caesar before
the Senate by his archenemy Pollio, who served with him in
Gaul. Listen to this. 'This bedraggled liar,' it reads, 'this faulted
memory, this recaster of deeds, this fading flower, this fraud,
has constructed a house of pure distortion.' "

We gaped like children.

"Here's an interesting one for you two—a piece from the
writings of Cratius, the world's first aesthetician. 'You see,' he
says, 'the splendor over all the manifold forms of ideas and
beautiful things. But amid all things of beauty we cannot ask
whence they came and whence the beauty. It can be no shape,

nor power, nor the total of powers and shapes; it must stand above all the powers, all the patterns. The origin of this must be formless—formless not as lacking shape but as the very source of every god-given intellectual shape.' "

"What the devil does that mean?" Olivia asked.

"Typical Roman rhetoric. But apparently Tertullian had no problem understanding. Listen to what he wrote in the margin. 'The meaning seems unmistakable—the act of creation. But is it possible? Could Cratius, so mediocre in all his other writings, have been referring to the subject of universal creation? I begin to think he was. For did he not say that within all of us, even the common, the spark of the genius must exist?' "

"That has a hint of, I almost hesitate to say it, Christian doctrine to it," Olivia said.

"The thought passed through my head, too," Don Ciccio, murmured. "If true, most intriguing. And I think it is true. Listen for a moment to what *has* to be a piece of diary written by Tertullian's wife. Her name was Phryne. I have no idea why such a private document was found amongst the scrolls Graebenhaecker stumbled upon. Maybe we'll never know. I suspect the cache had to do with police affairs."

We listened almost without breathing.

I have never found a man who is of no interest at all. Take John, that vexatious religious man whom Quintus considers his best friend and confidant. His intelligence is keen, even though bent by superstitions. For John is a member of that Eastern cult devoted to the confused teaching of Jesas, as is my husband, although Quintus has never bored me with his doctrines.

John is sinewy and tall, and when he sat at his weekly audience with me, which I forced him to make just for the perverse pleasure of it, he shrank and cramped his thin body. Then I slowly began to find him physically compelling. It seemed that he could not take his eyes from me. Why should he be different from any other man?—except for my own husband. Naturally he wanted to make love to me. But his cult abjures the flesh, and he abstained.

Still, this wiry, uncomely man kept watching me cautiously. He sweated, struggling with what he calls "sin." I wondered how to seduce him. I wished to do so because I knew how profoundly it would affect my husband, although the more I scrutinized John, the more I wanted him for the pleasure of it. He would be different from all the rest. How to seduce him? What did my teachers always say? A man is to be seduced through his convictions. So, in the second week, I commanded him to come before me every other day—in order to give me instruction in his faith. Within three sessions I had learned more about these followers of Jesas than I cared to know. And by the seventh session John was in my arms, breathing in deeply as I gently made him ejaculate between my breasts, speaking about "voices in the wilderness" and "rebirth." As I have found with so many hard and principled men, outwardly so arrogant, so impervious to beauty, once they have tasted me and I have suckled on them, they are captives.

John, the cultist, became my slave too much, seeking me every minute, confiding too much, saying that I had changed him. I had made him see that being too self-sacrificing was a mistake. He vowed that he would revise the chronicle of his faith—I call it a superstition—to reflect my views of humanity.

I told him one morning that since Quintus Maximianus was returning from his northern journey, he would soon have to leave my chambers. He turned pale as the sands and fainted *without a sound. My slaves carried him away. The physicians said he did not awaken for a day and a night, and when he revived he had lost half a measure in weight.*

Later he insisted on an audience. I didn't want to grant it, worried that his persuasion would sway me, for he was honeyed as a siren, but then I did. He bowed gracefully as he entered and smiled. He whispered, "Thank you, my lady." That was all. It was the last thing I ever heard him utter.

John remained in the palace. My husband's arrival was further delayed. Later I was informed that for the next two months John never left his carrel. He slept only three hours a day, and that in snatches. He ate little. He wrote prodigiously, filling reams of papyrus. They told me that he wasted away as if each page cost a piece of his flesh. Then, just before Quintus arrived, he died.

These superstitious souls act like none of us.

We sat silent for a long time. "Jesas"? Jesus? Not possible. And John? Not, I thought, John the Evangelist. Was it possible that Don Ciccio had cooked up an elaborate practical joke? No, that was like something I might have been tempted to do. The Don never joked about art. Olivia looked stricken. Later she told me that she was overwhelmed with anxiety when she heard Phryne's words. "What if it's *real?*" she kept asking. Curious. She seemed so shaken that I had to struggle to maintain my composure.

"Nice mystery," I said as blandly as I could.

"It's not just one," Olivia said hoarsely. "It's not just where the Tertullian Palace is or what condition it's in. It's Western civilization. It's a thousand mysteries. Ones that we might not want the answers to."

"But the bottom line to all this," I said, "is to find if it's there."

"I need your help," Don Ciccio said.

"To take a look is going to take one hell of a lot of money," I said.

"I agree. Say, ten million. Dollars, not lira," the Don added quickly.

"Hell, for that much and for a piece of the action—I mean, a share of what we might find—I'll throw in five million of my own money," I blurted.

Olivia sighed, I wasn't sure why.

"Excellent!" our host cried out. "We'll do it as partners. The larger the amount of money, the larger the share."

"You mean you're going to try to do this on the sly?" Olivia asked.

Don Ciccio stared at her as if she had gone daft. "Of course!"

"Can you simply do that? There are strict regulations against private digging. Won't the Ministry of Culture and the Department of Artistic Patrimony find out? What if we get caught? It will ruin us. Look, I like my reputation the way it is. I'm not sure I—"

"It will be just a modest probe," Don Ciccio said, trying to mollify her. "If we find anything promising we'll get in touch with the proper authorities right away. Waiting for official approval for a test could take years in Italy. I promise to be discreet."

I jumped in before Olivia could protest. All I wanted to know was where and when to start.

"Andrew, I find myself in an unusual quandary," Don Ciccio said. "I have no idea what to do. There are no clues even as to the general location of the Tertullian Palace. I can't think of a way to start."

"I can," I said. "We'll start with a guy I know. Jack Standish. His specialty is seeing under the earth."

"Andrew, please, no jokes now," Don Ciccio said.

"I'm not joking."

"Who and where is this Standish?"

"Egypt."

"This is surely a trick."

"No. Standish's whole life is to see under the sands. I'll call him tomorrow. Olivia and I will go talk to him. We'll visit Sicily and my villa on the way."

Olivia looked worried.

I HAD no real expectation of finding anything. I was just excited to get back into archaeology after so many years. The scheme was a long shot, but it was a game to play, a gamble. I had been a digger as a graduate student, in Sicily, at a place named Morgantina, where my villa is. I had almost stayed there, but as usual, I got restless. I told the Don the story of my first great find at Morgantina.

It was the second day on the trench, a wet, frigid day in March with Giovanni, my foreman, and fourteen workers. I'd marked out a rectangle about ten by twenty feet, and the workers had hacked away the first foot of dirt with picks. Then they worked with hand picks and trowels, patiently removing the black soil foot by foot. Late that afternoon, a third of a meter down, we hit something. It was entirely caked in mud and about two feet long. It seemed to be some sort of necklace. I recorded the location in my notebook, placed the object in a box filled with cotton batting, and raced down to our headquarters, where my professor was cleaning some previous finds.

He had on a rubber apron and rubber gloves and was submerging pottery fragments in acid just long enough for the caked mud to loosen. He gently lifted my necklace and immersed it in the jar full of acid. He had his back to me. I could hear him muttering the most exciting words over and over. "Now this *is* something!" he kept saying. I saw myself in the centerfold of the *London Illustrated News*. "Unique!" my professor whispered in awe. "What a discovery! My God!" He turned, holding my necklace in front of his eyes, and said, "You seem to have unearthed the world's earliest bicycle chain."

I had the dwarf on the hook until the very last line.

OLIVIA

When we received the Don's invitation to come to Naples, I was leery. The Don is so domineering. On our way out the door of our apartment, I felt sad, as if something were telling me not to leave. Now Andrew is convinced that the Don had more to do with our sabbatical than a grateful board of trustees. My husband is sometimes suspicious of my old friend.

I can't stop thinking about his unbelievable discovery and

about Herculaneum, about what may be down there, about the way those people's lives just stopped. The scrolls are unsettling. I want to know more. I can't relax, knowing what may be so close, but I am scared. It was good to get away to Sicily though Standish turned out to be certifiably insane.

In Sicily Andrew showed me things I'd never seen on my own trips. As we drove through the tiny town of Settemonti, he stopped and took me into the little city hall. The mayor embraced him as a brother! Then he opened a drawer and pulled out a bronze sculpture, about six inches high, of a young athlete. Greek. Fifth-century. It took my breath away. I thought the artist could have been Phidias himself, and there it was, tossed casually into a drawer in the middle of nowhere.

Then there was Andrew's villa at the site of the ancient city of Morgantina in the center of the island. It was lovely and desolate. The house, which straddles the ancient ruins on the corner of the old agora, or town plaza, is just two bedrooms, a kitchen, and a living room where Andrew's builder incorporated antique stones into the wall. But the terrace is splendid, spreading out on all four sides. One side looks out across the ancient agora, another faces the limestone ramparts of the acropolis.

In this secret place so far away from the turmoil of the museum and from Don Ciccio, Andrew had a chance to unwind. We relaxed into a long weekend of romantic lovemaking. Andrew needs to be relaxed, pleased with himself, completely amused, to become truly ardent. That weekend, all the conditions were met. We made the sweetest, gentlest love I had experienced in years, and afterward he didn't rush off. He hung around setting little amorous ambushes for me—wakening me in the middle of the night with an excuse to cuddle. I'm basically sort of inhibited, but that weekend with Andrew, I felt like

Phryne. I remembered her words about John and the way she seemed able to give herself completely over to pleasure. On our last morning in Morgantina, we made love for hours. I couldn't stop touching Andrew, and he almost became hysterical, laughing and saying that he would never recover.

We walked around the lovely site, littered with bits and pieces of dressed stones, pottery, and shiny green fragments of bronze. I found a silver coin, although it wasn't shiny, more a faint purple-lead hue because of corrosion. *My* first archaeological discovery!

I met Andrew's former foreman, Giovanni Puglisi, a man you'd almost think was endowed with supernatural powers. I invited him for lunch, and he came with several bottles of local fruity red wine, still "fuzzy" in fermentation. He insisted on remaining in the kitchen. Andrew says he considers himself too humble to enter the house. Later he took us to a huge ancient cistern, where he told an eerie tale. Years before, when it was found, it was filled with earth. The men had cleared out about twelve feet when Giovanni, who had been hoisting the buckets one by one with block and tackle, whispered to Andrew that before long, they would find the "dead people." Andrew, amused, listened to the quaint morality play.

Long ago, two friends, Giovanni told him, were exploring the ruins of the old city and had stumbled upon the cistern. There was hardly any dirt in it at all. They got a rope and some shovels, and one lowered the other into the well to look for treasure. He began to dig, and after several hours found an ancient vase similar to others found in the area, but filled with shining gold coins. Excited, he shouted to his companion to pull up the treasure. And so he did, but he didn't throw the rope back down to his friend deep in the cistern.

The man below cried out, "What are you doing?" And the

other answered, "Alas, I must leave you. For I love the treasure more than I love you. This is a hard country and a hard life. With this I can buy a vineyard near Palermo and a castle, too." The other pleaded with him, but his friend walked away. In the distance, growing fainter, he heard his cries. His shouts will soon cease, he thought. But the farther he walked, the louder the cries seemed to become. They changed from anguish to joy. Convinced that his friend had found more treasure, the other man rushed back and called down, "I was only playing a joke. I shall throw down the rope."

"And he did," Giovanni said slowly. "But the other, angry and vengeful, grabbed the rope and yanked, and the first fell into the deep cistern. Now both were trapped. They tried everything, even standing on each other's shoulders and jumping for the opening so far above. It was useless. The stucco sides of the cistern are scarred with their frantic scratching. And they died."

Two days later, when Andrew and Giovanni were removing the last meter of earth, they discovered—to Andrew's astonishment—the remains of a rope and two skeletons. The sides of the cistern were scratched, as if two wild men had attacked it with their fingers.

Although my husband seemed enthralled by the tale, I was disturbed by it. I kept thinking of Don Ciccio's face when he described Herculaneum. I wondered if he wanted it too much.

IN Cairo, the heat and bustle of the crowded airport terminal made me giddy. Mercifully, Standish had sent along his man Ahmed, who spirited us through immigration and customs like Moses parting the Red Sea. Later, we met Jack Standish, the man who could see beneath the earth, at the Safari Bar at the

Nile Hilton. He was bizarre, a younger and dissipated version of Charles Laughton. As soon as Andrew had asked, "How are ya, Jack?" he launched into a monologue on how the famous mummy of Ptah in the Cairo Museum had come down with malaria and had taken to shivering in his coffin, to the distress of the guards, who had vowed to go on strike unless the Pharaoh was cured.

After dinner he insisted that we join him at a smoke-filled bar on the island of Gezira to watch a belly dancer who had become the newest talk of Cairo. No wonder—her movements were hypnotic. When we returned to our suite at two-thirty in the morning, Standish informed us casually that we should meet Ahmed at the hotel entrance at five.

"Ahmed'll drive you out early to Sakkara to the stepped pyramid so you don't have to see it in the broiling sun," Standish said. "You remember Imhotep, the architect and history's first medical doctor. He was buried out there with two thousand dried-out alligators. That's how important he was. They'll serve lunch for you at the Ministry of Culture's rest house. Take an afternoon nap. When the sun starts going down, around four, Ahmed will saddle you up. Horses from Sakkara to Gizeh. Takes maybe two and a half hours. You arrive around evening. You'll join me for dinner—I'll fetch up a tent party, near the middle pyramid, Chephren's. Full moon. Then I'll show you my tricks."

The crumbling stepped pyramid was breathtaking. We descended down a long burial shaft, with a ceiling so low that we had to get down on our knees and crawl, to a pit that plunged a hundred feet down into the heart of the pyramid. But that paled compared to the horseback ride across the desert. No sign of contemporary life marred the vista. The trip had been timed perfectly. We arrived to find the pyramids silhouetted against the dark orange sky. Minutes later the first stars began to shine.

Standish greeted us, lolling back in a deck chair at the entrance to a spacious tent whose floor was made of three layers of carpets. The champagne was iced, and he toasted our ride as our horses were led away.

At midnight, Standish took us to his headquarters, a Quonset hut almost completely hidden in the sand behind some mastaba tombs near the Great Pyramid. Proudly he showed off his sonar equipment, which looked like air traffic control devices.

"It's simple, really," he said proudly. "I place sensing devices at intervals in the sand and a few on the pyramid, fifteen or twenty feet apart. They're small. Weigh almost nothing. I throw them from a jeep. They're battery-powered and they send out a ping, and these computers and screens show what they ping."

Standish threw several switches. The radar scopes began to glow. A large round screen ignited with a succession of small green dots. He clacked away at the keys of a computer keyboard, and suddenly superimposed on the scope was the ground plan of the three pyramids and the surrounding territory.

"These lines are the known passageways and sanctuaries within the Great Pyramid," he told me gravely, tapping each with a pointer. "And these dots signify cavities that no one had any idea existed, until me. And look here, off to the south side —these two blips are the cavities where those two solar boats were found. Here off to the west are two more similar holes. We don't know what's in 'em. The authorities are still hassling over where to go—inside the pyramid itself or to these holes. If it were up to me, I'd go inside. I've a feeling that old Cheops' treasure is still inside—there," Standish said, tapping gently at the pulsating green blip with his pointer. "But the king himself is buried here, *outside*."

Why would a Pharaoh want to be buried out in the open?

"He didn't," Standish told us, "except for one weird thing. Just before the pyramid was completed, Cheops' mother's tomb, a small pyramid nearby, was sacked by thieves. The son took her remains and ordered his architect to place them in a deep pit in the bedrock, which was then camouflaged. With that, I think the age of the pyramids came to a crunching halt—before the thing had been finished. I figure the king's body was never placed inside. I'll find it. I find everything."

He kept on insisting that we go inside the Great Pyramid, and before I could say no, he'd tossed some coveralls and hard hats at us. He brandished a picnic basket with champagne and *pâté de foie gras* and off we went. The climb up the eight-foot-high slabs to the entrance on the north side was spine-tingling. And the journey down the shaft, skittering on stones so smooth that I felt I was on an ice floe, was terrifying. When at last we had entered the central tomb chamber, with its peaked ceiling supporting the entire weight of the structure—billions of pounds—I had a sharp little attack of the willies, which Andrew cured with a hug and some champagne.

"It's the only cure for the sanctum-sanctorum creeps," Standish said, laughing. "Want to stay overnight? Napoleon did, and emerged pale and shaken. He never said a word to anybody about what happened. I've stayed a couple of times, and I never actually saw anything. Though I did hear things. Sounded like animals deep within the walls. Something. I'm surprised that Napoleon didn't bring some champagne."

At that chilling moment, deep in the empty burial chamber of Cheops, sipping champagne, Andrew told Standish what we had found on the scrolls. He didn't need much persuasion to agree to come to Naples. When Andrew warned that the tufa could be as much as twenty-five to thirty feet deep, he boasted, "My instruments will see through that stuff like glass. Hell, I can find any empty space!"

DON CICCIO

 I hadn't been to Sicily in years, and I had no desire to return to that land of aching poverty and Mafia madness no matter how glorious the monuments and antiquities. As I listened carefully to Olivia's enthusiastic descriptions after the Fosters' return, I was glad I hadn't left my Herculaneum.

"Now it's time," I told the Fosters after they finished their travelogue, "to meet a friend of mine, another eccentric. His name is Antonio Cartageno. He is vital to our investigation. He owns an olive grove on top of ancient Herculaneum. He will be, so to speak, our gatekeeper."

Cartageno's property is almost as beautiful as mine. Its hundreds of olive trees stand as if on parade, their silvery leaves shimmering in the light breeze from the far-off sea. The view toward the bay is perpetual, and Vesuvius looms through the haze to the southwest, imparting just the right air of danger.

As soon as we entered his gates, Cartageno popped up, a wizened man in his early seventies, dressed in hunting costume and puttees, an exquisite shotgun cradled under his arm. When he recognized me, he smiled and sidled over to us like a peasant.

"How honored I am to meet the American friends of Don Ciccio! We shall have a simple lunch and then tour my humble villa!" he said as he broke the shotgun smoothly and cradled it. It was not the gesture of a country bumpkin. He jumped nimbly into the front seat of my limousine.

The main house of his villa was not as large or as witty as mine, but it was an architectural gem, created by Vanvitelli.

"The property has been in my family since the time of the Ostrogoths, at least," the old man boasted, as a pair of servants served up a superior *pasta ai frutti di mere.*

"The fifth century?" Olivia asked in surprise.

"The records go back to that time," he said. "The barbarians never got this far south, so I presume my ancestors owned the land even earlier than that."

"Could some of them have lived in Herculaneum?" Olivia asked.

"It has always been an article of faith in my family that we were originally Oscan. We were living in Magna Graecia long before the Greeks came to colonize, and *centuries* before the

Romans arrived. Why doubt it?" His eyes glittered. Suddenly he burst into laughter.

We had *caffè* in Cartageno's spectacular salon, dominated by a Roman wall painting representing the Rape of Europa, obviously the work of a master. The muscular, snow-white bull breathed flames from his extended nostrils and rolled one great moist eye back at the beautiful naked woman, who didn't seem in the least frightened. It was comparable to any of the ancient paintings in the Naples Museum. Andrew and Olivia glanced at each other quickly and, they thought, surreptitiously.

But Cartageno noticed. "Ha! You *want* it for the New York museum, don't you? How much? Don't answer now. I might be tempted. No official knows that it exists. It was found deep beneath where we're standing, some hundred years ago. My grandfather tunneled through the tufa, obsessed with the thought that beneath our villa lay the original family seat. After months of tunneling his laborers came upon a room which miraculously had not been completely filled with lava. There they found this painting and a few other pieces. Come into the next room and tell me what you make of this next painting. It's about volcanology."

"In ancient Roman times?" Andrew asked.

"Why not? The Romans were keen observers. Pliny describes how learned men studied the hot springs surrounding the low hill of Vesuvius day by day. It was a hill then, not a mountain. Now look at my fresco and you'll see. And oh yes, the poem at the top is amusing."

The artist had depicted Vesuvius as a partly verdant, partly rocky phallus, erect and spewing forth a spray of fiery sparks.

"Goodness! It seems to be having an orgasm," Olivia whispered. "What's the inscription say?"

Andrew laughed. "Something like 'The mount which lies at the *summa*—summit—was a youth called Vesevo. He saw a nymph fair as a jewel. He fell in love . . . so much . . . that he belches out in fire.' "

Cartageno complimented him and explained that the other verses told bawdy tales of Vesevo enticing the nymph up to the crater, casting a sweet-smelling smoke around her, which made her limbs weak with passion, and entering her, erupting majestically, roaring with his love. He became fiery in his passion, so ardent that red streams of love spilled out, drenching the fields.

Olivia blushed as Cartageno chanted on. "The nymph adores the godly attention. Finally, Vesevo's passion explodes and in a mighty climax she is cast far out to sea. She became the isle of Capri, you know," he added.

"So that's why the place has such a reputation!" Olivia laughed. "How many more paintings like this may be down there?"

"Who knows? I think many," the old man said sadly. "The diggers didn't keep much of a record of what they saw. A series of tremors forced them to abandon the work. Two who could not tear themselves away from the treasures were killed. But they did describe one painting I'd love to lay my hands on, a vista of the city showing a series of palaces and villas. Many were identified by name—Lucullus, Julian, Tacitus, Procopellius, Tertullian. The last was most exceptional, the description says. It had hundreds of columns and arcades, dozens of porticos, courtyards, fountains, and pools, and hectares of gardens. Wouldn't it be wonderful to go back down there?"

I'm proud to say that not a muscle moved on any of our faces, not Olivia's, nor Andrew's, nor mine.

"Of course, that would be impossible. It is far too dangerous," Antonio said hoarsely. "There is nothing but death down there. Death, I tell you. The earth never rests. I hear the movements every night."

I saw Olivia throw her husband a quick, scared glance. I said to the Fosters, "I do hope you will forgive me speaking a short while to Cartageno in dialect. We shall join you shortly on the terrace."

They smiled and left us alone.

"My friend, I must seek a favor from you," I said softly in Neapolitan.

Old Cartageno gazed at me like an angel from some baroque altarpiece. He was "honored" by my asking a favor, "honored" to be taken into the confidence of a man as "illustrious" as I.

"A simple thing," I assured him. "All I ask is the use of your villa and property for ten days. That way a scientist friend of ours can test his invention, a kind of sonar device, good for trying to find minerals and the like. I can't say that I understand it, but I want to help for the sake of science."

The amiable gentleman nodded in approval, waving his hands in little circles. "It's a little thing, no? A new mechanism?"

I nodded.

"*Perchè no?*"

"I knew a man of your intelligence would understand," I said, relieved.

"Don Ciccio, as you know, I respect you highly." He smiled benignly. "And, as you also know, I am a man who is fascinated with the past, with archaeology, with my ancestors, with scholarship, with science." His voice rose with each word.

"Of course," I breathed.

"Excellent!" the old man exclaimed, patting the table lightly, and reaching over to clasp my hand. I reached out, but at the last second, he pulled his back. There was to be more singing, more poetry. I eased back in my chair and smiled and waited for the aria to end.

"But I wonder," Cartageno said and hesitated, then added quickly, "Only a small question . . ."

"What, my friend?" I made myself look as attentive as a firstborn son at the reading of the will.

"This device will in no way damage my land, my trees, or my house?"

"I assure you. These machines are lightweight, hardly noticeable. No damage to anything." It was moving to see how deeply the old man cherished his land.

"I am honored to be asked, especially by you, Count Nerone, as I have said. But why me? I mean, if your scientist friend wants to know if his listening devices work, he could more easily take them to the automobile tunnel over on the north side of the city and try them there."

"Dear Cartageno, my acquaintance already knows the machine will find tunnels and cellars. He—"

"What's his name?"

"Standish. Jack Standish."

"From where?"

"He's from Berkeley."

"I am not aware of him or this place. What does he really want?"

"Simple, my friend," I said, becoming slightly frosty. "Standish wants to see if his equipment can trace the existence of possible underground cavities at a known ancient site."

"What is Berkeley?"

"A large university in California."

"Rich? Does this Standish get paid by this rich university in America?"

Too late, I saw I had misjudged him. "I imagine."

"Then if I, a humble olive grower, asked for a little rent, he would understand and be able to pay?"

"It might be arranged."

"If this Standish does find an empty space under my property or near it, then what?"

"Then I would be interested in your help in obtaining permission to continue the experiment."

Cartageno bounced to his feet and walked over to me, studying my face closely. "You are keeping something from me, Don Ciccio. What is this Standish really up to?"

Clever old bastard!

I lowered my voice. "The fact is, Don Antonio, my friend Standish is a little, um, crazy. He dreams he has invented the perfect machine to see beneath the earth. He dreams it will be a great boon to archaeology. I'm not at all convinced. But since we're old friends, I just thought if you don't mind and could help me, I could, in turn, help Standish."

"I understand."

"I am in your debt," I replied. I was careful to keep any warmth out of my voice.

"One more little thing," he said, hesitating. "You know how sensitive I am to matters of my land and my pride. How long will this experiment take?"

"As I said, ten days. Less, probably."

"To be kept secret?"

"Completely."

"You're positive that the Superintendent of Antiquities will never learn of this?"

"Guaranteed."

"Fine. I'll do it."

"Good."

"But forgive me, Count, if I ask for a small payment. Call it a token for my beloved land. Times are not easy."

"What might a 'token' be?"

"Say, fifty thousand."

It was a pittance. "Assuredly," I told him.

"Dollars," he added.

"Ambitious, aren't you?" I said, a tinge of menace in my voice.

"For a secret mission? Not really. Perhaps it would be better if Standish went to the automobile tunnel, or to Pompeii."

"I see."

"And what I ask is not so much . . . especially if you're looking for something very special. And you *are*, aren't you?"

I realized I had lost the struggle. Containing further damage was my only concern.

"I think, Don Ciccio, you who are so intelligent and wise believe that there's something underneath my beautiful house, something that might become very valuable to you."

I gave him one of my colder stares, but he gazed back unflinchingly.

"Here are my terms," he said. "I want fifty thousand dollars deposited to my account at Bank Leu in Zurich, within two days. If anything is found—the slightest indication of anything —I insist upon an additional hundred thousand dollars. After that, if the authorities either seize my land or force me to rent it, I want your interests to match, twofold, whatever compensation the government awards me."

I inclined my head. "No," I whispered.

"Go somewhere else then. Try!"

Damn the old toad!

"I've heard you are a realist, Don Ciccio," he went on. "All I want is proper consideration. In money. And if there are excavations..."

The old gentleman was marvelous!

"My friend Don Ciccio, I want, in writing, *before* this American arrives, a contract that guarantees me fifty thousand dollars for the use of my land if there are excavations. And, in order that we keep this in the family, I demand the right to negotiate a monthly rent before you sign up with any other landowners in this territory."

I made some calculations.

"If you're not willing to agree..."

I sipped my wine. "I admire your resolve, Don Antonio. I must say, however, that I would feel better with the figure of twenty-five thousand, if we do find some underground hole. If not, then I am willing to promise ten thousand in cash. I want to avoid payments to Swiss banks. Their secrecy regulations have deteriorated."

I waited for my words to sink in. A twitch of pleasure came to his lips.

"And that's it," I said with all the firmness I could muster. "After Standish, and if something is found, then we pay fifteen thousand a month rent. And I demand certain guarantees. For one, silence. Second, I wouldn't want anyone else to be allowed on your property for anything to do with this unless I have a chance to approve."

"I'll give you sixty days to match whatever anybody else may offer," Cartageno said softly, licking his lips.

It was getting late. I was bored. "Agreed," I said softly.

"Agreed," he said.

We were about to shake hands on the accord when Cartageno suddenly stunned me with a rapid flow of words. His voice, low and raspy at first, began to run up the scale, ending in a kind of keening.

"There is death down there. The ground never rests. It is not wise to go down there!"

"Bless you, old soldier," I said, motioning to him my permission to kiss my hand. "You are truly to be honored. Bless you!"

What a tough and clever old bird!

"WHAT went on?" Olivia asked as we drove home.

When I told them about Cartageno's financial demands, Andrew complained bitterly that the kindly old gentleman could cost us a million dollars or more.

"But we have nowhere else to go," I told him as patiently as I could.

"What about the danger?" Olivia asked nervously.

"If we follow modern engineering techniques of shoring up the tunnels, I don't think we'll have anything to fear."

"But isn't the entire territory unstable?"

"There hasn't been a serious tremor in decades," I lied, and tried to change the subject.

But she would have none of it.

"He said there was death down there. Perhaps living here you tend to ignore the peril. Won't there be a problem of gases?"

"Olivia, no. The site is miles from Vesuvius."

"Cartageno, even from the little I could see, seemed genuinely concerned about danger," Andrew said.

I sighed. "All right, I'll tell you the truth. The fact is that the old thief is making it up in order to keep us away."

"I see," Andrew said. Olivia just stared at me.

"And you did hear him say that the room they found was —intact!"

"I almost fainted," Olivia said and laughed.

ANDREW contacted Standish, who cheered us by saying he'd come at once, the next morning. This good news was followed by his haggling over terms. He insisted on first-class passage, expenses, and a ten-thousand-dollar fee.

Furious, Andrew nevertheless gave in.

We returned to the scrolls to pass the time and found the most extraordinary thing. Andrew discovered it, a fragment of a record concerning Quintus Tertullian made by Nero's secret police. The record had been written in 65 A.D., and in flat, bureaucratic prose it described Tertullian as an accomplished hunter and a keen athlete who, in his mid-thirties, could box with professional gladiators who came occasionally to the palace for entertainment. He was an expert fencer, especially with the short sword, a polymath who was interested in subjects as varied as geography, physics, and astrology. All this in addition to running the extensive family farms, the vineyards, the shipping company, an arms factory, and what seemed an enterprise for breeding elephants.

STANDISH arrived a day late on the 23rd of May, tipsy and trailing eight cases of equipment. I had arranged for him to stay at Cartageno's small guest villa, which came with two servants and a spacious refrigerator.

His cases contained a bewildering array of devices, some new, others so dented they looked like junk. Standish's working habits were bizarre. He wandered from one probe to another, pulling behind him what looked like a golf bag. A headset was clamped to his ears, and around his neck he carried a six-by-twelve-inch aluminum box with a large central dial. Head down, he shuffled along, from time to time removing his earphones to wipe his brow with a large soiled red handkerchief. I followed him through one of his sweeps of the olive grove, wondering what if anything he was up to. "So! Got *that* one. Ah, now we're picking it up. One ping and two . . . ping me a solid sixty, sweetheart. Whoops! *Ouch.* That hurt! What the hell's going on? I just don't get it. On the one hand . . . then on the other. So, let's figure it out. Is it another false recurrence or . . . Let's triangulate, calculate, and *prestigitato!*"

At intervals Standish would return to his room and type on his laptop computer. On his fifth day, he brought out a different piece of equipment, a sort of metal detector that he held horizontally about a meter off the ground. He wended his way back and forth across the Cartageno property. After several hours of this he retired to his computer without a word. For three days and nights he didn't emerge. According to Cartageno, Standish didn't sleep more than three or four hours a night, and continually badgered the servants with demands for food and wine. On the ninth day he passed out and slept for a day and a half.

When he came to, he joined us for dinner. We were dying to hear what he had found, but he seemed in no hurry to bring the subject up. When he did, his words stunned us.

"I'm not sure. My instruments are sure acting strange."

"No dams, bulwarks, earthworks? No cavities?" Andrew asked tensely, leaning forward in his chair.

Standish shifted uncomfortably in his chair.

"For Christ's sake!" Andrew shouted at him. "In Egypt, those machines of yours showed a hole in the ground between every grain of sand! What's going on?"

"That's sand. This is tufa mud," Standish whined.

"What have you found or not found?" Andrew asked.

"I've got a pair of seismic disks," he said hoarsely. "See for yourselves. I thought I'd developed machines to give me a computerized axial tomographic picture of what's underground—yes, something vaguely akin to the CAT scan. My theory is that electronically induced seismic waves, like little earthquakes, can, after being analyzed by my computer, approximate the results of the medical scanners which give a precise picture of the brain. See if I'm right."

Standish dropped two floppy disks into Andrew's lap. "Good luck. Be in touch. Remember our deal. You still owe me some per diem, and if you strike it down there I get a chance to make a few picks. Time for me to get back to the more fascinating territory of the pyramids. I'll be hearing from you."

I escorted Standish to his car, taking care to pay him in full. I wanted no complaints later on from him about his not receiving his proper pay.

Once Standish had gone, we rushed to the computer room, where I ran the disks through a rapid analysis. We watched as across the screen came gray, then gray-black, then black shapes shifting, swimming past as if they were clouds of a terrible cosmic storm. When they began to disperse, the ink blacks started to lighten. The screen became gray and ghostly as fog. Abruptly the mists disappeared, and in the penumbra we could see an enormous architectural shape, not directly under the Cartageno land, but adjacent to it, a huge empty space criss-crossed by what seemed to be dividing walls forming hundreds of chambers of differing sizes. And to the northwest, toward Vesuvius, wasn't there something else? Giant bulwarks? No. I was imagining things.

"My God, there it is!" Olivia said. "The emptiness has to be the villa."

"But, how do we know it wasn't inundated by the mud?" Andrew breathed.

"We've got to try a probe," Olivia said. "But how? Do we do it on our own, or do we let the authorities in on it?"

"We should endeavor to do it ourselves," I told them. "Andrew, you're the construction expert—what might we need in men and equipment? For a discreet attempt."

"I don't think you can be discreet. This is big. For a decent effort I'd guess we'll need..." Andrew hesitated. "Ah, fifty men, two pneumatic drills, a bulldozer, enough steel to shore up a pretty big entrance tunnel, a backhoe, electricity, chain-link fencing, possibly some oxygen in case the air is foul, a first-aid station. I figure we'll need maybe ten to fifteen million dollars to start and maybe a quarter to a half million each month thereafter. If Tertullian's dams didn't work, you can forget about going further. To scrape that hardened mud out of the interiors would cost hundreds of millions."

I thought he was being conservative. My guess was that the project could easily cost as much as twenty-five million.

"You know, the two of us together probably could scrape up the funds," he said.

I let the remark pass. I could not let anyone know of my true wealth, even Andrew. I had never paid the proper taxes and flagging my wealth would only bring the government down upon my head.

"Well, obviously you can't pull off something like that without the authorities knowing!" Olivia insisted. "Look, this won't be some isolated crack at a tomb or a single narrow tunnel. What's the penalty if we're caught?"

"If I'm caught," I told her, "nothing more than a fine, a slap on the wrist. Night digging is a hallowed activity in Naples. If you two are caught, it would be an international scandal, a huge fine. Perhaps a token jail term. Anyway, a frightful rumpus."

"In any case, I presume we don't want to open up a tiny tunnel and conduct a 'budget' operation. We simply can't do this clandestinely," Olivia said.

"So do it the opposite way," Andrew suggested. "Let's make it a world event. Seek maximum publicity. But how do we make the government give us a role, even if we raise the money?"

It was a question I had been waiting for. "Why don't you two act as 'fronts' for the undertaking? Only non-Italians can get away with this. Foreigners, especially Americans—and two such celebrated ones—would be allowed to do virtually anything they wanted. The government would welcome you—and your money."

"I think not," Andrew said. "Being old museum hands, we'd arouse all kinds of suspicions. It would be assumed that we had a secret agenda."

"Which we would have," Olivia said. "Whatever happens, what if we do come across something astounding? How can we be sure the government will make a deal and allow us and the museum to have a share?"

"The right bribes will do it," I told them. "But we still need a front. The problem with having me as leader is . . . well, frankly, there is a misunderstanding between me and the Superintendent of Antiquities for the Naples region. He believes —inaccurately and unfairly—that I've abused the rules. There's to be an investigation. I'm certain it'll amount to nothing. And then there are rumors—allegations only—that I am overly sympathetic to the Mafia. No, I can't appear to be taking a leadership role, and I can't be visibly linked with the funding. An acceptable front . . . you know, when you mentioned your generous patron . . ."

"Al Stearns. Brilliant. He's the perfect one," Olivia said jubilantly. "He's got the money, he loves Italy, and he owns a historic villa on Capri."

"We'll tell him about Vesevo," Andrew said with a smile.

"What luck! He told us he's about to take his yacht, the *Esmeralda,* around Italy," Olivia said. "I'd be delighted to ask him. What do I tell him?"

"The truth," I told her. "Or a rough approximation. Tell him that we may have pinpointed the site of the richest treasure of all time and that we need an initial pledge of, say, ten million now and another ten or so later, if things work out. I don't think it would be wise to push right away for the full amount."

Olivia grinned.

"Stearns can afford it," I added. "I have it on the best authority that he netted two hundred million dollars in just the past six months on the sale of a part of one of his conglomerates. I wish I were wealthy enough to fund the entire project myself, or at least fully match your intentions, Andrew, but, as I said, I will pledge a goodly part of my savings, say five million. It will serve us well as a contingency.

"To the new archaeological team of Stearns, Foster, and 'friend,' " Andrew said.

THE next day Olivia reached Stearns by radiotelephone, and we were immediately invited to join him on the *Esmeralda,* which was in Taranto for a week's cruise through the Strait of Messina to Capri and into Naples. She told him we wanted to discuss his becoming involved in "an archaeological opportunity that will make Tut's tomb look like a kindergarten exercise." He had replied, "How much?"

"Don't expect a cheap ticket to immortality," Olivia advised.

I am not a yachting man. I have no interest in these immense private boats the rich all seem to own these days. What are they but expensive platforms for sunbathing? To my surprise I found the *Esmeralda* captivating. So excessively lavish! I must admit I began to think that in a few years, when I no doubt will become even more sedentary, I might actually enjoy bobbing around on such an air-conditioned floating island. I'd choose one like Stearns', a gold mine of electronic toys. There were launches of all types and sizes and a baby helicopter. Stearns gave us a tour, starting with the kitchens and proceeding to the staterooms, the gyms, the movie theaters, and finally the bridge. With special "windows" in satellites, Stearns was able to communicate anywhere in his far-flung enterprise without being intercepted.

"In absolute secrecy," he boasted. "The damnedest thing about these new yachts, and why they're so popular, is that this communication system is far more secure than anything you could get on land. Out here no one can possibly tap in to you. That's why I had her built."

Dinner the first evening was charming. Seated on the after-deck we cruised along at full speed under a full moon as we entered the great bay that approaches the Strait of Messina. I had never witnessed the American ritual of fund-raising. What a tribal dance! I had never seen Olivia so powerful or sexual.

Stearns was skeptical when we told him our plans. "Sounds great, but unrealistic. Look, Olivia, a character like this Tertullian was probably smart enough to move all his goods out to some safe place."

"But the dams are there!" she insisted. "And even if we find only an empty shell, it'll be the most exciting archaeological discovery in history."

"Empty shells are not my idea of excitement," Stearns muttered.

"Empty *Roman* shells are apt to be painted with hundreds of frescoes," she countered.

"Perhaps. How much is this project going to cost? Twenty million? More? How long will it take? Ten years? More? To find what? Fragmentary things that only *Archaeological News* will publish? And what about obtaining the government permits?"

Stearns began to pace the deck. "God. I've worked this country before, in steel, oil-cracking plants, nuclear reactors, apartment houses, resort hotels. Each time I've gone through Dante's Inferno! Red tape, strikes, bribes, kickbacks. Official corruption is in the air you breathe in Italy. My friends, I'd sure like to do it. Of course, I'll help, in a modest way, you understand. I'm talking about one or two million, which I'll have to match with another million in bribes."

Olivia looked so crestfallen that Stearns quickly added, "Perhaps a token more, just to start the project on the way. I'll give you four."

Before Olivia could say anything, I drew myself painfully from my wheelchair to my feet, a gesture that never fails to capture attention.

"I am blessed by being a member of one of the most exalted families in the history of Naples. I am doubly blessed by being a member of a family which has always worshiped knowledge, science, discovery, and the sacredness of ancient traditions. We Nerones have always revered classical antiquity. Because of our efforts over centuries, hosts of treasures have been preserved for mankind. The Nerone family is also blessed by having been moderately well off over a long period of time—we have husbanded our wealth. To spend it for good works is our motto. This project can become the greatest good work of all." I paused.

"We are sure to find this incredible palace," I lied. "It is sure to be jammed with treasures of art, literature, and philosophy. But Andrew has calculated that it will take as much as forty million to find it. For something so rare, I would say it's worth it. History will never forget the people who make this dream come true. I am willing, in secret, to match any sum that you, Mr. Stearns, are prepared to pledge for our initial investigations. The work will be arduous and unpredictable. But think of the glory. Think of your place in history. To find the Palace of the Tertullians. Follow your heart. For God's sake, man, join us."

Stearns sucked in his breath and burst out, "Forty. And I don't need your matching funds. How's that?"

"Princely!" I said.

"But I've got a condition. My name goes on this project. No one else's," Stearns demanded.

"Agreed."

"I've got a few other provisos."

"Yes?"

"I insist on being at the site, directing operations. I want a cut of the stuff we find. Souvenirs."

"Why not?"

"What's our first step?"

"It might be profitable to invite the Prime Minister here to the yacht to ask his permission to conduct an exploratory probe at Herculaneum."

"And what will his answer be?" Stearns asked.

"He'll say yes, depending, of course, on how much you offer him as a bribe."

Bruno Fanfano arrived by helicopter the next day. Tanned and sleek, he emerged from the hovering aircraft and jumped nimbly on the landing pad. He jogged across the deck and greeted Albert Stearns as if he were a political ally. "I have wanted to meet you all of my official life," he boomed. "I compliment you, sir, on all the benefits Italy has received over the years from your labors."

Stearns loved it. The memories of red tape, bribes, broken promises, and failed expectations faded. The PM turned to me, smiled, and shook my hand as if I were a rich uncle. He seemed about to embrace me but, thank God, drew back at the last moment.

"Mr. Stearns, I see your discrimination in people is equal to your legendary intelligence. Don Ciccio Nerone is one of our national treasures. Just the other day I was saying to one of my closest aides how fortunate a nation we are to have such a genius, a man of such accomplishment, sagacity, and incomparable taste."

Over lunch at anchor near the Blue Grotto, Olivia told a shameless tale of what her patron, "Albert," hoped to accomplish at Herculaneum "for the Italian people and to your enduring credit, excellency."

Albert, she told the Prime Minister, expected to establish a great foundation to encourage the creation of certain carefully chosen archaeological ventures which were so costly and so risky that the Antiquities Department would never and should never embark upon them.

"But what do you want me to do?" the Prime Minister asked.

"Permissions, sir," Olivia said firmly.

"That can be achieved only on the local level," the Prime Minister said, apparently indicating an end to the matter.

"But sir, you can order an overall permit," Olivia persisted. "Herculaneum is a political issue. If the olive growers who control the site suspected the government was about to embark upon even only a modest probe, they would block any local permit."

Then Stearns plunged in. "If I'm going to put up a lot of money, I want the assurance of the top guy. That's the way I do business. And since I'm going to be really perking things up in Naples, economically speaking, hiring quite a crew, perhaps, and if we're lucky enriching the museum, I would hope for a few small rewards, a few souvenirs. You can get that kind of permission for me."

Fanfano became chilly. "I appreciate your desire to help us in archaeology, Mr. Stearns. But I must tell you that what in America might seem a souvenir is considered a treasured article of history and scholarship in my country. We have suffered too long the depredations of tomb robbers, smugglers, and—I hope you won't think me rude—avaricious private collectors and certain unscrupulous American museums. It is a sensitive subject, a political one."

Stearns glared at the flushed politician.

Fanfano plucked up his glass of wine, studied it for a few

seconds, and said quietly, "I'll sleep on it. Mr. Stearns, let me say that whatever my decision is, I want to tell you you are a most compelling man—despite a frankness that others might take as threatening. I shall sleep on this."

The Prime Minister left after lunch the next day without a word to anyone about what he had decided. I was beginning to fear the worst when the steward delivered a note asking me to come to the bridge.

Stearns was there when Arturo carried me in.

"Late last night," Stearns began, "after I was settled, it must have been two in the morning, Fanfano knocked on the door of my stateroom." Stearns lit a cigar. "I let him in and the old bastard immediately lets fly with . . ."

I started to laugh.

"Yeah, you guessed it." Stearns laughed, too. "The bastard asks for three million dollars in cash. He said he'd see to it that I get first choice at what's discovered, though I'll have to pay up front. The transaction will be handled by a most trustworthy man, who will make himself known to me in due time. His name is Enrico Dorsoduro. The Prime Minister warned that his permission can be canceled in twenty-four hours, and he said that none of you should expect to be included in the arrangement."

"And what did you say?" I asked with a smile.

"I said, '*Deal,* buster.'" Who is this Enrico Dorsoduro, anyway?"

"Dorsoduro is an accomplished business executive in his early seventies who controls, with his three ruthless sons, all the significant illegal digging in the vicinity of Naples," I said. "His family have been in the trade since the eighteenth century. In the past, they have been suspected of murdering potential rivals.

Most of the highest-quality Italian antiquities acquired by the most discriminating private collectors and museums in the world came from the Dorsoduros."

"Sounds like Enrico is a player to watch out for," Stearns said with little interest. "But what can he do?"

"Not can do, will do," I told him. "As soon as Dorsoduro and the rest of his gang learn what we're doing, they'll move in. If we find the Tertullian Palace, he will begin tunneling in from his lands to the south."

Stearns looked at me, a gleam filling his eyes. "You're kidding. Hell, I think we can handle them."

THE permits were to be processed through the office of the Minister of Culture, and Andrew dealt with the minister himself, Giuseppe de Grazie. He seemed the perfect foil. He thought little of archaeology, calling it "a frightful waste of money and time." He preferred opera or ballet and confided to Andrew that he found excavators "mere clerks." But he immediately issued a provisionary permit for "a responsible probe of the site of the ancient city of Herculaneum on the property of one Antonio Cartageno."

To be sure the detailed documents would be rapidly processed, Andrew mentioned that he adored opera and would be delighted to make an anonymous donation of two hundred and fifty million lira for the *Turandot* that Minister de Grazie yearned for. But the donation didn't take us the whole way.

The complete permits were delivered to Andrew by his friend the minister, but they were quite different from the blanket permission we thought we were to receive. Our probes depended upon "finite and positive" discovery of objects and architecture that "might substantially prove" the existence of a prime ancient dwelling or of "any other important antique entity" and dictated "orderly and constant supervision by government specialists." The minister's covering letter instructed sternly that he was not going to allow the "Stearns Team" to continue tunneling if early indications of "a significant domicile" were not "thoroughly positive and tangible." The document warned that "all ancient property of any kind, from artifacts to building materials and any sort of embellishment, would be the property of the state." Our freedom was thus limited. We would be watched hour by hour by the antiquities bureaucrats.

The minister then hinted that in return for his signature, Andrew should fund an *Aida*. Andrew agreed, on the condition that we be allowed to submit weekly written reports to the office and dispense with the on-site supervisors. But nothing we could say could dissuade the minister from appointing Giulio Cassone, the Superintendent of Antiquities at Pompeii, our "continual partner and resident expert." Cassone had the right to visit the site at any time.

Stearns established an account in the Banco di Lavoro in the amount of ten million dollars. He rented Antonio Cartageno's villa for fifteen thousand dollars a month, and the old man moved into the "barn" Standish had stayed in. Stearns leased and purchased everything from miniature bulldozers to "splitter" drills, cement mixers, high-pressure hoses, and a majestic mobile crane. The more I saw him in action, the more I had to respect him. We took to having late-night meals together at Cartageno's or at my villa. We shared many fine bottles of wine and amusing anecdotes.

"What the hell are our chances? Really?" he asked one evening.

"Twenty percent we'll find something. Eighty percent utter failure," I answered.

"About what I figured," he replied calmly.

"How much do you want to lose?" I asked.

"About twenty."

I nodded amiably.

He smiled, studying me as if for the first time. "What's it like being a dwarf?"

The question made my heart skip a beat. Was this some sort of cruel test? I had no idea. I smiled casually and told him, "I am consumed by the mental anguish of it. I would do anything to change my appearance. Who wouldn't? Not a moment passes that I'm not reminded of what I am. Will I ever become accustomed? Never. Will I ever learn not to despise my condition? Surely not. Does it affect my thinking, my reason, my state of mind? Sometimes. Imagine being eternally burning with embarrassment, knowing that behind your back, everywhere and with everyone, you are being pitied, or joked about, at best tolerated."

"I expect so," Stearns said coldly.

OLIVIA

Opening Day. Squads of carabinieri in their dress uniforms were stationed around the Cartageno property. Thousands of Neapolitans crowded the bleachers Al had had constructed. Banks of flowers and yards of bunting festooned the stage where Cardinal Raniero prayed for our success. Holy water was sprinkled on the ground where the immense stainless-steel drill sat ready. The work began; the bit hummed almost soundlessly. All our machinery was powered by compressed air, and the massive engines needed to supply the power were located a mile distant at an abandoned quarry.

Every player performed faultlessly. I wore a chic excavating outfit I had never gotten to wear on my TV show. Andrew was dashing. Stearns had a special suit tailored to conceal his extra pounds from the television cameras.

"So, the most eagerly awaited archaeological excavation in the history of the world gets under way at an almost sacred pace," a grave American television correspondent intoned. "This is far from a circus. These are dedicated scientists, calmly at work. Expect no sudden discoveries. Put spectacular, instant finds out of your minds. Don't be fooled by publicity. This is serious, dedicated labor. What will the searchers find? No one can tell. But it's my guess, and I speak as one who's been close to the inside, that this team of scientists expects to discover something incredible."

The Italian television crews drummed up their own circus effects, superbly. RAI managed to generate some controversy by focusing on an anti-archaeological association, the Brotherhood for the Undisturbed Past. Some of its members carried placards with slogans: "Our ancients deserve the sleep of peace!" "Archaeologists are tomb robbers!" "Bury the Americans instead!" Their spokesman gave an emotional interview in which he suggested that the whole operation was a plot by Albert Stearns to "grasp into his greedy clutches for his own gain the ancient heartland of Italy."

Most of the Italian press and all of the foreign correspondents found the whole thing boring and left after three days of watching nothing but the grinding earth-screw and earth-moving equipment. I was bored, too.

But the drilling through the lava went faster than anyone

had expected. In five days, we progressed eleven feet into the rust-red, blackish lava. The material flaked away like dried-out dough. At twelve feet we cut through the lava layer entirely and entered the dried mud. We were all positive we would be able to plunge through the softer tufa virtually unimpeded.

We were to be bitterly disappointed. The tufa, which in the first meter was as soft as chalk, soon became a dense, cross-grained, concretelike stuff. Only then did our resident volcan-ologist inform us that sometimes in eruptions, lava mixed with the hot mud and produced a material as durable as cement. It took our sharpest drill an hour to penetrate six inches. Don Ciccio's rough calculations of the palace level indicated that we had to penetrate more than twenty feet. This might take years. Drills dulled and had to be replaced. Equipment began to break down. A vicious heat wave sent temperatures above one hundred. Morale plummeted, costs rose.

"Let's blast," Stearns suggested, "with surgically placed nitro."

"I will never allow it," Giulio Cassone retorted.

"What's going to get damaged?" Stearns protested. "A couple of millimeters of diamond-hard tufa?"

It was Andrew who prudently suggested a break. The heat and dust were causing respiratory problems. Everyone was on edge.

"Perhaps the Department of Health should come in and conduct tests," Cassone said.

Stearns uttered a curse.

"Mr. Stearns, if I did not appreciate what you have done for Italy in the past, I would throw you out of the excavation for that remark. I now order a cessation of all work—I have the authority—for five days."

"Why not make it forever?" my husband grumbled, but

out of Cassone's earshot. "At this rate, we'll never get anywhere near the level where the ancient buildings are."

The break lasted almost two weeks.

Andrew and I returned to Sicily. Stearns escaped to Rome. Don Ciccio remained. He refused to leave the site. When we assembled again it was supposed to be with a renewed spirit and heightened expectations. But I didn't feel renewed. I was even more anxious about the depth of Don Ciccio's obsession.

ANDREW

Sand, rock, heat, sweat, tears. After resuming work, we struggled day after day with the hard crust of tufa, grinding centimeter by centimeter. Our press briefings turned sour. The reporters began to publish discouraging rumors.

I became convinced that one of the Italian journalists was a government spy. He was too attentive. He kept pumping me about what Stearns and the Metropolitan Museum were going to get if we found something. I played dumb and told him to read the small print of our contracts, the section stating that none of us had any right to anything discovered. He got tired of hanging around and, realizing we were finding nothing, left, though I didn't believe he'd stay away.

The crews worked twelve, fourteen hours a day. But I soon got fed up with the farce. I arrived late or didn't bother to show up at all, which infuriated Don Ciccio. I'm just not good at waiting around patiently for anything, so I retired to the laboratory to soak and translate scrolls. I discovered three documents written and signed by Quintus Maximianus Tertullian in A.D. 64. Their contents brought me back to life. Hope returned.

. . . It was like thunder from beneath the earth, like the rolling drums at the start of the October chariot races. But it was terrifying. The earth's motion was playful at first, like the blanket-toss games of childhood. Then the swaying changed to violent crashing and the crackling of rocks. Burning oil splashed recklessly from the lamps, but fortunately it did not spread in our bedchamber. Phryne tried to make her way to the children, whom we could hear crying out in the darkness, but she passed out in the smoke. Alone, I crawled amid the furniture crumbling around my head. It was fate that nothing struck me. When I reached the children, I threw myself on them. I was worried, but my senses were keen, as they are when I am in battle. Farther off, I could hear the cries of the slaves and servants. There was a smell of oil, smoke, flames everywhere.

The earth shook for a minute, perhaps more. Then abrupt stillness. It was as if the world had stopped. My heart stopped too, or so it seemed. We huddled for a time together, waiting for more shocks. But the earth returned to normal. As soon as

I saw that the children were unharmed, I made my way to the superintendent's quarters and assessed the damage for the rest of the night.

Three Egyptian slaves, two males, are dead, apparently from fear. Five foundations of the south shops are rent asunder. There are cracks in the cement of two palms' width. Three marble statues in the grand gallery toppled and smashed, including the old athlete by Myron. I was surprised to see how well the frescoes and wall mosaics survived the earthquake. Minor cracks.

The great hall was unharmed. No colonnades are in peril. The fountains are secure. The kitchens have come through badly, however, and it seems that most of the pottery will have to be replaced. A minor matter. At first I feared that some of the horses might have been killed. But none were even slightly wounded.

Relieved to find the damage so minor, I was, nonetheless, deeply worried about the underground shrine. I yearned to rush below to check it but I had to wait until every freedman and slave finally retired. Then, with the chief of guards stationed at the first of the nine doors, I went down with my superintendent of works, the only other person left in the household who knew the nature of the contents of the secret depository. When I saw the fissures in the stones at the sides of the third, fifth, and sixth doors of the shrine I feared that greater damage must have occurred deeper down. But the tremors must have been stronger closer to the surface. The final portals were intact. Still, it was with anxiety that I entered the burial chamber. All was as it should have been. I was profoundly relieved.

What had happened? What does it mean? What will the future bring? The soothsayers were noncommittal—at first. Then Fabricus, said to be the most reliable in the city, informed me in a private audience that the quakes were a foretaste of bitter troubles to come—fire, hot stone, days of darkness, rivers of fire. I dismissed this at first as standard soothsayer fancy. But Fabricus informed me that the basis of his predictions was contained in volumes of ancient histories compiled by his ancestors over centuries. The earthquakes had come from Vesuvo hill, and a rain of fire and fiery rock would also come from those shallow slopes! He had found two ancient references to times when the placid old hillock had "opened up," to spew forth fiery rock and a sea of liquid mud. Old Fabricus accepted my additional money and showed me the texts. I have no reason to doubt his word that they are ten generations old. I was allowed to study them and spent a night with my tutor, Auricus, still clear-sighted at sixty-three years. He was able to translate them from the curious Greek.

Fabricus had not understood the full story. Perhaps he had been unable to decipher the Greek. The heart of the matter was in the account of a certain Antigon, a physician of hundreds of years ago, who had recorded the most astonishing phenomenon. In ancient times the entire verdant crown of Vesuvo hill had been lifted to the heavens and shattered into thousands of fiery rocks. Black ash had fallen for days. Tremors never stopped. One day the sun even failed to appear. Horses, cattle, goats, and people died. The terrible upheavals ended only when a river of molten stone and mud—fully seventy cubits wide—poured forth from the broken rim of Vesuvo, now a mountain, and descended to the sea!

I would have given scant credence to this if the account had not been written by so learned and observant a man, and had there been no traces of the event. A day after I had read the passages, I traveled with my superintendent from the top of Vesuvo to the sea. Since I knew what I was looking for, it was

*not difficult to see the old marks of a hardened river of stone
and mud. To my consternation, the river's path ran very close
to our palace. Later on, a study of the foundation walls of what
my forefathers had started as a modest country villa revealed
that the river of stone formed a part of the footings. Imagine!*

*What to do? I further consulted Fabricus and read J's
chronicles, but found no mention of an impending catastrophe.
Still, I had to wonder if soon that awesome prediction . . .*

With that puzzling phrase, the scroll was torn off, but the
fragment tended to confirm the theory that Quintus Tertullian
had constructed a system of land dams to protect his property
against something like the eruption of 79. What amazed me
was that he was such a sophisticated scientist. I found it astonishing that he had actually been able to track down the lava
flow. What had he been getting to when the parchment had
broken off? What had he meant by "J's chronicles"? Could this
have been Phryne's John?

"What we need is a Fabricus," Olivia said with a smile.

"We're on the very threshold of the ancient past. On the
very threshold!" I said. As an oracle might.

DON CICCIO

Andrew's joke about the threshold turned out to be prophetic. Shortly before five o'clock the next evening, the drill dipped suddenly forward and began to roar like a jet engine. The foreman shut the machine down just as it began churning into an orange-red material soft as chalk. From that moment on, the drill proved too powerful. It was easier to use pickaxes and shovels. How peaceful it was to sit by the side of the hole and listen to the soft sounds of the workers' picks.

But the work was slow even though the tufa was softer. We wanted to enlarge our hole now that no one was watching. We even used a little nitro. In the hands of an expert, which Stearns turned out to be, nitroglycerine can be used in such tiny quantities that one would think a skilled surgeon was at work. We used it at night under the supervision of Giovanni Puglisi, who had won the respect of the local workers, mine too, for his quiet leadership. During the most disappointing days, Giovanni had carried on the backbreaking labor, a one-man crew muscling heavy machines into place. When I was downcast, he would saunter over, thrust his sweat-streaked face close to mine, and growl, "If you continue to act as if the world were over, my men will do the same. We're close. There's something close —ten meters, say."

"What?"

"What you're looking, for, of course."

Within a week after starting through the orange-red tufa, Olivia saw it. Andrew recognized it. And I decided what to do about it. For starters I paid off the workers handsomely and except for Giovanni dismissed them all.

It was red, very red, like a slice of Chinese lacquer embedded into the tufa. Puglisi took a stainless-steel hand pick and worked along the sides of the object and underneath it until he had recovered it in three pieces.

It was a curved piece of red terra-cotta roof tile. Shortly after we had removed it, we found another, and then half a dozen more. Some were crushed. They must have been broken when the hot mud had surged across a roof. What roof?

Only hours after we found the tile, there was another remarkable event. A half a meter deeper, we discovered ten square feet of perfectly preserved roof tiles. We realized then we were standing on the roof of an ancient building that had been preserved in the mud-tufa for nearly two thousand years.

"What now?" Olivia asked. "Break through?"

"No. We find how big the roof is and enter through a window or door. Cassone would throw us out if we smashed through. And, for now, we don't tell a soul!" Andrew said. "Make the hole larger, work our way down gently. We must keep this a secret from the press."

"And from Cassone, too," I added. "Although not reporting it will be a violation of the permit."

"A technical violation," Andrew said.

We spent a week enlarging the hole and discovered something even more astonishing. We found the end of the tiles, which meant we had come to the edge of the sloping roof. Giovanni, my personal servant Arturo, and Andrew dug out around the supporting wall, and within hours they had penetrated some two meters down to the cobblestones of a street of ancient Herculaneum. Where were we? What would the building turn out to be? Could we get inside? The questions raced through our minds.

It couldn't have been a coincidence. Several days after we had made our way down to the cobblestones and had laid bare the pitted stucco of the side of the ancient building, I received an invitation from Enrico Dorsoduro asking me to join him at his villa to discuss "long-term goals of mutual benefit."

Enrico Dorsoduro, in his early seventies, tall and willowy, was a master at camouflage. His rustic villa in a thick grove of cedars near the summit of Vesuvius concealed a host of structures that obviously had little to do with a traditional "fattoria." Inside the farm buildings was a series of pillboxlike structures —armed, I'm sure. A battalion of workers and farmers milled around the central compound, which was protected by stout walls. One could hold off an army of carabinieri from the redoubt.

Dorsoduro looked like a gaunt version of that marvelous movie actor of the 1950s Vittorio De Sica. He had the same hollow cheeks, aquiline nose, and white mane. He, too, was genial and soft-spoken. Friendly. I was wary.

We met alone. He had insisted that Arturo excuse himself. Once seated in his study, its walls ablaze with ribbons won by his prize Arabian horses, Dorsoduro wasted no time.

"Fascinating, isn't it? Digging. You may have heard that I, too, am something of an archaeologist. My family has controlled property here, at the south end of Herculaneum, for generations, and we have also conducted private excavations. Have you discovered anything of note yet? No? I'm sure you will. It's a shame you had to become entangled with the government bureaucracy, although I suppose one has little choice. But it's too bad that you had to approach those Americans. I would have been so eager to have become your partner. Perhaps it will be possible to allow them to make a few initial discoveries and then we can proceed on our own. I can be of help. My men have great expertise. What kind of arrangement would you want?"

"None. It is in good hands."

"You mean you intend to do this . . . by the book?" He was taken aback.

"Absolutely."

"Nothing for yourself?"

"The pride of discovery and the widening of the boundaries of human knowledge is all I want," I answered piously.

"Are you saying no deal at all?"

"I regret I cannot."

"You are proud of your name and reputation, aren't you, Count Nerone?" His voice was harsh.

"Justly."

"The family name . . . Nerone . . . it's a pure one, no?"

"Yes, at least from the early sixteenth century."

"Not exactly."

I shrugged, indicating I was ready to leave. I had no interest in discussing my genealogy with Enrico Dorsoduro. But he stood up, came over to where I was sitting, and stared down at me coldly.

"Your illustrious name is pure, but not as pure as you believe," he muttered. "Have you ever heard of an Austrian general, von Richter, also known as Florian Graebenhaecker?"

"Never."

"Ah. Well then, let me tell you about him. He married into my family in the end of the eighteenth century, passing away under mysterious circumstances during an excavation at Herculaneum. His wife, Judith, bore two children by him, twins. One of the boys married into your family, Don Ciccio. So we are related. Your noble family is our own."

"Slander."

"Don't worry, I won't spread the word—for the moment."

"What exactly do you want?"

"To help you in your efforts. In any way you can think of. Whenever you wish."

"I don't need help."

"I've already helped you. How do you think you stumbled on those antique scrolls you've been deciphering?"

I struggled to stay calm.

"They were mine," he continued. "They've been in the

family for years. I had them sold to you by Bonfante, one of my men. I knew you could translate them with your clever machines."

"Absurd! You could have done it yourself!"

"No. I am a man who knows my limitations. Besides, why should I do all the work?"

"Since you are so free with speculations, let me balance it a bit with truth," I said. "I have in my possession a dossier on your archaeological and smuggling activities. It could bring a storm of indictments down on your head."

"Make it known." Dorsoduro smiled. "One word and you'll find you'll be ousted from your operation abruptly. I have the power. But think about how valuable my help will be. By the way, I have equipment that can slice into tufa like a knife through mozzarella. Understand, cousin?"

"I do understand. Clearly. When I need you I shall alert you. You'll know," I told him. He smiled thinly.

His men escorted me and Arturo out. All the way home I thought about what the old fox had said. Well, well, so the lowly Dorsoduros were related to the exalted Nerones. Through the General! So I had been tricked by Dorsoduro into buying the scrolls! A clever move. If I made him a partner, he was way ahead. If I spurned him, he would continue to track me, moving in when we found something. But that meant he would have to eliminate me. How? And how could I eliminate him? He had to go. I'd have to figure it out.

I gave my friends a somewhat edited version of the encounter.

"What if we do find something?" Andrew asked. "You really think Dorsoduro and his gang could dig all the way in from the south and enter?"

"He might have other ways. Perhaps he's allied with Cartageno. Remember, he's been at this business a lot longer than we have. Perhaps the idea of tunneling in is not so farfetched."

OUR anxieties over Dorsoduro were soon forgotten when we made an extraordinary discovery—an ancient wooden, bronze, and iron double door with great iron brackets and stout hinges and an enormous iron lock. It is thousands of years old and intact. It came to light about two meters down the stucco wall. The rugged portal is made up of nearly a dozen thick cedar planks. It is embellished with two massive bronze pulls in the shape of two roaring lion heads, velvety green with corrosion. God, what treasures will we find behind them?

We agonized over what to do next. Should we enter on our own, or must we alert Giulio Cassone and the antiquities authorities? At first we were all determined to go in straightaway. But the more we thought about it, the more we saw the risk. What if we did find the empty spaces that had been protected by Tertullian's great system of dams? If we were caught, we would be thrown out for all time. The fear of being detected forced us to go to Cassone and tell him that we had carried out a little more work than we had described in our reports. We figured he would be irked, but with the prospect of monumental finds, we thought he would soon forget the minor breach. Actually, he was quite ugly. He glowered in silence, but then startled us by telling us that he already knew. His spy had been more alert than we suspected. Cassone blustered about how we had "violated" our contract and trust by not alerting him "at the first instant" we had found the roof tile. What we had done was illegal, he said. We had dared to flout the rulings of the department. We had deceived the Prime Minister. How could he and his colleagues ever again trust us to maintain an "appro-priate and professional" record of our discoveries? What right had we to work "in a clandestine and secretive manner"?

Stearns blew up and told him to shut up or he'd have his friend the Prime Minister fire him. He pulled a copy of the permit from his pocket and insisted that we had acted within our rights. " 'Significant discovery,' " it says," he quoted. " 'Sig-nificant!' " That's when we have to alert you. Do you think a bunch of roof tiles and an old wooden door is 'significant'? Well, I don't. It was a judgment call. When things were in order I called you. Okay?"

"You Americans think you own this property. You think you own our head of state. And our country. Try getting me dismissed. I'll throw *you* out of this country."

"A commie! Christ, we've got a *commie!*" Stearns mum-bled. But, thank God, Cassone hadn't heard him.

WE had to delay the opening of the portal for a week; the area had to be enlarged to allow room for the television and film crews. During the time-out, Al Stearns was filmed chatting with hosts of political, cultural, and scientific celebrities in front of what he was already calling "my door." By the end of the week virtually the entire world knew something about Herculaneum and that door.

Finally we were ready to see what lay beyond.

Conservators, supplied by Cassone, skilled in picking an-cient locks, worked in the glare of the television lights, fussing for the greater part of an hour before telling us the lock could be opened. But before we could enter, another hour passed as scores of television crews lined up for close-up shots of the lock as it was unlocked. Another hour went by as the cameras—I counted fifty-four crews—were repositioned for long shots of the opening of the double door.

Stearns and Cassone occupied the stations of honor closest to the portal. Just behind them stood Andrew and Olivia, and behind them were Giovanni Puglisi and two of his men. It had been decided that the excavators would have the first glance at the interior of the chamber without any television lights. When they were ready to reveal to the world what they had found, the spotlights would slowly and dramatically come on. One camera had been designated to film the event.

The scene could not have been more dramatic—near darkness illuminated by two small lamps held by Stearns and Cassone. Silence broken only by nervous rustling and coughs. Cassone took hold of one of the lion handles and pulled gently. After the slightest hesitation, the door moved easily. The ancient hinges crackled like dry leaves. Was there emptiness? Yes, there was. Then Stearns took hold of the second lion and pulled the second door open. What now? Stygian blackness! Or so it seemed. Good! Together Cassone and Stearns moved forward with their lamps to illuminate the interior. They never made it.

What triggered the riot we'll never know. But every spotlight in the area was ignited at the same time. The camera crews and correspondents rushed forward to catch sight of what lay behind the doors. People stumbled, and some fell. Fists began to swing. The excavators were squashed against the door. The rush was halted only by the physical power of Giovanni and the bellowings of Al Stearns. Cassone threw himself at the first wave of reporters and pushed several to the ground before those following close behind halted. Stearns howled a string of curse words at the mob in surprisingly good Italian. The mob stood glaring at the team.

"So, for Chrissakes, what the hell's inside?" someone shouted.

Only then were Cassone and Stearns able to turn back to the portal and peer inside.

What did they see? Not emptiness. Inside the doors there was a barrier of mottled stone. When he saw it, Stearns began to pound at it with his fists. Giovanni dropped in defeat to one knee. Andrew and Olivia fell into each other's arms.

Much as I wished to have Arturo carry me there, I held back. A closer look would have exposed me to the reporters, who were already barking questions at the confused members of the team. Olivia appointed herself spokesman.

"Hey, professor, this means that the hot mud got in, right?"

"Sadly, it would appear so, yes."

"And solidified?"

"It would seem so."

"You mean these dams didn't work?"

"Apparently not."

"How much money have you people sunk into this operation?"

"A great deal."

"As experts, do you think you've been stymied?"

"For the moment."

"How do you feel?"

"Crushed."

"Is there absolutely no way of cutting or boring or grinding the stuff away to see if the room has anything inside?"

"It would take years."

"What's next? Abandon the work?"

"There would seem to be no other course of action."

"Can we have a statement?"

"We are, I'd say, proud—I want to emphasize that—proud and fulfilled, too, to have come so far. I believe I can speak for the whole group in saying that none of us has any regret. The work was arduous. The chances were always slim. We all knew that. It's simply..." Olivia fought to keep her composure. "It is not so easy to be confronted with such disappointment."

"Would you characterize this blank wall as a total failure?"

"Well..."

It was Andrew who answered. "The answer is yes, it's a total failure. There's nothing more to be done here. We obviously cannot hack or grind our way through that stuff and won't try. We have found the door of an ancient building, now a tomb, one that will be sealed forever."

We received condolences from all over the world. Archaeologists from important institutions sent their sympathies. Governments dispatched letters praising the excavators for their attempts and commiserating over the demise of the project. But not everyone was so polite. There were editorials mocking our efforts, calling the project "archaeological hype," "fraud," and "hapless, silly waste." There was no word from the Prime Minister. My sources informed me that he was delighted at our embarrassment.

Al Stearns, grimly philosophical about "another dry hole," left for Rome the next day, after having withdrawn all his funds from the bank.

Andrew, Olivia, and I, left on our own, were faced with the depressing job of cleaning up the site, filling it, and closing it down forever. The costs turned out to be far more than I had figured. Faced with the depressing financial news, Al Stearns proved less than stalwart. He sent me a telegram telling me his lawyers would be in touch to discuss "the proper payments in light of the failure of the operation."

IT was many nights before I could sleep very much at all. When I finally did, I dreamed that Giovanni Puglisi's craggy triangular face, flanked by Andrew's and Olivia's, was taunting me.

"Wake up, Don Ciccio," I heard Olivia whispering. "Giovanni has found something you must see. Now."

I awoke with a start. There they were, the three of them. Giovanni's face was impassive.

"What?"

"You've got to come with us."

"For God's sake, where?"

"To the door."

"What time is it?" I protested. "Call Arturo."

"I'll carry you," Andrew murmured.

"Whatever for?"

"This you must see only with us."

I hesitated.

"Do as we say," Andrew commanded, and I let him have his way. They helped me into my excavation coveralls and a down jacket, and Andrew swept me up in his arms. We drove to the dig and descended to the level of the cobbled street. Seeing the open doorway and that barrier of hardened mud filled me with sadness. What kind of torture was this? "This is futile!" I cried out.

"Giovanni, show Don Ciccio what you think you found," Olivia said calmly.

"Excellency, after everyone left, I stayed behind," he said.

"I looked more closely at that wall. There is something about it. Different than the hard lava. . . ."

He grabbed a pick, walked over to the portal, and aimed a fierce blow at the hardened mud. The pick recoiled as if thrown back by a charge of dynamite. Giovanni gazed at me placidly. What was I supposed to think? I was still too foggy with sleep to comprehend.

Shrugging, he once again slammed the pick against the hardened mud. This time a chunk about the size of his fist fell to the cobblestones. For a second I was still confused, then it dawned upon me what it had to be. "Carry me over to the doors. Quickly!"

As he held me up I examined every centimeter of the surface of the mud. There was something curious about it. Unlike normal tufa, which was filled with stones of random sizes and shapes, this tufa was full of chips almost the same size.

"Take a look at the bottom," Olivia said.

Only then did I realize, and I gasped.

"That's what we think, too," Andrew said.

"Is it concrete?" I asked in astonishment. "Is it Roman concrete with an aggregate of chipped stones just as you see throughout Pompeii?"

"We think so," Andrew said.

"Which must mean that Tertullian filled an outer section of the palace—presuming this is the palace—with concrete as further protection."

"That's what I think," Andrew exclaimed. "This door is in a structure that's only one story high. That's hardly the height of a private palace. But it is fine for the storerooms and shops that most often surrounded even grand houses. I figure that Tertullian dumped a load of cement in these shops."

"What next?"

"Either blast through the stuff, which I think would be stupid, since it would attract a lot of attention, or dig out more of the roof and find out if there's another wall higher up. Then enter there. One thing has always troubled me about this street we found. It's much too far below the modern surface. My guess is that the larger Tertullian complex stands there to the east, adjacent to this. It must be at least three levels high."

"Foolishness!" Giovanni cried out suddenly. "Do it my way! Andrew and Arturo will help me . . ."

"Do what?" Olivia asked.

"Dig out a tunnel down there!" He pointed. "Through there. It will be hidden. We shall go in there, through the stucco wall, through the concrete, until we enter this building."

"Do you think you can get in? How long will it take?"

"Not long. I shall do it."

"This is getting crazy," Olivia murmured. "What about Cassone? Or Al? Or spies?"

"Plenty of time to tell them," I assured her. "Al cut out. Why suffer through another embarrassment? Let's let Giovanni, Arturo, and Andrew make a probe. If we find the place filled with dried mud after all, we can close down forever. If we do find something, then we can decide what to do."

"No one will ever know," Giovanni said. "My tunnel will be easy to disguise. I will kill the spies."

And so Giovanni, Arturo, and Andrew began to carve out our own private tunnel through the tufa. And it proved to be surprisingly easy to make. Only two days of chopping away.

The stout Roman concrete has been another matter. It started flinty, made up of compact stone chips, but then turned into mortar embedded with large rocks. To remove the rocks, they have to pry them out with crowbars. We desperately want to use pneumatic drills, but are afraid they'd attract attention. I want to avoid tipping off Antonio Cartageno. As the days pass we despair of ever coming to the end of the concrete. The farther we penetrate, the larger the stones become. Andrew and the others work hour after hour, paying dearly for each inch of progress. Often it takes hours to loosen, jimmy, wriggle, and free a single stone. At times, the three men seem to move in trance.

A WEEK after we had started the tunnel, I was interrupted by the buzz of the intercom. It was Andrew.

"Come quickly. We've found another door, and what a door! And we've punched through . . ."

"And?"

He said nothing.

"For God's sake, tell me!" I commanded.

"Arturo will bring you."

Never in my wildest imaginings could I have predicted what they had found. As I hung on to his neck, Arturo scrambled down the low, narrow tunnel and entered a makeshift antechamber which Andrew and Giovanni had hacked out of the concrete fill. At the end of this space was an enormous black hole. Andrew motioned us to enter. They had set up a series of floodlights but had not yet lit them.

"Where are we?"

"It appears that a sort of corridor separated the shops from the villa. We are standing in front of a wall faced in marble and . . ."

Arturo put me down gently. The floodlights were illuminated. Directly in front of me six feet away, set into a wall made of rectangular buff marble blocks, was one of the most beautiful portals I had ever seen. Far from the rude doorway we first encountered, this one is a delicate piece of architecture with a sculptured entablature and a pair of harmonious scrolls at each end. Two graceful Ionic pilasters flank the portal. There are two doors, each sheathed with silver plates. On the plates set into the four corners are hippocamps in heavily gilded silver. The doors are barred by two pieces of thin rope with the end of each fastened to a gold ring on the inner frame of each door. At the center where the ropes are knotted together is a large lump of red wax with letters surrounding another hippocamp device. I took the wax into my hands and read what was written on the seal: "Quintus Maximianus Tertullian."

Before anybody could say a word I took a small knife from my pocket, cut the rope, and pushed the door open. Boldly I entered. I will never forget the aroma. It was, surprisingly, of pungent leather! Rich, heady leather. The longer I stood there, the more powerful the odor became. It was sweet, thick, so pervasive that I swore my mind was being affected by it—and, of course, it was.

"Quick, a flashlight," I rasped. Arturo placed the light in my hand. When I turned it on, I gasped.

"What can you see?" Olivia asked tensely.

" 'Wonderful things,' " I said with a laugh, echoing Howard Carter's first words at the discovery of Tut's tomb. "Do come in."

"Right away!"

A stillness. A quiet. An uncanny feeling of peace. These were the feelings that came over me as the others stepped into the void, circling the chamber in which we found ourselves with their lights.

Arturo fetched my wheelchair and set it down on a floor

made of earth pounded perfectly flat. Although there wasn't a hint of anything threatening, Olivia and I instinctively drew close. It wasn't fear—that would come later—it was a feeling of awe, awe that we were standing where no human being had been for over two thousand years, a place suspended in time. We were overwhelmed by a sense of expectancy. I imagined the sounds that accompany the beginnings of a new day—bells clanging, the thud of clay pots in the kitchen, the rustling of brooms, the whinnying of horses, the commands of foremen. Every object looked as if it had been left carefully in its place only minutes, not thousands of years, before.

"It's as if there was a fire drill all that time ago . . . and no one returned. It's perfect!" Olivia murmured.

What we saw stacked before us was familiarly domestic, yet so amazing that tears came to my eyes.

Hundreds of objects and utensils are neatly arrayed in the large chamber, which is about fifteen by forty feet in size. We were in what is apparently a tack room—not unlike one you might encounter in a stately English country home. The only difference is that it dates to the time of Christ! We saw dozens, hundreds, of objects and implements, beautifully crafted and tooled saddles, bridles and harnesses, straps, fittings, wooden forms, lengths of shining bronze, silver, and gold, studs, rivets, and tools. What incredible tools! My God, I thought, were we in that stable I had read about in the scrolls?

It was a long time before any of us could say a word or begin to carry out the precise plans we had made in the event of such a discovery. Andrew had brought along a videotape camera with a sophisticated measuring device which can calculate the measurements of any interior, any object, and the distance between each object. These tapes can be fed into my computer. We had also prepared a conservation kit, worrying that the objects would begin to decay rapidly once exposed to today's atmosphere. (That fear will almost certainly prove groundless. From the first minutes of our entrance and from then on, it has been obvious that no object, artifact, or work of art has deteriorated in any way; everything should be as durable now as it was then.)

I should not give the impression that we acted as unemotional technicians, plodding through a chamber of miracles the likes of which the world had never seen. We remained in something of a state of shock as Andrew videotaped the room and its contents. Then we all went berserk, shouting and embracing. At last we gathered ourselves, and began to think rationally.

Olivia and Andrew scouted the contents of the three long tables on the far side of the rectangular room.

"A workbench. For the chief craftsman," Andrew called out.

"What he was working on when he left is unbelievable!" Olivia added. "Come, look at this!"

It was a large harness and bridle, over three feet high. Although unfinished, it is a masterpiece. The leather elements are magnificently tooled and inlaid in silver with rosettes and images of horses galloping.

"I've found something," Andrew shouted.

I raced my wheelchair down the aisle. There on a wooden armature was a chunk of buttery-yellow gold—it must be half an inch thick—inlaid with purple enamel which flickered in the light of my head lamp. The enamel is formed in the shape of the hippocamp. This harness and bridle have to have been intended for very special functions. The leather itself is thin, pliable, polished to a patent-leather finish, and embellished with alternating gold and silver decorations depicting colts.

Sitting on the table near the harness was an eight-inch-tall carving of a horse's head in ivory. Obviously it was made to be mounted on top of the bridle-headdress itself. The horse's head is thrown back, the nostrils flare wildly, the billowing mane is thrust upward in a spray carved out of the thinnest ivory strands. The wide eyes are subtly edged with delicate accents of inlaid ebony.

"Look here!" Andrew announced when he held it. "It's signed."

There on the lower left part of the sinewy neck we saw the Latin words *Capretius me fecit,* meaning "Capretius made me."

"Wait till you see this!" Olivia called. She had wandered off down the long table and was coming back holding something in both hands.

It was another solid hunk of gold, beaten and incised into a Gorgon's head. The writhing snakes surrounding the grimacing face with dead eyes seemed to be shuddering in the agony of death. Their skins were fashioned out of a translucent black enamel. The eyes of the thing are rubies, garnets, sapphires, tourmalines, or jagged pieces of rock crystal.

We were even more impressed with the workaday implements strewn about the room. Capretius' tools, laid out neatly on the table, are made of polished bronze, steel, and bone. Their ivory and dark-wood handles are of truly fine workmanship. Capretius' fingerprint is clearly visible on one scalpel-like knife, so fresh that the artist might have laid the tool aside only moments before. Life crackles from these everyday objects like electrical charges.

We came across dozens of mundane harnesses, each with its own Roman numeral branded into the leather, and hosts of wooden saddles. Yet, according to historical "fact," the saddle was not invented until the early Middle Ages.

We remained in the tack room for hours having the experience of our lives. The more we found and marveled at, the greater was the temptation to dash pell-mell into other chambers. The abundance didn't slake our appetites. It made us ravenous.

Our surroundings were pristine. Everything seemed fresh and whitewashed. What we first thought were dirt floors are in fact wooden, covered with a thin layer of beaten mud mixed with grain fibers. They are comfortable underfoot and, no doubt, cool in the summer. At first we didn't notice the walls— I think we can be excused for that. From a point about a foot above the level of the tables to the ceiling, they are painted with lively patterns in green, vermilion, and cerulean, depicting stars, rosettes, and triangles within triangles interspersed with garlands. To me, this was the biggest surprise. The ornamentation is profuse and vivid, quite unlike our stereotypical notions of classical restraint.

The wooden and iron furniture is fascinating. Few pieces of ancient Roman furniture have survived. Despite being entirely utilitarian, this furniture also carries lavish decoration. The six-foot-long benches have low backboards carved into a variety of vegetable shapes, and the short legs of low stools have been worked into elegant fluted columns.

When we ventured through the portal at the end of the tack room, we found ourselves in a corridor with a barrel-vaulted ceiling some twenty feet high. The corridor has a host of doors. The first room is large and square and is divided down the center by a row of fifteen stout stone columns painted lurid crimson. Along each long wall—approximately sixty feet—are storage cubicles, six on each side. The entrance to each is shrouded by a linen curtain. Inside we found a melange of machinery—blocks and tackles, wooden presses, sluice boxes, sieves, levers and fulcrums, bellows, screw-jacks, wooden pallets with iron runners, and measuring devices, each item meticulously carved. Nothing like this has ever been discovered before.

Imagine getting excited about a laundry! But if it's two thousand years old, why not? It is huge—fifty by thirty feet with enormous copper vats, tables for pounding the clothes, channels in the floor for drainage, and even bars of yellow-gray soap which smell like cedar and charcoal. There are piles of clothing of all kinds, cotton shirts, shorts, and trousers.

Suddenly I noticed what seemed to be a ghost walking toward us from the dark. Olivia shrieked. It was a man wearing a shirt, leggings, and a pair of shorts. It was not, of course, some ancient brought back to life; Andrew had dressed up in Roman clothes.

"You bastard, you scared me to death!" Olivia lashed out at him. "You make it seem . . . trivial!"

We were exhausted. We had been in the palace almost the entire night. As we headed back to our entrance tunnel, Olivia spotted something beneath the workbench near the bridle and parade halter, a small parchment book held together with two silk thongs. It was a sketchbook in silverpoint with a series of drawings. On one page is a study for the ivory horse head, and several sketches, clearly from life, of snakes' heads. On another page we found an amusing caricature: a bearded, middle-aged man squinting at a piece of parchment held tightly in his two hands, obviously an artist examining a student's work. Capretius, of course. On the last page is a quick sketch of the torso and head of a man in his mid-thirties wearing a toga and a laurel wreath.

"Tertullian, I'll bet," Olivia exclaimed. "What kind of man was he, I wonder."

We left just as we were about to collapse from exertion and emotions.

I AWOKE the next afternoon completely refreshed, eager for another night's work. Andrew and Olivia joined me in my private rooms for supper. What were we to do now? I asked them. Alert the authorities?

"Hell no. Let's go in alone as long as we can," Andrew insisted. "You know they're going to take the whole project away from us sooner or later. Let's have the palace to ourselves for one complete run-through and get it all down on videotape. Then, when we're ready, we can turn the place over to Giulio Cassone or the Prime Minister himself. For our brilliance and labor I want something for myself!"

"What about Stearns?" Olivia asked.

"Let's decide when we see what else we find!"

"I can go along with that," Olivia agreed.

Of course, I went along with that.

How many chambers will we find? Hundreds? Quite possible, if one believed Pliny's description. What stunned me those first few days was the realization that we had come in through what I supposed to be the servants' quarters! What will we encounter when we reach the quarters of the lord and his lady? Have the dams and bulwarks protected their rooms?

We all find it almost impossible to grasp the flawless condition of the objects, especially since we are all accustomed to seeing nothing but fragments from antiquity, marbles with broken arms and noses, bronzes caked with corrosion or silver tarnished a blackish-purple, wall paintings cracked and pitted with age.

We know we have embarked upon the most exciting and dangerous journey any archaeologist has ever made. It is like ascending a mist-shrouded magical mountain, encountering surprise after surprise. It would be impossible to describe anything more than the highlights of what we have found so far.

In the car driving back to the villa at the end of that incomparable first night, the shock of what we have actually done hit us. We became giddy, as if we had drunk a bottle of champagne apiece. In the midst of the merriment, which was punctuated by loud whoops from Andrew, Olivia, who had gotten quiet, suddenly spoke out. "I have this feeling all of a sudden," she said, looking like an ancient oracle, "that this place is going to become our curse."

"Baby, you've seen too many movies," Andrew said, throwing his arms around her. But she never really got back into the celebratory spirit that night.

On the second evening, the palace seemed far more alive. The fresh air filtering in from our tunnel lightened the atmosphere, and the battery of portable lights and headlamps we brought down eliminated the tomblike feeling. Olivia had been fearful we might encounter some skeletons. But why would we? Everyone escaped—they must have perished outside.

After that we didn't exhaust ourselves by staying all night. We would come just after dusk and stay until midnight. Then we'd have a champagne supper to celebrate the "find of the day." Sometimes that find was something silly, like brooms.

It might seem that a storeroom filled with hundreds of common wooden and straw brooms could not come near the experience of finding a parade harness with gold and ivory trappings, but it was. Imagine a slender, smooth, well-worn handle, darkened by handling, carved with a Roman numeral and a capital letter, plunging into a bed of wiry cut straw slightly longer on one side. Somehow the ordinary things sang out a hymn extolling the infinite creativity and durability of all humanity.

Imagine how it was to be wheeled through a portal into the darkness, holding your breath in expectancy, leaning forward excitedly as the lamps went on and seeing parked in front of you five grandiose chariots including one eight feet tall entirely covered with gold plates! And what gold! No mere veneer these panels. There are over two hundred of them, each an eighth of an inch thick, each having repoussé scenes from a hunt, scenes of tigers, lions, deer gazelles, and wild boars. The hunters are having the time of their lives, shouting with joy at the thrill of the adventure.

There are all types—even a pair of buffoons. The most entertaining is a dandy, looking like a popinjay in an outlandish leather hunting costume covered with hundreds of feathers. Trying to cope with his oversized bow and arrow, he has managed to tie himself up in knots. His feet are tangled in the reins. The horses have bolted, so the fop is being catapulted out of the chariot, feathers flying, hair streaming, wearing a comical look of outrage and astonishment.

What struck me was not only the sophisticated style of the beaten and chased gold panels, but the sensitive treatment of the subject matter. The hunted animals are not being butchered en masse. They are shown as more than equal matches for their hunters. Some of the more clever ones have even escaped. Others, having fought with singular bravery, are being allowed to go free. No matter how well the hunters perform, this hunt is for one hunter alone. He seems to be everywhere at once, forcing his chariot to go faster than any of the others, making record-book shots, instructing the others where to place traps and nets. The man is youthful and handsome, identical to the man in the silverpoint drawing we found in the notebook of Capretius' apprentice. His armor bears the distinctive hippo-camp crest. It has to be Quintus Tertullian.

His "state" chariot is a true wonder, imbued with a sense of festival and pomp. It looks as if it were moving even when still. The oak frame is sleek and practical. The wheels, about a meter high, are sheathed by polished steel and inlaid with brass decorations.

The rest of the chariots are lightweight, crafted from thin wooden pieces pegged or held together by a series of clever hinges. Every part is sealed with pitch and wrapped tightly with twine soaked in resin and overlaid with silver wire. The technology of the wood-and-gut springs is highly advanced. When Andrew climbed into one of them we expected it to bend under his weight. But it didn't so much as creak.

Near the "garage" is a blacksmith's shop, where we found a heap of ashes and burned-out coke in the smelting hearths and a pair of pincers and two hammers obviously thrown aside in a hurry. This was the first sign we saw that the warning to leave the palace must have been sudden. One of the more singular sights in the smithy is a ten-foot-high bellows with the leather intact. When Andrew stepped lightly upon the floor pedals, the bellows wheezed and a rush of air made the millennia-old ashes blow into the air.

We found a series of cubicles with terra-cotta and stone jars containing enough foodstuffs for a small army. Here are grain, wheat, barley, and a crude brownish flour that tastes bittersweet and curiously like citrus. There are also jars for wine —hundreds of them—containing nothing but a pasty blackish-red residue. Giovanni warmed up some water and poured it in.

Olivia tasted some and pronounced it too sugary. On one of the four-foot jars is written the word "Falernum" and the date of the vintage. We calculated the year to be A.D. 68.

The longer we stayed underground in the dream world of antiquity, the farther we penetrated into the labyrinth of rarities, the more we seemed to become a part of that timeless environment. Surrounded by the ancient objects, hypnotized by them, addicted to the excitement of never knowing what would appear through the next door, behind the next curtain, or around the next corner, we became the masters and slaves of the place. Our discipline faltered. We began to wander alone through the seemingly unending series of rooms. Andrew or Olivia always managed to videotape the contents, but the exploration gradually became less and less organized. I holed up in the workroom of the palace locksmith, tinkering with his tools and fiddling with the keys and broken or half-assembled locks sitting on the workbench. I have to admit to being rather seduced by them.

Andrew and Olivia said they felt possessed by the place and its memories. We started to slow down, to accommodate, I suppose, the pace of life of two thousand years past.

I don't remember who can be accused of doing it first. Soon we fell into the habit of taking a small object or work of art when we left at midnight. Whatever it was, we always returned it, or almost always. We didn't consider it stealing. It was, more accurately, a sort of temporary loan for the purpose of closer inspection. I wanted to see how the ancient things would look in the modern world. The first object I took out was a handsome ebony-and-ivory gaming table inlaid with gold strips. The game is equipped with playing pieces of silver and turquoise in the shapes of animals, four solid gold dice, and a pair of throwing cups made out of rock crystal cut so thin they almost seem invisible. I kept it for a week and then returned it, keeping a turquoise cat. Who would miss it? I never did manage to figure out how to play the game. Who else would?

As we found chamber after chamber off the vaulted corridor, we realized that the palace is much larger than we had imagined. There is a second corridor, similar to the first, with its own chain of rooms, and then two more alleys with shops and storerooms, some filled with concrete like the first one we encountered. The first or ground floor turns out to be an enormous rectangle measuring some three hundred by four hundred feet, honeycombed with passages, closets, rooms, and cubicles. Naturally there is an armory with neat stacks of swords, daggers, spears, greaves, breastplates, and helmets in bronze and even steel. Since I'd first started to read Caesar's exploits in Gaul at the age of ten, I'd dreamed of holding a Roman short sword in my hands. I'd longed to feel the heft and weight of the weapon that had literally conquered the known world. When I plucked one from its rack and touched it, closing my fist around it, I felt I was reaching into time. It weighed no more than two pounds. What an exceptional design. Despite its heavy appearance, it was so balanced it seemed featherweight. No wonder the Roman infantryman could stand for hours poking that short sword ahead of him.

The armory also contains a spacious hall, filled with tables and benches, which looks like a clubhouse. Hanging from pegs on the walls are different types and sizes of crossbow. Some measure more than six feet across—siege bows, most likely. Others are small, portable models, made either for the hunt or for reconnaissance patrols. Straw baskets filled with iron and bronze bolts are arranged against the walls.

Adjacent we found a shooting gallery, about eight feet wide, with several dozen small windows now sealed off. The gallery is about seventy-five feet long. At the end stands a target with a man painted on it. Andrew found some small crossbows on which the gut looked strong and pliable, and they worked. By God if he didn't even hit the target.

We each acquired our favorite section. Mine changed each day, though at the beginning it was a medical clinic with three wooden operating tables fitted out with basins. Bleeding must have been in vogue. I was astonished to see a host of glass bottles set on small coal burners or on lamps with long wicks obviously made for sterilization of the surgical instruments—scalpels, small saws, tweezers, and needles.

I found rows of glass vials filled with alcohol. Who would have suspected that Roman physicians used disinfectant? On shelves lining the walls I saw jar after jar of medicines, principally dried herbs, carefully labeled according to variety and use. The walls of the clinic are decorated with a series of frescoes in white set against a dark red background showing the anatomy of male and female bodies, clearly based upon actual dissections.

The kitchens are gloomy caverns, black holes with little light or ventilation, cluttered with dozens of braziers and iron pans that look like oversized woks. Beneath the kitchens we found half a dozen grim dungeon cells with nothing on the floors except some straw, not a chair or pallet in sight. Three meters below this level Andrew came across a series of furnaces with ducts for heating air and water. The fuel, peat and wood, is stacked in tunnels that once must have been filled from the street level.

In a storeroom leading out into the street, we made a discovery which would have made Louis XV jump with joy— luxurious sedan chairs. They are as grand as anything that master of the cluttered Jean Henri Riesener would have designed. These stout, pompous limos were embellished by craftsmen who had graduated from the *horror vacui* school of embellishment. We had a good laugh over them.

Every centimeter of their exteriors is carved or painted with every imaginable detail from the classical repertory—bead and reel, egg and dart, dentiled entablatures, colonnettes and columns. Ionic, Doric, and Corinthian applied capitals are used lavishly. For some inexplicable reason the decorative plan, when it isn't simply a catalogue of stray architectonic details or hybrids, revolves around sea creatures—dolphins, sharks, eels, crustaceans of myriad variety, snails, crabs, periwinkles, and phalanxes of amusingly theatric hippocamps strutting their stuff with webbed feet pawing the air. Top hats and canes wouldn't have surprised me.

The interiors are equally ludicrous, with exaggeratedly puffed leather upholstery stained hideous colors in frightful combinations—cerulean next to pink, cream side by side with a faux tortoiseshell. One "limo" is painted a mustard orange, and its hippocamp crest is purple, of course. Another, covered with a latticework of polished brass, twinkled in our lights like a Las Vegas neon sign in eye-popping madder with its double hippocamp crest slathered in lemon yellow. The garish opulence of the Tertullian transportation equipment made us wonder slightly about this oh so artistic lord's level of taste.

"If the scholarly world caught sight of this junk," Andrew burst out, "they'd want to get rid of the evidence. Wouldn't it be fun to take one of these limos out of the palace and offer it to a dealer in antiquities? He'd think it was something from a Mardi Gras."

Despite their vulgarity, the sedan chairs are obviously the latest models. Their windows have wooden panels that can actually be wound up and down—something more advanced than such equipment in Model T Fords—and are adorned with small square panels of remarkably clear mica for spying on passersby. In Limo One, as Olivia dubbed the orange one, we found a vanity case on the backseat containing an ivory comb and a silver hairbrush, both decorated with bands of putti flying through the air.

The Tertullians must have spent every night out on the town. One room contains a number of torches, every one of them new, most six to ten feet tall. They look like something out of a Jean Cocteau film, for the baskets on top of the poles have been fashioned into all sorts of fanciful, surreal shapes—fishnets, crinkled acanthus leaves, bunches of berries, naked arms raised in the air in salutes, and alternating grinning and frowning satyrs.

Then, all of a sudden, we felt a tremor. It was nothing as dramatic as Quintus had experienced, no soft swaying that built to a crescendo. I barely noticed it at first. I thought perhaps I was a little shaky. But then I saw Andrew's startled face, and somewhat to my puzzlement, he leaped to grab Olivia and pull her to the ground. Then I heard two muffled cracks followed by a shimmying or shivering that lasted a good ten seconds. I waited for the dust. Nothing. I gazed up to see if any of the objects were jiggling. None of that. The quake seemed almost supernatural, a sinister phenomenon unrelated to our surroundings, a message sent to our souls. Since then I have never entered the palace without a small moment of dread.

Olivia clung to Andrew, and for the next few days she had nightmares about being trapped underground, buried alive in this "paradise" of treasures. She seemed to expect some sort of disaster, some punishment for our disturbing of the past.

I took the precaution of fitting us with portable sensors of the type miners use to detect tremors and more serious distur-

bances. These along with Andrew's powers of persuasion induced Olivia to return to the world below.

A FEW days after the tremors, we exhausted the service areas.
We climbed the circular staircase two flights up to the next level
and into an immense central hall. Its vaulted ceiling rose some
forty feet over our heads. Our first clear view of it by a set of
klieg lights made us gasp. The entire vast surface of the vault,
a hundred feet long and forty wide, is covered by mosaic. The
figural array that floated above us, captured in glinting tesserae
as numerous as the stars in the Milky Way, is amazing. A mere
ten square feet of this mosaic would be considered one of the
singular art discoveries of the century.

The theme is abundance—pure, untrammeled, bursting
abundance—of flocks, crops, vines, the fruits of the sea, human
beings, and gods. Four heroic-sized figures blaze across the
immense stage, each symbolizing a fecund harvest. Neptune,
surrounded by a regiment of sea sprites and water nymphs,
brandishes his trident at the far right. His purple-red beard
crests like a tidal wave; his wide-open arms beckon his subjects
to gather around him. From fingertip to fingertip, the distance
between his massive arms must be more than twenty feet. Every
detail of his anatomy has been rendered meticulously. Rubens
could not have portrayed the sea god in a more flamboyant
manner. The workmanship of the thousands of stone tesserae is
fine enough for an oil painting. The myriad sea creatures, sped
by a tempest, surge forth from the foamy water and up into the
air to surround the giant god like comets orbiting the sun.

Beside Neptune, Ceres, goddess of the crops, springs forth

from the bowels of the earth, arms upraised in the triumph of rebirth. Her expression suggests complete carnal pleasure. What is especially striking about the artistry of this mosaic is that even from the floor one can see every splendid detail! The colors are a bit garish—a spectrum of green and yellow tinged with violets for the fish scales, brunette seaweed that seemed made of velvet, and silver wings on flying fish so translucent you could make out the sea spume through them. I could even see dozens of "painted" scallop shells on the shaft of Neptune's trident.

The third figure at center stage is Bacchus, bulbous, pink, dripping with vines, splashed with red wine. Stinking drunk, he is supported by four nut-brown satyrs with grotesque grins pasted on their goaty faces. Behind the tottering group is a waltzing orgy. A host of voluptuous girls cavort with a gang of satyrs who have thrown them to the ground. The daisy chain is inventive and vivacious!

We couldn't identify the fourth character—a female wrapped in a diaphanous white gown which reveals every part of her body. A nymph perhaps, or a minor goddess in the Roman pantheon; her very stillness, compared to the others' frenetic activity, makes her all the more impressive and dignified. Yet even she pales compared to her chattels. I admire, perhaps too much, the animal painters of the baroque period, such as Snyders, Rosa di Tivoli, and Baratta. I collect their works when I find choice examples. None, absolutely none I possess, comes close to the creatures depicted in the mosaic.

I counted over two hundred creatures and at least four dozen different plants, flowers, and trees. This mosaic is far more than mere decoration, it is an encyclopedia of what I suspect was much of the known flora and fauna in this region of ancient southern Italy. Not only is the entire hall ceiling covered with the glistening stone tesserae, mosaics cover the arches and their pilasters. The twenty-four arches on the long side of the room and the twelve on the ends are completely covered with tesserae of flaming reds, bright yellows, and some subtle rusts. Under one's feet the mosaic becomes gardens and vineyards with small orange and lemon trees, miniature palms, dwarf cedars, shrubs of a hundred varieties, ripened flowers, and tangles of thorns—all rendered with the most exceptional realism.

So clever is the simulation that we became slightly dizzy trying to figure out what was mosaic and what was real. Perhaps I exaggerate, but at a distance I could have sworn the floor was three-dimensional. When we drew near, the impression became an abstract series of colored patterns, a Persian carpet. I have never experienced anything like it before.

OLIVIA

Am I dreaming? No dream could be as troublesome and blissful. I'm worried about keeping this secret. What we are planning may lead to serious entanglements. Not that we should tell the authorities, but I'm scared we'll be caught. And afraid there will be another earthquake.

Each of us sees this place differently. For Don Ciccio it is a treasure of art. Andrew loves the machinery and the documents. I am haunted by what is not there, anything human. I've sometimes had the feeling that around the next corner, through the next closed door, someone will be watching and waiting.

Last night we found ourselves in a mosaic-floored courtyard which is surrounded by four aisles and dozens of small rooms, cubicles, really, which made me think they were living quarters for the freedmen and a few elderly slaves. Andrew and Don Ciccio admired the mosaics, and I gathered my courage and went exploring. I had to make myself push open each wooden door. I felt like a sneak thief, a feeling I never got over inside the palace. Casting my light around, I hoped I wouldn't encounter anything awful and didn't even pretend I was investigating carefully. I didn't take out my videocamera to make notes. Taking pictures seemed like another theft.

I can't remember how many rooms I entered. One was crammed with tables, their tops cluttered with scrolls and codices bound in rough deerskin. It must have been a scholar's room. There was a writing desk on the wall opposite the entry, its surface covered with bronze and clay oil lamps. A single scroll stretched across one of the tables, and three quill pens were thrown casually on it. They had handles of ivory and ebony strips fastened by thin gold bands, and each was neatly inscribed "Stephanus."

The scroll is decorated with a beautiful drawing of a riotous procession through the streets of a Roman town—Herculaneum. Scores of people dance through the streets. Hundreds line the thoroughfares. Banners are hoisted in the air, some painted with grotesque and amusing creatures: baleful donkeys, grinning tigers, an elephant with a giant head and a tiny trunk.

I grasped the wooden spools at the ends and rolled them back. The street festival disappeared and there was the face of a young boy, perhaps eight to ten years old, with soft large eyes, dark short hair, and a smile wrinkling his thin long face. Would a child of mine look like this?

I kept unrolling, passing dozens of sketches of the same boy moving through handstands, cartwheels, and back flips, which he didn't seem to have mastered. In one sketch, he is vaulting straight up in the air with his arms stretched out and his genitals whipping around like a pennant! He has a mischievous grin, a grin like Andrew's. As I continued to unroll the drawing, I found the boy standing at attention, walking stiffly, walking loose as a cat, duck-walking, and arching himself backward into a supple bridge. I saw him in dozens of dashing—and, I might add, provocative—poses, strutting like a dancer, and trying, vainly, to form the alphabet with his sinewy body. He had to be the son of the house, of course.

There are other studies of this gorgeous boy, sketches of him sleeping on a cot with the thin sheet revealing his body, close-ups of his head buried, but for an ear and a tousled mane, into an overstuffed pillow. Who was the gifted draftsman? His tutor Stephanus? No. The scroll is signed by someone else, Lavinius. I deposited the scroll in my shoulder bag. No one would miss it. Now what? I thought.

The next room in this suite is a neat bedroom with a wooden bed high off the ground on spindly iron legs. Its mattress, thick and stuffed with horsehair, bristled and creaked as I sat on it. Next to the bed is a small table with two lamps and a wax tablet and stylus hanging on a string. Stephanus had inscribed a few sentences in Latin, but I couldn't decipher them.

The third room of the suite is only a niche, measuring only about four by five feet. It is empty except for a small shrine hung on the center wall. Shaped like a house with a peaked roof, the shrine is flanked by platforms holding two gilded bronze statuettes. The images are spectacular. One is Zeus enthroned. I have never seen energy like that in such a small bronze. The heavily bearded face seems wise. The second, of Hercules, is less than a foot high but seems much larger. The hero is leaning exhausted on his club, his face tired. I ran my hands over his tight curls and hooded eyes. The pupils are highlighted by two dabs of silver. I loved the shrine's vivid crimson color and the statue—a robed, seated goddess that looks a bit like Queen Victoria.

As I was leaving I came across a small parchment book with writing exercises. The boy—I was sure he was Tertullian's son—was having a terrible time with the upstrokes and diagonals of W and K. He apparently had spat on the parchment and rubbed a finger into the wet spittle, whorling and looping it into a wave. Suddenly I found myself kissing the page, and then, without thinking, I turned toward the door, expecting the boy, home again from his outdoor games.

I found his basic geometry primer, an astonishing *geography* scroll with dozens of gouache drawings also by the gifted Lavinius. They show the Mediterranean and the delta of the Nile rendered in great detail. The margins are filled with pen drawings of animals and birds—cats, dogs, and monkeys, a pair of ocelots in leather harnesses, camels, rhinos, a hippo, and birds of exotic species. Twelve inches of the scroll are devoted to drawings of a crocodile. Every ridge and craggy peak on the alps of the ferocious reptile's head is painstakingly delineated. Lavinius must have seen the real reptile. I unrolled a few inches more of the scroll and got the proof.

In one drawing, the croc is chained tightly to a post in the corner of a tank inside some sort of room. The drawing provides a strong clue to where it was made, a small window shaped like a keyhole, identical to those I remember having seen in the Cairo Museum. Specifically (I have a photographic memory) they are found in Gallery XXV on the second floor. That's also where you find the charming wooden house models which the ancient Egyptians placed in their tombs.

Lavinius' rooms are infused with the gentle, faintly sweet aroma of oil from the lamps. The oil shows no sign of crystallization, and the lamps are not corroded. I lit one, and the smell was poignant beyond imagining.

Later, I found myself inside a cubicle no more than six by four feet. It sort of unsettled me. The walls seemed freshly whitewashed. I have read that when someone died, it was customary to whitewash his room. I wanted to run back to Andrew and Don Ciccio, who were still wandering about looking at the mosaics. But then I shone my flashlight into the next door. What I saw made me stop dead in my tracks.

An easel stood near the center of the spacious room. As my light caught it, I knew, though at first I refused to admit it. I cried out for Andrew and Don Ciccio.

"Coming!" Andrew yelled. They were by my side within seconds, Don Ciccio in Arturo's arms.

"You cannot believe what is sitting in the middle of that room," I said, and I laughed a bit hysterically.

"Jesus!"

"Get my chair, Arturo, quickly. I . . ." Don Ciccio was terribly pale.

The unfinished portrait is one of the most compelling images I have ever seen. The man seems three-dimensional. The painting might have been executed with a brush with a single hair, so delicate are the details of the hair and eyelids. He isn't handsome. His hairline is too high and his nose is as crooked as a gnarled finger. This is no idealized "classical" mask. The face is arrogantly intelligent, and cruel. Icy. Patrician. And disturbing. But, God, it is as fine as the best Rembrandts. It has the delicacy and dispassionate candor of Goya.

At the bottom of the portrait: Quintus Maximianus Tertullian.

"My God!" Andrew cried out. "How I'd like to get that into the Met! Can you imagine what that's worth? What a coup!"

Don Ciccio inched up to the picture. As he lifted himself out of the chair to study it, I could see that his face was covered with moisture.

All at once his head fell back. He slumped unconscious, his left hand shaking. It was a terrifying sight. He had always seemed healthy, even robust, considering everything. I had come to take his complaints as hypochondria.

We got him above ground as quickly as we could, afraid that he might fall into a coma. The limousine was equipped with a telephone, and his doctor and two nurses were waiting when we arrived at the villa. They swept him up into a fully equipped hospital room off his salon. The next day his doctor told us that our friend, "owing to some deep shock," had suffered a mild stroke. He would be bedridden for at least a month and was forbidden alcohol of any kind.

"Ridiculous! I'll stay in bed a week at the longest, and you must transmit your explorations on video, live, as you go."

Andrew objected. "Forget it. I'll be damned if I'm going to allow some piece of video to kill you. We'll brief you every morning. You've got to relax. No more high-wire acts. Play it by the book. Just to keep you happy, I'll leave you *this*."

Andrew had brought the portrait from the palace. The Don almost burst into tears.

We decided to slow down. We stopped dashing all over

the place. Instead we explored together, taking proper notes, making a videotape record. We found more chambers off the great mosaic-floored court than I can count, as well as two sizable barracks. From the rude straw-packed pallets and the scythes, whetstones, and hoes, we figured they were the field gangs' rooms. The foreman of the operation was apparently the perfect Roman administrator. He kept orderly lists of male and female slaves and freedmen nailed neatly to every available space on the walls of his four spacious rooms. On one wall, displayed for all to see, we found a citation of excellence, apparently presented to the foreman, written in the crisp handwriting of Quintus Maximianus Tertullian himself:

To Carolus, on the eve of his fifteenth year of service to my father, an award for his devotion and tirelessness. To him the proper praise and a change of rank and uniform shall be granted. Hurrah!

Carolus was apparently a rabid fan of gladiatorial contests. Andrew thinks he might once have been a gladiator. Where there weren't rosters of slaves (oddly named, some like vegetables, some like beasts, still others after colonies or countries: "the cabbage," "the Caananite," "the Alban Hills") or work schedules (my God, how these poor souls had to labor, twelve hours each day, six and a half days a week!), he plastered his bedroom with diagrams and sketches of footwork exercises for gladiators.

Some of the most vivid sketches are by Lavinius, the house artist, it would seem. He captured the gladiators fighting to the death. The wounded are portrayed gushing blood, screaming, their mouths wide open at the sight of their bleeding bodies.

The fighters cry for mercy; some are shown weeping and groveling, but all are doomed. I acquired an indelible aversion to that Roman sport.

Lavinius was superb. Later, when I returned to his rooms, I found some female nudes, beautiful sketches. He fondles the female form with a silhouette line of consummate tenderness and seems to have been in love with his principal model. Her body, of which she seems justifiably proud, is beautifully proportioned. His delicate line winds its way flawlessly around her anatomy. I marveled at her deftly placed ear, her sculpted lips and swelling breasts, her nipples so perfectly positioned that I just burst out in laughter, I was so delighted. I've rarely come across anything comparable—maybe in a few pencil drawings by Ingres.

I look upon those days alone in the Tertullian Palace as a combination of intense, unexplainable fear and poetic serenity. I remembered the dreamy, slow-motion feeling of gliding below the surface of the waves when I used to scuba dive. The exotic majesty of Herculaneum produced the same sense of never-ending surprise.

I found the room of the family nurse and inspected her tools—a comb made out of bone, two ivory hairbrushes, and a tightly rolled scroll with an hourly schedule. It details a series of things to do with "the baby, Antonia," the daughter of Quintus and Phryne Tertullian—wash times, naps, play times, and bed, which was to me surprisingly late, at ten o'clock. Ah, the decadence of old Rome.

I found Antonia's well-scuffed leather cat with one ear chewed off. It has a squashed, Oriental look about it, as if it fell from some caravan that had arrived from the China silk road. I couldn't help myself. I slipped it into my shoulder bag.

That night, I broached the subject of what we were going

to do with the place at a late champagne supper (against doctor's orders) in Don Ciccio's suite.

"Don't give it a second thought," Andrew said brightly. "What's to say that we can't get away with it always, going and coming as we please, borrowing whatever we want, without anybody ever finding out? We've managed perfectly well up to now. None of us is ever going to say a word. So far no one has a clue, not even that spy. And Cartageno doesn't seem to have the slightest idea that we're burrowing beneath his feet. When we were at his villa last week, I had Giovanni go down into the palace and rummage around, deliberately making more noise than we do, and I heard nothing. Since we enter only after dark and the entrance is in our own backyard, there's no chance any official will catch us in the act. How would they know how to get in? Giovanni's disguised the door. I see no reason why we shouldn't keep it to ourselves forever."

"I heartily agree," Don Ciccio said. "Although I believe we are certain to be nabbed. But getting caught doesn't disturb me. Here in Italy all I'll get is a slap on the wrist."

I was doubtful. Cassone seemed to me very much an inquisitorial, even vengeful, sort. I played devil's advocate, emphasizing the importance of the find to scholarship and learning, but I didn't make much of an impression on either of them. Andrew and Don Ciccio both jumped all over me, accusing me of being naive. All they wanted, they said, was "a short-term private deal" which could not conceivably harm anybody or anything.

I didn't want to give up, for I thought they were both wearing blinders, but there was little more I could do at the moment. I was annoyed that I had not insisted before—the day after we had made our first entry—that Cassone be alerted to the discovery. We would have been severely reprimanded for having broken in on our own, but I think we would have been allowed to remain. Now, if we're caught or if we admit what we have done, I'm afraid we'll be thrown out, possibly prosecuted for some kind of trespass. Although I'm convinced that the palace isn't something for us to play in as long as we like, what to do about revealing its existence mystifies and deeply troubles me.

I also admit the palace gets more and more interesting. The next day we came across a group of workshops, factories really, and their contents had us reeling. We found ourselves inside an enormous gold smithery, bursting with jewelry and art objects. Once our discoveries are revealed, the entire history of Roman embellishment will have to be rewritten.

Scholars have taken it for granted that the Etruscans, who lived in Italy centuries before the Romans, fashioned the most complex and delicate gold jewelry in history. Their artisans were noted for filigree and droplets of pure gold, a thousandth of an inch around. Etruscan gold bracelets were decorated with a blizzard of perfect round globules. In Etruscan filigree every "flake" is exactly the same, spread equally apart, the depth uniform. Another thing that is astonishing is that these balls of gold are so small that several hundred can easily be spread out on the nail of your little finger!

Etruscan jewelers—and this was in the seventh and sixth centuries B.C.—were famous for their inventiveness, skilled in fashioning entire menageries of fanciful animals including hybrid lion-bird combinations and outrageous griffins. No one has ever been able to explain how these "primitive" Etruscans could possibly have created such minute things without magnifying glasses. And the special craft of filigree is said to have died out with the Etruscans themselves some time in the late third century before Christ. In that gloomy jewelry "factory," set up so casually in the Tertullian Palace, we learned that all these suppositions will have to be corrected.

We learned that the Romans did not merely carry on the filigree technique, but invented it and taught it to the Etruscans! The technique consisted of blowing molten gold through an iron machine which resembled a miniature Bessemer converter. The gold was heated until it melted, then was blown through a leather funnel onto mirror-smooth polished squares of steel which had been fixed with a flux of some kind. Apparently, when an artisan got the precise temperature—to the tenth of a degree—and blew with just the proper velocity, the liquid gold, flowing through the narrowing funnel, burst out into droplets of exactly the same size. And we found magnifying glasses, five of them at the bosses' desk, fashioned of six-inch-wide roundels of rock crystal.

The work stations are filled with objects at varying stages of completion. This wasn't an assembly line. The artisans—we figured there were around twenty-five—were apparently allowed to invent and work on what they wanted. Of course there was some duplication. Earrings shaped like jars with a single band of filigree—not the luxuriously encrusted type—were apparently produced by almost everybody. Another specialty was a bracelet fashioned from a dozen gossamer strands of spun gold wire held together by regularly spaced vines with clusters of gold drops tucked into them, the whole thing dusted by filigree.

I slipped one of the bracelets into my bag. Then I did something I haven't ever told Andrew or the Don about, something I hesitated to mention even in this private record, which, like Andrew, I began at the urging of Don Ciccio and have been adding to periodically.

That weekend Andrew and I went to Rome to relax. I

took the bracelet with me, and one afternoon, without telling Andrew, showed it to an old friend, Professor Orazio Cellini, who at eighty-one is considered the most skilled forgery detective in Europe, even by his enemies. Tall, lean, and composed, he is the image of an Old World patrician until he sees a work of art. He seizes the object like a turkey buzzard. All the more so if it happens to be a piece of antique jewelry. He really homed in on the bracelet. He clutched it in both hands and held it within millimeters of his eyes, one of which he closed slightly. He got so close to the bracelet I thought he was going to bite it, and so he did, a furtive nibble to test the gold. He was obviously enchanted, or at least that's how I interpreted his exhaled breath. Cellini glanced up quickly at me, fixing me with his eyes wide with astonishment and suspicion. Finally, he sighed deeply.

"Ah, my dear Olivia, for an instant there I thought you had something miraculous! A shocker, it's so good. But no, it cannot be true. After I allowed myself the initial burst of hope I began to see the anomalies. Look, one sign is the astonishing perfection of the filigree drops. They're much too small to be antique. Too mechanical. Machine-made. And here! The color of the gold—far too buttery. And here . . ."

And then Cellini, the "infallible," gave all the reasons why the bracelet was a clever, yet all-too-pedestrian, very recent fake!

Slightly numbed, on the way back to our flat in the Piazza Navona, I had a mad idea. Had Don Ciccio made it all up? Was Cellini right? I laughed at the idea, but it still made me nervous.

Back in the palace, the two grandest masterpieces of goldsmithery in the Tertullian factory went a long way toward convincing me that what we were seeing was genuine. They are pieces a Benvenuto Cellini might have envied and an Orazio Cellini would also have condemned. One is a necklace, the other a solid gold table fountain.

I've never seen a necklace like this anywhere on earth. It's less a piece of jewelry than a slice of life. Dozens of horses and men are scattered in bands and sections about two or three inches wide. In proportion, delicacy of detail, vigor of anatomy, sheer drama, and sense of unity between men and beasts—almost a kinship—this is a sheer miracle. The small gold sculptures were achieved completely in the round, a technical *tour de force* I'd never seen before.

When I studied the necklace a second or third time, small things emerged that I'd missed at first. The action takes place on meticulously rendered golden terrain. Grasses, shrubs, and a series of small flowers sprout through the thickets and brambles. Everything is captured with perfect realism. Who could possibly have worn the thing, or would have wanted to? It weighs over twelve pounds. The necklace is larger, finer, better made, more exuberant than the only other masterpiece I know in the world that is faintly similar to it, the famous "horse" necklace in Kiev made by Greek artisians in the sixth century B.C. Of course, we took the necklace home with us for Don Ciccio to gloat over.

He stared at it for a long time and sighed. "I believe I covet this more than anything I have ever seen in the world. Now there is a good lesson here, no? Imagine what would happen to this if the Italian authorities were in charge? The world would see it for at most a month, and then it would go into some cellar for decades, or maybe it would be pilfered. What do you think it's worth? Twenty million? More? How wonderful it is! Why bother to return it? Of course, I'm only joking. Naturally, we'll take it back, promptly tomorrow, or very soon anyway."

We kept it for two weeks and then put it back. After that I began to be concerned that when the officials finally entered —after we decided to allow them in—our tracks may easily be detected. But Don Ciccio calmed my anxieties. The next group, he said, would be as awestruck as we'd been and would have no way of knowing the original positions of things. I agreed. Still, from then on we made a very specific video record of everything we touched or moved or borrowed. We didn't leave fingerprints. I would tease Don Ciccio that I'd mislaid my purse down there or that Andrew had dropped his calculator and couldn't find it.

The other golden object, the table fountain, is made of gold and ivory, chryselephantine, as the ancients called the technique, which Phidias used to create his giant statue of Athena in the Parthenon. Chunks of ivory were softened and rehardened for the goddess' flesh. Most historians dismiss the claim that ivory can be made malleable. Well, it can. The artists responsible for Tertullian's fountain did it.

Imagine a pile of solid gold about three and a half feet tall, embellished with the finest, purest ivory, decorated with hundreds of diminutive figures attending a musical extravaganza. Nothing like it has ever been seen—or dreamed of—before. It has four large spigots in the form of dolphins' heads set on four balconies, and on the balconies are many figures robed in togas, himations, short gowns, parade armor, veils, cloaks, and even shorts. I counted over three hundred characters, each one with a distinct personality.

In the upper balcony there is a thirty-man orchestra with lutists, harpists, drummers, and men playing strange percussion instruments. Most intriguing is a curious banjolike instrument with a whole section of five players to itself. The squadron of Lilliputian performers and admirers must have commemorated a real event that took place at the palace. There in a lofty parapet, brilliantly clear, unmistakably, is Quintus Maximianus Tertullian, his hard face turned slightly up with a fixed smile. Next to him is a beautiful woman in a gold gown, her white shoulders gleaming. That pert, heart-shaped face, even if it is only two centimeters in size, is certainly Phryne, Tertullian's wife.

One evening our earthquake sensors suddenly began to beep. This time we beat a fast retreat from the palace before the palpitations began to swell. From outside, the noise was unlike anything I had ever heard. Then came the tremors as volcanic gas swelled around us. Then it got still again, and we edged our way back in. I had to summon up all the courage within me to join Andrew and Giovanni, both of whom held my hands.

At first we thought nothing had been disturbed, but when we went back inside, we found that the tremor had opened up a section of rooms which had been sealed off for some reason, either by Tertullian or the eruption of 79. I recognized the place instantly. There was the jagged hole leading up through the lava and the shattered fresco depicting ancient Herculaneum. The sense of foreboding came too late. We recoiled as we saw two skeletons, crushed by piles of brick, their bones splintered under the fallen wall. We realized that these were the remains of the diggers whom Cartageno's grandfather hired a century ago to find his "ancestral" seat. We were shaken, of course, though we were nowhere near as frightened as we might have been if we had encountered skeletons from Tertullian's times. In my fantasy the ancient inhabitants of the palace never died. They are like their objects, intact and perfect.

We rushed back to Don Ciccio.

"So old Cartageno wasn't talking nonsense," he said. "Thank God I had the prescience to arm you with the sensors. Now that you see that they do work, your fear of being trapped should disappear." The Don did not skip a beat as he changed the subject. "In my solitude," he continued, "I have come across something of very considerable moment. It's a police report on our lordship! Listen, what do you make of it?"

The document added another mystery to the welter of those surrounding him.

Tertullian is being scrutinized as of this day. The undertaking is risky, because of his power. Therefore if our agent, who has been well placed in the palace, is discovered, we have a difficult problem.

A group of suspicious people from the East have been coming and going in large numbers. Two have spent as much as a fortnight as guests. One is the Palestinian rabble-rouser and another is a Greek who is said to be another original member of the conspiracy. The wealthy seem to have fallen prey to most of these "fakirs" of the growing number of Eastern mystery cults.

Once a record of Tertullian's meetings with these characters can be established, then a charge of treason can be lodged. And then the Emperor will gain all the Tertullian possessions.

"The most seditious crowd of all in the first century were the Christians. You don't suppose Tertullian . . . "

"That arrogant nobleman?"

I wondered. Was he more than a stiff-backed Roman patrician? There were so many mysteries, so many questions. Who was this man? Who was his wife? What would happen to them, to us?

ANDREW

I have a growing suspicion that the dwarf is planning to dump us when we have explored the whole villa and either take control of the place himself or turn it over to the authorities and become a hero. I'll have to figure out a way to head him off. Meanwhile I'm having the time of my life. And the fun is just beginning. We found a bunch of documents in the carpentry shop, and though most are merely instructions for the artisans, two thin books contain snatches of the history of the palace which make my mouth water. The land around the palace was, according to the documents, purchased for a handsome amount—far more than it was worth—by the honored Caeius Tertullian, who wanted to be generous with the natives, a group of mixed Romans and Oscans. Caeius, a twofold *triumphator,* that is, a celebrated victor in war—most unusual, considering he was an engineer, not a soldier—described his plans and wishes in his usual precise manner:

The climate and the views are incomparable, so I purchased enough land on the most prominent outlook to guarantee that my successors (long may they hold wealth and power!) will gain great profits from the sale of the lower hectares. The establishment of a memorable family seat demands lavish sacrifices. I made them. One must create a majestic plan, one for a thousand years, or more. I did. I supervised as the perimeter walls were planned, drawn, and built just as I did with the hundreds of military camps I built. I prayed my sacred family's house would grow, the gods of Prosperity and Luck willing, into a palace, if that is what my followers desire. I myself seek only a pallet, a simple straw mattress, and a clay cup to piss in at night.

The work began with a team of oxen and the help of an Oscan farmer, who later became my estate foreman and never cheated me beyond the accepted amount. We labored three days in the heat to furrow out a trench with a newly forged bronze plow I had dedicated to Zeus, Demeter, and Vulcan. We formed the trench in the exact dimensions of the exterior walls. Then I designed and erected the foundations, the defensive walls, and finally the interior defenses. My foundations were copied from those I invented for stone bridges over those raging Eastern rivers. I sank them deep in concrete boats for stability, as the region's peasant legends include tales of times when the earth shook. I took these charming stories as fact. One tale, however, which I tried to forget, lingered in my mind. It described how over a long expanse of time, Vesevo, the low verdant hill to the northeast, had grown to the height of Mount Olympus and then over a dozen lifetimes had sunk back into the ground. Not likely! I scouted the gentle hill, saw it was perfect for vines, and bought the property. In time, my wine became a legend. In time, so will my architecture. My floating foundations will be effective for buildings tenfold the size of my humble house. I thrust them so deep that even a second story could be built someday despite the moving of the earth.

From what I could gather, the next "master builder" of his lordship's family seat appeared to be the gifted Marcus. In roughly 210 B.C., Marcus razed everything that had been built before him and, in concert with a member of the family called Princess Diana the Great, built the grand central court, the world-renowned pools, the interior menagerie, the golden, painted portico decorated by Epictetus the Third, the private baths, and the picture galleries with the abundance of old master mosaics, paintings, and sculpture that Lady Diana had collected.

The Tertullian house was fortunate to have survived the civil wars at all. Everything on the third level, where the private family rooms were located, was burned. Yet certain treasures were preserved, including the inlays in amber, which were the pride of the family, the "map of the world," and the gods by master Phidias.

It took a generation for the survivors of the wars to amass sufficient wealth to repair what was left of the palace. Yet finally, fueled by the booty accumulated during the Eastern wars, the greatest period of expansion and refinement began.

Lord Maximianus, the Clever, commissioned from Livinius of Rome the triple temple with its golden doors, the four towers with their statues of Hercules (the name Herculaneum having been coined by Caeius), the treasury, the second painted portico, the observatory, the inner gardens, the state triclinium, and the libraries. No age of the palace had ever been so filled with inspiration and accomplishment.

Equal to the prodigious efforts of Maximianus were the works of his father and his grandfather, who made the "towers shine and the halls sing in triumph." The palace was apparently never so beautiful as under these Tertullians, at least until Quintus.

Would it still be as beautiful? Or would we discover that the upper stories had been smashed by the mud or the lava? I woke in a sweat many nights, thinking of a myriad disaster scenarios.

About the time we walked into the third room of this incredible place I began to compile my list of the objects and works of art I was going to demand as our share. I immediately thought of that gorgeous gold-and-ivory fountain! Puts Fabergé into kindergarten. I can't keep my hands off the thing. It's as complex as a symphony. I'm impressed with the fountain as an art work, but even more as a slice of life with witty comments about the Romans. The thing is equal to a dozen histories and social studies. Aristocratic Romans *reveled* in ceremony, theatrics, feasting, and drinking. No one from Gibbon to Hollywood has ever really shown the depth of their hedonism. They virtually lived for ostentation. One had to be, and could be, profoundly rich, in the Rome of QMT. "Hail profits!" was the motto of the times. Showing off was not simply expected, it was the "right" thing to do. The social structure was hewn from granite. Cries for moderation, restraint, or morality were quickly forgotten. The powerful did exactly what they pleased. The frank, completely uninhibited sexual activity intrigued and puzzled me.

There's no doubt about my wife's eye. She immediately spotted Tertullian's sensual Phryne as the painter's model. I plucked the tiny statuette off the top of the fountain and compared it to the woman in the scroll of nude drawings Olivia had found in the artist's studio. The plump, succulent ladies are the same. The vellum pages I found under Lavinius' bed prove it. He's got his tongue stuck six inches inside of her, and her ladyship is performing the damnedest gymnastic move, shouting in pleasure.

In another drawing, she's given him a blow job and his sperm has exploded all over her smiling face. Her energetic tongue is lapping it up and both her hands are scrambling to get his cock going again. His little sketchbook is a howl. Lavinius depicts himself in a quill-pen drawing, half on his bed, his lower body slipping to the floor. His expression is part bliss, part agony. He's cradling his balls tenderly in both hands, a wiped-out stud. I wonder if we'll find anything to indicate whether Tertullian knew. And what about her ladyship's go with "John"?

Old Caeius was one smart guy. The infrastructure of the place obviously dates back to him and has been only slightly reworked by later generations. It's easy to date Roman concrete and brickwork. In the years before Christ, within a Roman foot, which is roughly the extent of an average man's hand plus the other palm set above it like a T, there are invariably four stout bricks and six inch-thick mortar joints. Later on, the number of bricks per foot increases as their thickness diminishes. By the time of Constantine, the once-solid masonry has degenerated to seven or, occasionally eight, wafer-thin bricks. In the good old days, the concrete was as fine as dough. Later on, when the Empire slipped further into decadence, the concrete became softer and more pliant. In the palace both the brickwork and the concrete date to the end of the first century before Christ. The ony exception is a curious round section of ashlar masonry off to the farthest northern side of the furniture workshop, which is older than anything else I've ever seen.

Something else I had never seen was a Roman toilet. There are lots of them, and not just in the grand public rooms. The quarters for freedmen and slaves have plenty, as well as showers and basins for washing. They aren't primitive outhouses, either; a rudimentary flush system was provided. Giovanni swore to me that once a large enough water hose is installed in the palace, he can fix the plumbing so we can use one of the toilets and a bath. I told him to go ahead.

One of the wittiest technical achievements in the place—this has got to be Caeius too—is a couple of "fireman's poles" located near the main public dining room. The waiters would apparently run the food up three narrow staircases and then, to keep things moving, would plummet down the poles back to the pantries to rush another series of dishes to the dining chambers. I came across the banquet menu on a pantry table. It included fifteen different courses, including duck, lamb, mutton, veal, oysters, clams, lobster, "sweetmeats," nuts, something I couldn't translate but may be insects, greens of all kinds, and a half-dozen varieties of fruit. There were eight kinds of wine, plus something called *tartolla,* which I took to be some kind of grappa or fruit liqueur.

How did the noble guests get to the third level? Surely not by sneaking up narrow stairwells used by porters and waiters. I figured the main staircase had to have been outside, curled

158

against the facade of the palace, overlooking the sea. But we had no choice but to use the servants' access. We ascended, ready for anything. Olivia had resigned herself to rubble; I was prepared for grandeur, hoping for the best, but steeling myself for disappointment.

We emerged from the depths and set up a battery of flood-lights.

Unlike those explorers of the past who turned a corner in a rock tunnel and were suddenly confronted with the beautiful gates of Petra, "the rose-red city half as old as time," or the first man to set foot on the moon, whose spontaneous words had been rehearsed for weeks, we reacted with silence.

Neither of us could speak. I sank slowly to my knees. I couldn't even blink my eyes. In that first split second, it was someone else's words that came to my mind, not any of my own: "When, out of my delight, the refulgence of many precious stones lifts me from the material to the sublime in an analogical lift from earth to heaven itself."

They were spoken by Abbot Suger, creator of the royal church of Saint Denis and soaring Gothic, when he first saw the stained-glass windows in the apse.

What we saw was a vast antechamber, a semicircular colonnade of lofty Corinthian columns with tops carved more like gemstones than marble. Inside the chamber, it felt as if a pair of welcoming arms had opened wide to embrace us. The stone was painted ivory. The cupola soared fifty feet or more above our heads. That dome of heaven is exactly that, the firmament. On the cerulean surface of a deep, crystal-clear night, every star visible in Quintus Maximianus Tertullian's time is depicted. The sky is millions of pieces of cut lapis lazuli. The stars are lumps of pure gold, surrounded by shining rock crystal. The

Milky Way is a spray of gold dust. Interlaced in wires of silver are the signs of the Zodiac and the most prominent constellations.

The effect staggered us. The very idea of such a cosmic subject was terribly moving. I cannot think of anything like it in all of art. It was more ravishing than the tomb of Galla Placidia in Ravenna, even Venice's San Marco itself.

Think of it. A visitor's first sight inside the luxurious Tertullian Palace was a view of heaven itself. By entering, one ascended to the height of the gods! When I consider what we encountered after that, it seems fitting that we were greeted by the splendors of the infinite!

Olivia's reaction concerned me. I had to coax her. She seemed confused. "The heavens are supposed to be soothing, hospitable," she finally said. "But these skies are so perfect, so alien. They scare me."

Probably nothing more than a momentary downer, I thought. I must admit that the palace has frightened me from time to time, too. For people like Olivia and me, it is the kind of discovery one only dreams about. It's beyond imagining, and I have, I think, a great imagination. I wonder if it will desert me.

The oval-shaped antechamber with its slender Corinthian columns leads directly into another wonder, a rectangular hall some two hundred feet long and a good fifty wide. It reminded me of an early Christian church. Its line of enormous double Ionic columns, some forty feet tall with ocher shafts and gilded capitals, supports a beamed roof. At intervals, semicircular niches appear, eight to be precise, and in each stands something no one has seen since the last of the pagans' original Greek sculptures. There are few true Greek works in museums or still in their proper place anywhere in the ancient world. And even the best-preserved—in the sculpture of the Parthenon, the Hermes of Praxiteles at Olympia, the bronze charioteer at Delphi, the Pergamon altar in East Berlin, and the two bronze warriors of the fifth century B.C. from Riace—are deteriorated. The delicate painted surfaces have been lost, and the bronzes have shed their subtle patina.

Not these. The first statue in the first niche is a crouching Venus—the so-called Anadyomene—by Alexander the Great's master of masters, Lysippos. Up until that moment, no one had seen an original Lysippos since, say, the fifth century after Christ, when his last surviving marble was melted down for lime.

The piece is dedicated to Alexander himself and signed *Lysippos epoiesen,* "Lysippos made me." It captures the goddess of love, kneeling down, holding her knees tightly together as if she's been surprised. Her slender arms cover her breasts. But her face is at odds with the chaste pose. She caught my eyes in hers, soft brown with speckles of green and hazel, and they reached out toward me. Her smile caresses. Her hair is golden, and damp. Her milky skin too seems moist. She has just emerged from the bath. She is like a closed flower about to open.

Across the hall, in the niche opposite, is Hercules, her spiritual and physical antithesis. Exhausted after his labors, he leans on his immense club, which is actually a fair-sized tree. Poor, old, sweaty, battered Hercules is by Scopas, the genius of the mid-fifth century B.C. In seconds I saw that everything I'd read or was taught about him was nonsense. Neither a classicist nor an idealist, Scopas was a down-and-dirty realist. His giant old fighter, marvelously painted in enamel, doesn't glisten with sweat. Hercules' battered face is striped with dirt and perspiration. A couple of fresh cuts and scratches still ooze blood. I almost reached out to clean them off. The wounded look in his eyes. Sad animal eyes, sad to have seen the horror of the world, perhaps.

With a consummate mastery, Scopas animated his marble effigy with raw details—sweat-matted, tangled, filthy hair, crusted blood, and dried spittle. In places the flesh is scraped raw. Perhaps this is Hercules the son of sorrows, seen as a sympathetic and surprising image of humanity on the edge of a defeat greater than death, a state of numb hopelessness.

Olivia laid her head against my chest. "I haven't ever much liked Greek or Roman art, although I never had the nerve to admit it," she said. "So heartless, distant, chilly. But I can't feel that way any longer. He's so incredibly beautiful. And to think that he was actually the victor. He's the symbol of this place— Herculaneum, his namesake, and more, this palace. Two thousand years later this house is still victorious."

In another niche we found a slightly larger than life-sized seated portrait of Emperor Nero inscribed with a long, official greeting Tertullian himself composed for his leader. "Powerful Lord and High Priest," it reads, "victorious defender of our lands, overseer of our lives, the god, Nero. May your glorious reign be long and may your sojourn to our proud house be happy. To thee we sacrifice a perfect pair of bulls and present you with the small painting of the dice throwers by Polygnotus you so admire. Bless you, Lord of Lords!"

Olivia wrinkled her nose. "Christ, Polygnotus was the finest Greek painter of the entire fifth century! Tertullian had to give that to that pig?"

The statue makes the degenerate Emperor look like a saint. His smile is benign and his hands are stretched out in a gesture of friendship. Yet his lips are incarnadine and his cheeks rouged. However, the Emperor wasn't effeminate. In his role as

Pontifex Maximus, chief priest of the land, makeup was necessary. But no matter how skilled the carving, the statue is lifeless.

Not so a pair of life-sized painted marble portraits depicting Lord and Lady Tertullian, in the niches closest to the entrance to the next chamber. It was our first chance to see Phryne in full scale. What a stuck-up, nasty little bitch she must have been. But gorgeous. I'm convinced the sculptor wasn't trying to flatter her, either. That face, those almond eyes, the lush body of perfect round plumpness, the delicate hands, would have caused a sensation at any time in history. But her look is one of cruelty and selfishness. She has the face of a spoiled brat. She looks no older than her early twenties. No wonder she made Quintus suffer. The sculptured dress is a marvel, as if five layers of diaphanous fabric were laid on top of one another. It is a startling *tour de force*. Tertullian is nowhere near as good, far too rigid.

The other niches house an extraordinary variety of sculpture. One is the original *Spear Carrier* by Myron, in perfect condition. No doubt that he was carved from life. The athlete seems about to step forward. The surface of the marble is flawlessly painted. Every pore is shown, every hair on his body is depicted. He is literally shining, for he has apparently just anointed himself with oil.

I have to say that I'd always thought that there was nothing in antique art duller than Myron's *Spear Carrier*. I found nothing human in the pectorals like platters, the stomach muscles that look as if a turtle shell had been stamped in his midriff, or the all too perfect positioning of the feet, which art historians loftily call "the ponderation." Not to mention the rotund arm muscles, the tiny head with trim, cropped hair, or the handsome, vapid face. I've loathed the thing since school days when every day I had to pass by a plaster cast of the standard Roman version. There was nothing like having the canon of manly Greek proportions standing in front of a bunch of skinny schoolboys to instill in them all a lifelong hatred of it. But I take it all back. The difference between the original and the copies is staggering.

The architectural decoration of the hall is fine. Everything is carved in stone. There isn't a centimeter of stucco or plaster in the place. And the stones I found far more accomplished than even those meticulous carvings produced by the Renaissance master Andrea Bregno. The free form of the volutes, the vibrant tension of the tendrils tucked between the sweeping orbs of the Ionic capitals—the work is as good as a drawing by Leonardo.

The feeling of luxury is almost suffocating to the modern taste. The human body, always perfect, is worshiped, not just admired. In yet another of the niches in the Great Hall we found a magnificently painted life-size marble of the Three Graces. I was surprised to see them depicted not as personifications of grace at all, but as prostitutes!

I can only describe what we found in the chamber after the Great Hall by comparing it to one of the most famous objects in the Naples Museum—the grandiose mosaic representing Alexander the Great in battle at the River Issos, wearing silver armor, astride his war-horse Bucephalus. His face is in stark profile, his staring eye exaggerated. Alexander is shown in the epicenter of the work, impelling himself forward, so eager is he to thrust his lance through his prey—King Darius, the Persian—who is shown in full rout in his chariot. Darius' face reflects terror and Alexander's shines with triumph in the moment just before the grand climax. Scholars have written about the fragmentary mosaic in hundreds of publications. Most have theorized that it was copied much later from an illustration in a lavishly illustrated scroll made during Hellenistic times, probably not long after Alexander's death in 323 B.C.

Wrong. The "splendid" mosaic is a mediocre, confused, ill-conceived, and badly executed bastardization of one tiny section of a tapestry that is part of a giant series of tapestries. Yes, tapestries that outstrip in quality every tapestry we know of—those in Angers, or Raphael's monumental series in Saint Peter's, or the unicorns in New York. We found them in an oval hall off the Great Hall—a series so finely woven they look like silk embroideries. There are dozens of them. Each one measures some twenty-five by fourteen feet.

I put my hands on the surface of the first tapestry. It seemed that a surge of electricity coming from deep within the age-old fabric rushed through my body. Imagine, a work of art from the time of Alexander the Great. I cast my light eagerly over wall after wall of gleaming fabrics, so fresh, so silky that they shone like mirrors. The entire complex history of Alexander, the greatest military leader in history, is here.

I saw Alexander's birth with his adoring father, Philip II of Macedon, watching gimlet-eyed as the midwives presented the babe to his mother, Olympia.

I saw his education by Aristotle.

I saw his first trials at the time of the assassination of his father.

The drama surges across the picture plane in one uninterrupted frieze. No decorative or achitectural motifs hinder the pace as the creators alternate the mood of the vignettes between tumult and calm. I was impressed with the calm moments, the scenes of Alexander's schooling under Aristotle and the long waits between battles. Alexander appears to be a student in awe of his tutor, an exceptionally robust, handsome lad of ten or twelve who sits hunched at the feet of the philosopher, scrutinizing a tablet. The respect and affection between student and teacher are obvious.

In the episode depicting the assassination of Alexander's father, Philip, the actual murder isn't shown. Instead, the tapestry designer recreates the moment when Alexander brings the news to his mother, who sits in a private chamber, illuminated by only one lamp. The scene's eerie light is reminiscent of Caravaggio. Alexander appears as a youth brought to maturity suddenly, in one awkward, painful moment. The artist shows Alexander, perhaps even more deeply moved than his mother, trying to disguise his feelings for her sake as behind him a spray of shining silver threads symbolizes his glorious future. Some shadows portend trouble as well. This is the work of a seasoned storyteller who seems to know that the tale itself, so singular, so filled with intriguing chapters, calls for a restrained manner.

Alexander's coronation in 336 B.C. is shown as a ceremony of religious piety and athletic fervor, with the participants in the games—the runners, wrestlers, jumpers and discus throwers—lining up to be embraced by the newly crowned king as they receive their laurels. Alexander is several inches taller after his coronation.

I found myself gawking at the mastery with which the weavers rendered a runner whose lithe body has, in falling, stirred up a cloud of dust. I marveled at the realism of a lion's pelt casually thrown over our hero's shoulders as well as the details—the remnants of a banquet, a silver wine jug, and a few golden goblets.

I was struck by how different these scenes are from the standard life of Alexander. Remember the Gordian knot, which, according to legend, the young warrior split open with

his sword? In the tapestry he is depicted as painstakingly unty-
ing and unraveling what looks like dozens of feet of tangled
ropes. That is much more like the Alexander I imagine, someone who might have relished solving the puzzle of Rubik's
Cube as much as planning the intricate steps needed to lay siege
to an enemy city.

The tumultuous crossing of the Hellespont shows a thousand boats bearing men, horses, and equipment. The landing is
more a parade than an assault. Throngs of Persians prostrate
themselves on the ground before the invader, who is obviously
quite bored with the proceedings. Not long after the placid
landing, Alexander's army is attacked by King Darius' advance
guard at the River Granicus and utterly destroys it, turning the
stream into shades of blood so varied, so freely "painted," that
it looks like the product of some abstract expressionist.

That victory opened the whole of Asia for Alexander, and
he seized it. Unable to tear my eyes from the row of tapestries,
I watched, transfixed, his passage through Miletus and Halicar-
nassus like a rider of the Apocalypse. But he does not destroy
the cities. The troops, with iron self-discipline, make careful
inventories of every item they capture, every citizen they en-
slave. The booty is equally shared by foot soldier and officer.

Alexander's invasion of Syria—in 333 B.C.—brings his first
encounter with Darius, a surprise meeting with Alexander for-
aging alone except for a pair of bodyguards. Darius, the King
of Kings, clad in silver armor to which a series of lavender
ribbons were tied, gazes at the young man with intense curiosity
and admiration. Clutching a bow and arrow in one hand and
the reins of twelve horses in the other, he appears capable of
handling anything, like a master. But he realizes that this is not
the moment for a contest. His opponent is isolated and vulner-

able. There would be no glory. So with a cavalier wave, he turns away. The next time they meet, Alexander will be the son of Amon-Ra, the sun god.

In the next panel, the setting abruptly moves to Egypt, which is not seen in the standard classic way. Here is no ordinary barren desert scene strewn with pyramids and colossi. Instead the oasis of Siwa where Alexander was deified is shown as luxuriantly verdant, with soft, rising dunes. A sacred well lies at the center inside a grove of palms near an impressive temple with a series of pylons and row of sphinxes. Beside the temple are tents, as large as half a city block, decorated with lively paintings depicting Egyptian deities.

Alexander doesn't become a god at one sitting. The colorful ceremonies go on for days and include purification rites, countless sacrifices, and a baptism, in which the nude Alexander is carried into a pool by four priestesses, who do not appear to be vestal virgins. In fact, in the next scene Alexander is shown later that night in a large bed with the two pairs of ladies.

A virtually interminable series of sacrifice scenes follow. These efforts to placate the gods were costly; the panels make it clear that the newly anointed "Son of the Sun" had to pay for the scores of unblemished white bulls. But it seems worth it; in the climactic scene, Alexander is taken into heaven for a union with Amon, who actually makes him a god.

Alexander's divine rebirth into the world marks the center of the tapestry series and the apex of his life. Then the action builds once more as the army marches back to Mesopotamia to prepare for a second encounter with Darius. In all the standard histories of Alexander, he won the second conflict. Not here. Darius tricks him much the same way Harold was fooled by William the Conqueror at Hastings. The King of Kings pretends to see the entire front break away before him; Alexander, accompanied by only a few men, gives chase and corners his quarry in a box canyon. Suddenly Alexander is trapped as the entrance is sealed off by Darius' personal guard. Alexander is taken prisoner! But he is not put to the sword. Darius greets his captive as an equal.

Alexander is next seen kneeling in homage to the Persian despot. This is followed by a sumptuous banquet during which Alexander and Darius drink to each other's prowess and courage. At dawn Alexander and his men are released and return to their armies. But Darius and Alexander are never again to meet. One of Darius' generals, furious that Alexander was set free, assassinates Darius.

Alexander goes on a rampage, slaying the murderer by cutting his throat. Raging through Persia, he grants no mercy, laying waste to Babylon, then Susa, then the sacred city of Persepolis. The style of the weavings becomes violent, highly emotional. The earlier steadiness segues into confusion, and the scenes grow harsh with fire and blood.

It seemed to me that Alexander's decision to march his exhausted troops back into Bactria, which caused the death of many men, had led the artist to change his attitude about Alexander. The artist stops idealizing Alexander and begins an "honest" portrayal of his life. Alexander starts to deteriorate; his body gradually shrinks; his face fattens and slowly loses its golden hues. His troops want to return to their homeland, but he thirsts for one last great venture in Asia. In a sort of last hurrah, the hero charms the dispirited and hostile band into following him. But despite victory after victory, the troops are fading. Tired, aging, world-weary, they become little more than brigands. Morale slips. Discipline disappears. On the long march into Afghanistan, one soldier robs another and a petty quarrel ends with a murder. For the first time there are gallows and executions for the transgressors. Now, when Alexander speaks, some men turn away, others laugh or yawn, and others don't look up from their dice. They don't get the plunder they came for, and the land, parched and uncompromising, is scorched before them. Death follows them, not in the guise of the glory of battle, but furtively in the form of fever and disease. The horses begin to falter and die.

While his men go mad, sicken, and die, Alexander seems to gain strength. But the stronger he looks, the more the men resent him. Finally he is surrounded by a rebellious crowd of officers and men, who beat him. He gives in to their demands to retreat.

The army turns south, marching through mountains and wastelands to the edge of the Persian Gulf. Alexander broods in his luxurious Egyptian tent or, while on the road, in Darius' war chariot drawn now by four emaciated palfreys. He dresses himself in Persian garb. A fleet of small ships is constructed, and after a stormy passage in which half the army is lost, the survivors reach not safety, but another desert.

Alexander, with the consummate guile of a madman, manages to trick his gullible men once again. He promises them lavish booty if they will follow him just one more time. They go. The tapestries chart their invasion of India right to the edge of the River Jhelum, farther east than any Greek had ever been. Here the landscapes grow lyrical: India is depicted as a warm, sweet land with placid rivers.

As I walked along the immense expanse of the final series of tapestries, I was soothed by the exotic trees and plants. Acres of beautifully tended farmlands lie at the border of the jungles. Lakes and streams ensure the never-ending fertility of this promised land. And the people who live here, tending the fields and caring for the bountiful flocks, are handsome, far more attractive than the Greek invaders. Simple, trusting, friendly, and curious, they come forward to lay gifts at Alexander's feet. This is not how conventional historians like Arrian or Plutarch describe Alexander's Indian campaign. To them, Porus, the Indian satrap who ruled the area, was a tyrant who enticed Alexander into the beautiful place and then attacked without warning. Not so, according to the creator of the tapestries. He shows Alexander as the aggressor, tricking the guileless and hospitable Porus into meeting at the Greek camp without his bodyguards. Porus is promptly slaughtered.

Flushed with this massacre, Alexander tries to persuade his men to continue deeper into India. They will have none of it. Alexander has lost all contact with reality. By now he believes he really is the son of Amon and dresses himself up to look like the god. While his men pretend to tremble before him, they mock him. At one of these ceremonies, he falls into a fit, tears at his hair, and cries uncontrollably. Then, suddenly, he seems to regain his senses. He stares at the group standing shocked before him and berates them, crying out, "What do you do? Why these trappings for me, a mere soldier, your comrade in arms?" Tenderly they take him in their arms, strip him of the clothing of a god, and bathe and anoint him. For a moment, Alexander seems the beautiful young man of yesterday, the youth who unwound the coils of the Gordian knot, the warrior who defeated every army that stood in his way. But the hero is in fact dying. As the sun sets on the third day of his deliverance from madness, Alexander commits suicide! He appears in front of his white silk tent and falls upon his lance.

I found the climax of the tapestries melodramatic and disappointing. There are too many funeral games, sacrifices, banquets, speeches, and parades. Of course, the legend of Alexander grew from these occasions, with all the stories coming together in a grand historical cover-up. As testimony after testimony was given and praise was heaped upon his name and deeds, the bitter truth was gradually expunged. Alexander never failed in any military adventure. He never lost control of himself.

The tapestry cycle concludes majestically in a spray of gold with fires of light as rich and tumultuous as a storm on the surface of the sun. In a crescendo of colors, Alexander's body, restored to the glory of youth, is literally lifted to the sun by a phalanx of genii. His face is turned upward, eyes heavenward, as the sculptor Lysippos portrayed him.

AS Don Ciccio's health improved, he began to make a nuisance of himself. Our videotapes had made him ravenous to return to the palace. I managed to persuade his physician to let him be more active. The Don's a weird duck, but he *is* one of the most perceptive people I've ever met. Within minutes after entering the antechamber and the Great Hall, he pointed out to me things we had overlooked.

He was particularly taken by the carpets. In the rush we had neglected to tape them. They are smashing. The carpets seem to cover every inch of the floors, carpets in delicate, muted earth colors intermixed with light greens and a stunning rose-red, predominantly abstract in design, with meander patterns or a series of linear trapezoidal and pyramidal shapes. The borders are rich, naturalistic floral designs.

When we wheeled Don Ciccio slowly in front of the row of tapestries, he was silent. I was afraid he was going to have another seizure. But he was struck dumb by the beauty of the works. When he finally spoke, he gripped my arm fiercely. "His

followers, the generals who apportioned off the world he'd conquered, *had* to change the story, if only for their own legiti-
macy," he whispered. "I'd guess Seleucid, the fellow who won
Persia in the casting of lots for the empire, commissioned the
series. Doesn't it strike you as odd that of all the hundreds of
lieutenants, only Seleucid and his tribe of officers are always
constantly shown in the best light? Always. Here, take me back
to the beginning! See?" Don Ciccio cried out excitedly. "He's
always placed in the front; always shown saving the day, advis-
ing the great man on what he should do next. Of course, Alexander always follows his instructions and prospers.

"What a catch for the Met *those* would make, eh?" the
Don needled. "How much would you be willing to pay? A
hundred million? More? Can you believe that we are the only
human beings who know they exist? We are the only ones to
have seen them in almost two thousand years. Does anybody
else really have to know? If this palace is ever opened to the
public, what will the millions who come to ogle really get from
these magnificent things? Will they become closer to God? Will
these things offer them insights into human nature? Will they
become better parents? You know the answers. Obviously, masterpieces such as these should be left to the true connoisseurs
and savants. Us. Ever since I first saw the Sistine Chapel, I have
been convinced that hoi polloi should never have been allowed
in."

THE luxury of the Tertullian private baths surpasses anything
I have seen in any palace of any civilization anywhere in the
world, from Versailles to Topkapi in Istanbul to the fabled
retreats of the Punjab. Only one place I know can compare in

the slightest way, and that's the bath complex in the palace of the Sultan of Brunei.

The walls, floors, and ceilings are fashioned of magnificently fitted slabs of porphyry, lapis, sardonyx, amber, malachite, and a marble so pure that Michelangelo would be in awe. The purple porphyry is unblemished. The lapis has not a single carbuncle in its vast expanse and glows silkily. The malachite is equally amazing. Not even the Kremlin has malachite as solid as this; it rang like bells when I tapped it with my fountain pen.

The designer arranged the stones in the bath much the same way an *ébéniste* might match an assortment of rare woods. The result is both architectural, with the marble and amber setting off the darker colors, and lyrical, in the way the purples, flashing greens, and lapis blues clash, then blend. Within the fields of the lapis and porphyry, a myriad of semiprecious and precious stones are set into gold and silver frames. It creates the impression of some Fabergé construction the size of a house—an enchanted piece of jewelry one could soak in.

The bath, following the standard Roman canon, includes the *calidarium* (very hot water), the *tepidarium* (tepid water, as it sounds), and the *frigidarium* (the coldest water, created with blocks of ice and barrels of snow packed all the way from the mountains). Chambers for massages, exercises, and beauty treatments are located next to the main salon, where the floor is covered by four layers of carpets. Unlike Persian carpets, these carpets are woven from fabric of muted colors—a spectrum of pastels, beiges, and early-morning hues that serve as foils for the thunderous colors of the porphyries and lapis lazulis. They are almost ghostly and were woven rough—deliberately and enchantingly.

We were enchanted again by a profusion of everyday objects, including a set of silver wine vessels—a large mixing bowl and two dozen cups—which I covet and which are patterned after the motif of the Corinthian capital. The rich volutes and fully ripened acanthus leaves are heavily beaten chased silver, two inches thick in places. I also admired the lavishly gilded bronze furniture which is arranged throughout the chambers and which repeats the graceful motif of the acanthus leaves of the Corinthian capital on the lounges where the guests once reclined in luxury.

How amusing that the Romans used towels! But they were nothing like the soft ones of today. The coarse linen towels stacked near the different baths were obviously made to stimulate the skin. I was also astonished to find a profusion of perfume bottles—over three hundred of them placed like parade soldiers on shelves or side tables. The bottles, all glass, are in a large variety of shapes and colors. Many were dipped in molten gold or have been patinaed with some sort of artificial iridescence. We had a good laugh at the idea of offering a hundred or so to a local antique dealer. We'd be run out of the place for trying to peddle fakes. Some bottles are shaped like Roman buildings. A precious few are miniature temples. One depicts a triumphal arch in blue-green glass, covered with tiny applied figures in silver. We also found a number which are caricatures —gaping Moors, self-satisfied Gauls, slinking Persians, and comically inscrutable Chinese. There are animals as well: elephants with war towers stacked high on their backs, lions and tigers, foxes, birds, and deer. The finest are signed by their maker, a certain F.C.

I put a couple on my list of things I intend to take with me before we turn the palace over to the authorities. What if we have the same things on all our lists? What a hassle! I'll work out the proper apportionment. Plenty of treasures to go around!

DON CICCIO

My illness was phony, of course. I wanted the Fosters to have full run of the palace, to become obsessed, to fall so in love that they could never let go, to anyone. I was getting worried that Olivia might feel impelled to go to the authorities. She frets so much about her precious reputation. She doesn't know what's important.

Sometimes I regret the necessity to have the Fosters involved at all. But how to get rid of them now, so late in the game? It would be wonderful to be alone in my magical rooms, alone in my perfect world. If I ever have to admit defeat and share the discovery with the authorities, I have a plan for us to maintain control for at least as long as I expect to live. I will create an international foundation to care for the palace and put the Fosters in as "fronts" for what will one day be the finest archaeological laboratory in the world. If we are discovered and authorities try to take over, I know how to thwart them. Using my eminently respectable Americans, I will retain exclusive visiting rights and the privilege of having wonderful things like the Alexander tapestries on private loan. I don't intend the general public to enter my hallowed shrine. I shall guarantee that for conservation reasons, like the ancient caves of Lascaux, the palace is never invaded by the mobs. I'll pay for these rights. Gladly. What kind of endowment is needed to keep the palace in good condition forever? I estimate the amount at a quarter of a billion dollars. To anybody but me, the task of raising that fortune might be daunting.

But for me, no cause could possibly be more worthy. Although it took weeks of intense bartering and an exhausting secret four-day trip (during the time I was confined to my rooms by my physicians), I have succeeded in selling all my holdings in a European corporation that is controlled by English agents working for the three highest members of the Politburo. When my computers first uncovered the Soviets' secret deals to raise the money for the natural gas pipeline, years before, I wheedled my way into a central position by seeing to it that one of my banks was an early funder of the project. Then I took steps to ensure that the American National Security Agency was permanently thrown off my track.

I have placed my tidy "Russian" profit in Eurobonds. From it, I have amassed around three hundred and fifty million dollars, conservatively speaking. Immoral, perhaps, but what enormous wealth has been acquired without breaking the rules? Some persons collect Picassos with their ill-gotten gains. Some cruise the seas in the yachts they make their private worlds. The Palace of the Tertullians is my Picasso, my private world. If everything goes right, this treasure will be mine alone.

In addition to getting the money together I have found the one man who can guarantee me control of the Tertullian Palace whether or not we remain undiscovered. That man is the Superintendent of Antiquities, Giulio Cassone. He appears to be completely reputable. He seems to have avoided the financial entanglement that eventually corrupts every archaeological official in Italy. Initially that made me doubly suspicious of him. But the only hint of impropriety I have uncovered is an "independent" income which he banks in Switzerland and which began around the time the Dorsoduros smuggled a large number of antiquities out of Italy. I also discovered he once served in the intelligence branch of army headquarters. If there is one Italian governmental entity that is ethically spotless (or virtually; there was one tiny transgression in the late 1970s involving a gambling scheme), it's that unit. I was surprised to learn by accident that Cassone is *still* in army intelligence. Is he assigned to Naples to look after me? I was alarmed, so I risked the exposure of my Soviet dealings and a damaging tax inquiry and penetrated his unit's data banks to see what I would find.

The work was chancy. Intelligence is the only organization besides mine that has developed sophisticated warning devices against trespassers. For the first time in years, I took personal charge of my computer's journey through the maze. Quickness and sensitivity were required. I was almost trapped a couple of times. The most dangerous trap was a "corridor" in which I was supposed to think that their machines were inefficiently programmed because they repeated the same questions three times in a row. But I realized that their machines wanted *my* machine to assume they were inefficient. I spotted the trap with just nanoseconds to spare and waltzed away from it.

Once through the "barbed wire," I moved easily to Cassone's personal files. I had misread the man and his mission. He was attempting to expose the same crooks I was. Cassone had worked his way into the inner circles of the Dorsoduro operation to become a trusted *capo*. He had made a small fortune from his cut from this operation. It came to three hundred thousand dollars a year, all of which was punctiliously accounted for and desposited in a government account.

I was fascinated to read that Cassone's mission was to bring down not only the Dorsoduros but all the art dealers, private collectors, donors, and museum curators who had made illegal acquisitions through the Dorsoduros or their middlemen. I saw now that he was ready to pounce. The inventory of the treasures which had left Italy illegally for Switzerland, Germany, Japan, and America would stun the art world.

I was amused to see that the Dorsoduros were by no means Cassone's only prey. The Prime Minister himself was a target. The investigation was nearly finished, and if the Dorsoduros had been the sole targets, indictments and arrests would have already been issued. I possessed the missing link that would form a chain of indictment and conviction. If Cassone, the purist, would agree to my keeping the palace for as long as I wanted in exchange for the information necessary to trap the Dorsoduros and the Prime Minister as well, then I would have done it all.

The one disturbing piece of information in Cassone's files was that the Dorsoduros suspected I and the Fosters had found something, though they were not sure it was the palace. The news was disquieting. What would Dorsoduro do? I was sure he wouldn't wait long. I had less time than I had thought.

So I tried to hurry Andrew and Olivia along. "Don't lag," I cried. "Come along. Don't linger over that. There's bound to be something far better through the next door." I tried but I failed. The palace deserves the blame. How can anyone race through a reception hall decorated by fragments of the ancient Seven Wonders of the World or an ancient music room complete with the orchestra's actual instruments? How can one hurry through baths decorated with semiprecious stones or a miniature temple dedicated to the Roman gods or a chamber completely sheathed in amber? That was the "public level" of the palace alone. So, instead of speeding up, our adventure took more time, and the longer we lingered transfixed, the more anxious I became that my finely honed plans, which required precise timing and perfect execution to succeed, would falter.

The magisterial hall of the tapestries leads into a vestibule with such a low ceiling that even I found it oppressive. Then suddenly the confined space explodes into a vast vaulted ellipse, painted in white, blue, and gold. The most remarkable series of objects I have ever seen are displayed there. One of the Tertullians collected fragments of the ancient wonders of the world. These wonders differ slightly from those mentioned by modern historians. Each is placed in its own painted stage setting, the fragment slipped in so cleverly and the *tromp l'oeil* painting so convincing that you can hardly see the difference between real and the artificial.

A fragment of the Great Pyramid is there, and what a fragment—its solid gold pinnacle. About three feet high, it is the symbol of the eternal sun. As a *mise-en-scène* a painter has depicted the pyramid itself as it looked then, entirely covered with highly polished marble veneer that disappeared ages ago.

The waters of the Nile lap up almost to the paws of the brooding, noble Sphinx, which is painted in vivid, lifelike colors.

"It's not imaginary, is it?" Olivia exclaimed. "We're actually looking back in time, aren't we? This simply could not have been invented."

Andrew ran his hands over the polished golden pinnacle. "Can you imagine what this thing is worth? And how many millions would line up to see it? This beats everything else we've seen!"

The second and third wonders are the lighthouses at Alexandria and at Rhodes. The Tertullians had what appear to be genuine segments from both and paintings of each. The Pharos, or lighthouse, at Alexandria is represented by its huge brass oil lamp.

The painting captures the lighthouse as it would have appeared if sighted from the sea. It also presents an enchanting panorama of the quays and walkways surrounding the Pharos, and much of the city.

Alexandria, a city dotted with pleasant squares, was also the home of another wonder, the low structures, embellished with Ionic porches, which formed the legendary library. Captured here in the moments before Julius Caesar burned it, the library seems like the soul of the city. No temple is so prominent as this library with its alabaster facades. It is clear that the Alexandrians respected human learning above hollow gods who, jealous perhaps, sent Caesar to destroy it.

The next "wonder" is a model of the bronze Colossus of Rhodes, the antique world's least aesthetically appealing monument. The colossus, a giant naked youth with his two feet planted on opposite banks of an estuary funneling into a harbor, almost made it to modern times. But it collapsed when the land on one of the banks shifted. For many centuries the giant lay fallen in the mouth of the harbor. Finally in the middle of the seventeenth century, a Levantine scrap merchant sawed up the green corpse and carted it away. A pity? I don't think so. The thing was overblown and silly.

As I was thinking about this, there was a sudden sharp earth tremor. There had not been a peep from those worthless sensors. Instead, what followed was a hideous noise much like an enormous branch breaking high in a tree. I fell out of my wheelchair. I smelled the stench of sulfur. Would hellfire come next? The walls of the chamber palpitated as if alive. But it was all over quickly. In all my life in Italy, I hadn't experienced anything like that. Thank God Olivia had returned to the villa early.

"Andrew, we must never let Olivia know about this."

"If she'd been here, I think she might have packed it in and gone home. You might not have suspected it, but she has to talk herself into coming down each day." He looked ashen. "Don Ciccio, what do you think? Is this the shape of things to come?"

"If I thought so, I'd be in Paris or in my garden," I told him with my usual confidence. "Look, the little tremor did *some* good; it split the middle of this wretched painting of the Colossus. Suddenly he looks like an aging athlete. What a ridiculous wonder! I'm beginning to question Tertullian's taste."

Frankly, I found almost all the wonders boring. I think Pausanias, who made the list, intended it as parody of bloated monuments and inflated art. I might be wrong—the fourth wonder and the life-sized reconstruction of it are, for me, worth everything else we have discovered so far. The object is a hand. Yes, nothing but a hand. But such a hand, in ivory, almost two feet high and more than a foot across. It obviously belonged to a sage or a leader under stress; it is gnarled and aged. It manifests a great calm, yet one senses that this is a hand that could reach out in anger and destruction. It is tinted ever so delicately, and its subtle creases are marked with thin wires of solid gold. This was the ivory-and-gold hand of the great chryselephantine statue that once graced the temple in Olympia. It belonged to Zeus, the king of gods, and was part of the statue created by Phidias, sculptor of the Parthenon. Completed in the year 436 B.C., the Zeus of Olympia is one of history's most exalted works.

Wonders five, six, and seven are horrible. They made me so tired I'm not going to bother to explain them. But the eighth wonder is so spectacular it made me short of breath. Veering away from Pausanias' list, those quixotic Tertullians had chosen their own eighth wonder. Far larger than the others and placed in a more prominent spot is a piece of the original head from the Trojan Horse, about six feet long! It is fierce, primitive, ugly, and menacing, with lips curled back to reveal a crooked line of teeth. The eye is wild, fearsome.

The ancient designer of the *mise-en-scène* went all out; it is, after all, the climax of the exhibition. Troy is dark, evil-looking, a series of ramparts of truly unscalable heights. The walls of the buildings—dozens of them—bristle with thousands of warriors. This city could never be taken. The Greeks are shown in retreat, miles off on the shoreline, like clouds of dust in the still, hot air. The horse, its freshly cut wood still sticky with resin, stands stiff-backed, straight-legged, leaning slightly to the left, set up on a makeshift pedestal with broad skids fastened underneath. I was mesmerized by its sinister aura. I wanted to cry out, to warn the Trojans, who were peering down over the battlements at the mysterious ex-voto, wondering what to do. There is this stillness. The banners are limp on their poles. The only hint of the impending destruction is, far back in the center of impregnable Troy, a ribbon of black smoke, rising in the sky.

The discovery of the gnarled totemic head of the Trojan Horse had a great effect on my determination to keep the palace and its contents under my complete control. But, unfortunately, the attitudes of the others have solidified as well. Andrew told us that he has come to the conclusion that we should each choose an appropriate number of works and writings for ourselves and remove them from the palace. Then we should seal off our entry, disguise our tracks, and tell the bureaucrats about the palace in exchange for a series of blockbuster exhibitions to be held at the Metropolitan. It strikes me as an extraordinarily naive idea, but there is no deflecting him from it.

"Look at it this way," he exclaimed. "Can you imagine the furor this stuff is going to make? Christ, think how much money we could make from a world tour of just the wonders alone. I say let's finish our exploration of the rest of the chambers, take what we want, and then activate my scenario. Unless we get legal guarantees, the Italians will have nothing to do with us when the existence of the place is revealed. Oh, they'll thank us profusely, give us a banquet, and a medal—and an audience with the Pope—and then say, 'Bye-bye.'

"I suggest we act prudently, cautiously, and with the proper degree of self-interest," he went on. "We all agree that our ideal goal is to keep all of what we've found for ourselves, to use in any way we want short of doing anything that might get us into legal difficulties. My advice is to continue, make lists of what we each want for our own personal reward, and feel out the situation day by day."

Then Olivia stunned me. "I think we should tell Cassone and the authorities and let them in on this right away. We have no right to control, appropriate, borrow, or own any of this. It is the property of the whole world. Our compensation should be in knowing that we were the ones to discover it. I'm frightened. I'm terrified that an earthquake is going to destroy all of it. I have nightmares that we will be sealed off down here."

Olivia was weeping now, and Andrew led her gently away to their villa. She never lost control like that again, and later on she insisted that she had come to her senses. Eventually she agreed reluctantly with my plan to proceed in secrecy. But Olivia's a consummate actress, and her determination is steely. From that moment on, I have been convinced she is plotting to foil my scheme and hand over our discovery to "mankind." What should I do? How to head her off? I don't know yet.

And Olivia isn't my only worry. My sensors detect someone tunneling far off to the south, moving toward the palace, and Arturo has been able to pinpoint at least ten workers with drilling equipment coming from the general vicinity of the Dorsoduro lair. If they proceed at a steady pace, they could be at the Tertullian Palace in just over a month.

ONE recent evening, without the Fosters, I received Giulio Cassone. He seemed contemptuous at first, utterly casual about my exquisite menu and the superb wine, which he could hardly have been accustomed to. He sat silent, watchful, seemingly immune to all pleasures. That made me triply cautious, but by the time dinner was finished, I was ready to broach the issue.

"I want your unofficial reaction to an idea of mine," I began, and he waited. "I'd like to make a major investment in our dig. I want to start up again. I want to carve out the hardened mud that must have inundated the rooms."

He raised an eyebrow. "Have you any idea what such an undertaking might cost or how many years it will take to clean out but a single small room?"

"Yes, I do. I have some inkling from accounts of the work in the mid-nineteenth century."

"That work was abandoned soon after it began," Cassone observed quietly.

"I know. Sad. But today we have equipment that can do the job far more efficiently—high-speed dentist's drills, microwaves to soften the stone, laser cutters that can go through the tufa like butter."

He shrugged and continued to wait.

"I'd like to obtain two things from you. One, permission to proceed, and two, a new contract, one that allows a foundation established by my world-respected friends the Fosters to care for, financially and administratively, whatever is unearthed —in perpetuity."

"You mean total personal control," Cassone asked, "over what could be the most important archaeological discovery in history. You don't ask for much."

"I'm not one to mince words—I say what I want. But mind you, the foundation would guarantee that anything discovered would always be available to scholars. As for the general public, there would be certain conditions."

"What conditions?"

"The public would come in once a month. In groups of, say, a dozen."

"You are saying that you do not want anybody else to know about or be able to see what you and your American friends discover?"

"Well, not until we are gone, by which time we would have arranged for the site to be handsomely maintained in perpetuity. At no expense to the government. You see, in exchange for allowing us the run of the place for what would be just a few short years, possibly decades—none of us is getting any younger—the state would be solving a very large problem —the financial burden of the upkeep of whatever we find at Herculaneum."

"I see. Does this mean that Signor Stearns will be involved?"

"No."

Cassone's eyes flickered with amusement.

He studied his clasped hands for a long time. "No. I cannot permit private citizens to control state archaeological property or artifacts."

"I'm talking about a major financial investment," I protested. "Something close to a quarter of a billion dollars. We mean to strip away the tufa from the interior of this edifice, come what may."

He shrugged again, but this time allowed himself a thin smile. "Such a commitment suggests to me that you have very good reason to be confident," he said. "Am I right?"

It was my turn to shrug.

Cassone gazed coldly at me. "No. I think it may be time for me to ask my superiors to investigate your efforts to close down your project, which seems to be taking a long time," he said quietly, starting to rise from his chair.

"I wouldn't do that," I said calmly. "I want you to be a willing partner in the next phase of our task. You mentioned superiors. Which ones, might I ask? I know, for example, that you have more than one set. One is, of course, the Department of Antiquities. The second—now let me be blunt—is Enrico Dorsoduro."

"Slander!" Cassone growled.

I handed my considerable dossier on him over to him. It is more than a hundred pages long. He received it casually and barely glanced at its contents.

"You will see that it proves that for the past two years, at least, you've been active in the illegal antiquities cartel of Enrico Dorsoduro and have received numerous payments from smuggling operations. Awkward, huh?"

"Well, this seems to put us on equal terms," he said evenly. "You see, Don Ciccio, I have some interesting information about you as well. Perhaps our secrets can cancel each other out and we can forget about all this. And, by the way, it's still no to your request."

"I think not. I also happen to know about your third set of 'superiors.' "

Without betraying an ounce of emotion, he opened the dossier again, flipped to the back, and squinted at it. Silence. His face reddened as for five full minutes, he scanned the computer printouts. Finally, he gave out a long, soft sigh, closed his eyes, and inclined his head toward the ceiling. Another minute went by. Suddenly I was surprised to hear him chuckle.

"My compliments, Signor Conte. As a mark of my respect for your powers of detection, I shall have delivered tomorrow, if I may be permitted, a copy of my file on you. It's against regulations, so I beg you to be discreet. Don't be concerned— your secrets will not be divulged."

"Of course," I said casually. "Might I have some idea of what you have discovered?"

"All."

"My . . . uh . . . financial apparatus?"

"Yes, to the extent that we know of your considerable wealth and power. No, if you mean how you have managed to amass such a fortune."

"So you understand that I am capable of continuing the dig, under the terms I outlined."

"You want total control. Until you die. In exchange for your arranging to maintain the place permanently," he intoned.

"For all mankind," I said.

"I understand your philanthropic nature," Cassone said gravely. He leaned back in his chair and gazed at the ceiling for a minute or two.

"I have some vital information that will significantly contribute to your investigation of the Prime Minister. Significantly."

"Funny how one's memory works," Cassone said. "I do now recall certain precedents for the arrangement you and the Fosters seek. I think I can agree to your terms. With one proviso: that ultimate control over every object that might be found remain in the hands of the state. Be assured that the state will assert its control only if there are gross improprieties and negligence on the part of the board of this foundation of yours."

I smiled.

"I sense you need time to get your project under way, " he went on. "I will make the appropriate amendments to your original contracts and have them to you within two days." A crafty smile appeared on his face. "In the meantime, you have my permission to . . . ah . . . continue with what you have been doing. A question. What have you found? Are you sure it is this palace?"

I smiled reassuringly.

"The Dorsoduros are on the move," he said.

"I know."

"When you are ready, please tell me what I should say—and when—to our mutual friend Enrico."

"Tell him to keep coming."

We shook hands on what we had agreed upon. This man will go far. I will not be at all surprised if, with my help, he attains very high levels of government. And, naturally, he understands that I sense his ambition.

THE Fosters decided to go off to Rome for a week. Delightful. I relish my privacy. I spent the time in my gardens and in the laboratory processing the final batch of the scrolls. One night, rather late—just after two—after a pleasant romp with a young lady appropriately named Andromeda, I was scrutinizing the remaining materials, which had already been sent through the translator. I brought them up on the screen and saw nothing but a batch of tax records. I was about to switch the computer off when I saw that a new document was being revealed. It was obviously a copy of something Quintus Maximianus Tertullian had written himself. No doubt the imperial spies had obtained it from the original. They were more efficient than the KGB.

Sometimes I feel like a fugitive from all my words. I am truly a stranger and afraid in a world I never made. Only the promise of salvation and eternal life sustains me.

My father's death brought me responsibilities beyond reckoning. Every freedman and slave added to my burdens. Then my father's household spies approached me, servile and menacing, to tell me about my wife. Had I any suspicions? None that I cared to give voice to, but I had no doubts about the truth of the messengers' stories. None at all. The woman, a piece of corrupt flesh, my contracted wife-to-be from childhood, the mother of my children, has shamed me, her children, our name. A lover? No. Two? No again.

I wanted to execute the spies. To think that my father, an honorable and moral man, would have countenanced household spies! I had them tortured and interrogated. But I did not execute them. Nero would find out and use it against me. He suspects my association with the faith. He watches me closer and closer. They had me in their grip. I do not care about my life. To give it for the calling is blessed. But the vile Emperor will also destroy my children, my house, and my shrine. I fear for the children and for this house where my family has gathered the most treasured objects of our civilization. I suffer far more than the martyrs and confessors. Their flesh was raped, but despite the agony they perished in joy with the name of the leader on their lips. My burden is heavier. I live on and allow the sins of my wife to continue.

I live in fear that the Emperor knows everything about the faith and is waiting to pounce when he sees the opportunity for the utmost cruelty. But that deranged man has his worries, too. The most disastrous harvest in threescore years and his profligate expenditures on his arts and building projects have begun to annoy the Guard and disturb the mob. Perhaps he will be swept away like carrion.

Christianity, Petrus says, is "not for the wealthy." He quoted the parable which states that for the rich to enter eternity is as difficult as for the proverbial hawser of hemp to pass through the needle's eye. I told Petrus that to be poor and lazy does not assure a place in heaven.

Petrus is dirty. His Latin is a disgrace. Half the time I cannot fathom what he is saying. When he raises his voice to me or mumbles on about the wealthy and educated being cast out of the congregation, I remind him of other types of sinners, those who lie and deny. Petrus, a brute only partly tempered by the faith, once flung himself at me, shouting in Aramaic. Only my skills as a boxer made it possible for me to avoid injury. I knocked him cold with a blow to his stomach. I gazed down on the dirty, sweat-streaked face of this oaf of a man in wonderment. He was so stupid, so much a bully. What had the leader seen in him? Why had he chosen Petrus to be the foundation of his Latin church? Why not J, the intelligent philosopher? As Petrus came to, I realized the burden of loving one's enemy. Petrus was gruffly contrite. I forgave him. Or at least I told him I did.

"It's hard to forgive you, too, Quintus," he told me. "But I do. Your tongue hurts. You use it like a knife. Have you ever denied? Or lied? I think you do it all the time. You have even met the 'god' Nero. And you didn't tell him you are of our congregation? No? For shame! I try to forgive you all your wealth, your chattel, your pagan idols. I find it hard. How different we are. You, the wealthiest man in Rome. Me, one of the poorest. You, living in fear, unable to speak out, a slave to your wealth. I will die soon, and you will live a long time. I bet I'll be happier. You should leave all this, this filth, the corruption, the death of your soul. And you should publicly proclaim the faith and join me in Rome and blessed death."

"Petrus, you say your mission is in Rome," I told him. "Mine is here. It is to lay the lasting foundations. You know what I feel about martyrdom. One does not seek it. It comes. If it comes to me I shall receive it. You chase after it like a hunter. How do you know you should hunt it?"

"I have been chosen. The lord called me. He awaits me in Rome. I know it," the brute insisted.

The faith can lead certain men to believe they are "chosen." Petrus, I'm sure, has not been called to a lofty mission. He is an ignorant man who hears false things. But he is also passionate. He has lived with the leader. He has been changed by his words. Is this enough for martyrdom? I cannot say. J has also lived with the leader. He, too, was chosen by him to establish a bishopric. But not through strife or martyrdom. Why? J and I have talked so many hours of our goal: to strengthen the congregation. Flesh and faith are strongly bound together.

Petrus comes from the wild messianic side of the congregation, the side of that true madman Paul. These zealots preach the crucifixion and the physical resurrection. Do these events represent the true teachings of the leader? I do not know. They say that in our world these days people want to believe in messiahs, not lawgivers; magic, not ethics; necromancy, not fact; the afterlife, not the sacredness of a pure faith.

I am not one of these. I came to the teachings and the congregation because I was moved by the moral and ethical principles. Having been trained as a Skeptic, I found the ethics appealing. When I met J and heard his rationale I was convinced. The long hours I have listened to him quoting Jesas fully convinced me that, despite the difficult dogma, his teaching will cleanse the world. By "difficulties" I mean the teachings about the poor, the helplessly crippled, criminals, and, of course, women. J believes that our congregation will achieve ultimate victory if we permit women, even those unmarried or widowed, into the faith. Jesas, J told me, said, "My teachings come from my mother; women must feel free in my congregation." I do not care to argue with J. On certain matters, he is as stubborn as Petrus.

Petrus has betrayal in his blood, and he will betray me. Ignoring my pleas, he has taken to teaching the lessons to freedmen in the Basilica and the amphitheater. Word is bound to reach the Emperor's police. I begin to fear for the safety of our small groups, all highborn, with much to lose. If the teachings of Jesas are not to reach the learned and the prosperous, how will the foundation of the congregation support us?

THERE has been another dangerous row with Petrus. This time J stopped the argument before we came to blows. This time I might have hurt him. J and I banished Petrus from Herculaneum, Pompeii, and Naples.

"Go northward to Rome, seek the destiny you insist upon," J cried out. And bad-tempered Petrus did as he was told. He left with an imprecation.

"Your faith is weak," he shouted. "The congregation is to be built upon blood and the mysteries, the idea that Jesas died and came back to life, after ascending to heaven. It is impossible, but that is why it is the great truth which I believe, and the congregation will prevail only through those who believe as I do. You silent ones, you poets, you rich, will soon not be heard or listened to. I go not because of your pitiful order, but because I have heard the call. My martyrdom is at hand!"

He departed. We are both relieved. Once again I turn to the task of disseminating the teachings.

PETRUS has been brought to trial in Rome, convicted, and executed. True to his word, he became a martyr. He asked for death by the cross. It is said that he insisted upon being hanged upside down.

Such a fate would be none too good for my wife, a consummate actress, a gifted liar, a brilliant dissimulator. She kisses me, croons to me, pampers me, and cuckolds me daily. I, too, am an actor, pretending to love her. In one regard Phryne's escapades have benefited me; her sexual technique has become exceedingly inventive. But once I leave her chamber and retire to my room to read, she waits and sneaks out like a rodent—to whom? I no longer know. But I hear stories. When she's tired, she stays at home and cavorts with Lavinius. I have thought often of exposing him and putting the entire blame on him. The spectacle of one of her lovers being tortured to death in public might put a halt to her scandalous acts. But I cannot do it. His works are intriguing.

It might seem curious that I would hold the work of a mere craftsman, a decorator and painter, in such regard, but Lavinius can capture a likeness! Even hers. I had brought to me in secret the drawings he has made of her, and I felt immediate physical longing. He is working on an image of me. It is, if anything, too realistic, too similar to the portraits of the Republic. I commanded him to render it with more dignity. He did, changing it from the direct frontal view to a more sedate profile. The most admirable work of this impudent Greek slave is his series of the history of Jason. The wall paintings are the talk of the city. The secret of the strange glow and polish, Lavinius told me, is that he has mixed the finest marble powder into the layer of paint just below the final surface.

Phryne claims to know, and I believe her, every piece in the palace, everything gathered in for the hundreds of years the family has collected art. She has had everything repaired and cleaned. I appreciate certain of the treasures. The ancient stones from the two temples in Athens that my great-great-grandfather traded for two loads of grain. The quaint weavings of the history of Alexander commissioned by another ancestor, a military adventurer who served Alexander. The old master statues and paintings. But I am fascinated by these objects mainly because of their place in the history of our family.

Despite all the evil Nero has committed, one thing can be said on his behalf: he is a master of connoisseurship. His desire to acquire puts my ancestral holdings in danger. He is determined to have them. Should I join the conspiracy to assassinate this monster? Should I, a member of such an illustrious clan, bloody my hands with regicide? For this is what it truly would be. Should a member of the congregation and a bishop contemplate taking a life, even the life of one so worthy of death?

J argues no. The leader forbade murder. Love your enemy. Punishment is for the higher one. Besides, J reasons, if a Christian is known to be one of the murderers, the next mad Emperor—for Jesas predicted they would all be mad—might uproot the congregation. I know what Petrus would say: "Plunge your aristocratic sword into his belly and confess!" He would be right. What a quandary! If I do nothing, Nero will conjure up charges, and I will be arrested and killed without mercy. My children will be banished or slaughtered. Phryne will linger on, pleasuring the beast until he grows tired and sends one of his black messengers to cut out her heart. If I join the conspiracy and it doesn't work, even more horrors will come to pass. The thought of being tortured for months is terrible.

One of Nero's most gifted torturers has developed a way of flaying a man alive for a full month and a half, keeping the wretch living in howling agony. The ghastly skinning—and concomitant salting of the ragged red wounds—is performed by teams so that the victim never really sleeps or falls unconscious. I know. The Emperor has commanded my presence. "I have willed you to be here because it will do you double good," he said. "As our largest landlord and wealthiest citizen, you should learn the new technique of torture. And the spectacle— better than theater—will make you think. I like my aristocratic subjects to think." Suspecting that this was the way I was going to die, I watched. I do not know who the man was. The team had been ripping the skin off him for ten days before my "invitation." The fellow could have been of any race or nation. His face was the only part of his exposed body that had not been scraped or tugged by the flaying forks. His hair was bright red. I was astonished at that until the Emperor whispered into my ear that he had made the decision to dye the man's hair.

"Pretty, isn't it?" Nero said so very gently. I could easily hear him over the high-pitched whimperings of the victim as the skilled torturers ripped back the skin on his stomach ever so slowly.

"What was his crime?" I asked, careful to seem offhand.

"I don't know. Does it matter?" Nero shrugged.

Such is the mark of a god.

I was struck at how clean the victim was. A group of four slaves did nothing but wash away the blood, quickly stopping the flow by scattering handfuls of powdered salt on the flesh that had just been exposed. As their hands moved, the man twisted in screaming agony. His whole body, except for his head and the area around his genitals, was a raw, pulsating wound. The climax, the Emperor proudly told me, would come when the skin was scraped, very slowly and deliberately, from his face, scalp, and neck, and the skin cut and pulled back around the man's genitals.

"It is difficult to say which is more entertaining," Nero said, "the 'music' that comes with the tearing away of the eyelids or . . ."

I was forced to stay for that. But there was a catastrophe.

The man expired at the first cut. Nero flew into a tantrum and ordered the flaying of the entire team of specialists. Such is madness. The unknown man never confessed. Perhaps there was nothing to confess.

What a chronicle! I was repelled by it, but I couldn't put it down. Nero's taste for human suffering made for gripping reading, much as I hate to admit it. Tertullian knew and loathed Nero! He also knew Saint Peter and had disliked him, even joked about him! Who was J? He was, I suspected, John the Evangelist, but I wasn't going to come out and say it even to myself until I had found more documents. I wondered whether Tertullian would join the conspiracy.

After the first portion—the text is a fragment—the tone of the diary changed. For the next twenty pages Tertullian carried on about his estates and land. Not that the information isn't interesting—it is—but it is more a subject for a doctoral dissertation. Yet there are some compelling nuggets. Tertullian nourished an affection for anything experimental involving agriculture or animal husbandry. Although the computer translation became at times virtually incomprehensible and I didn't have the advantage of the original Latin throughout, I *believe* I read that Tertullian was responsible for cultivating a maize that would grow far faster and be more hardy than earlier varieties, making it easier to preserve on long, damp sea voyages. I'm also positive that Tertullian established an elephant-breeding ranch in Africa.

Who would ever believe that our first pachyderm foals would have emerged from their mothers' wombs so perfect and so eager to greet the world? The pygmies started shrieking as, one by one, the oily, gray, wrinkled little bodies squeezed forth! They had never seen anything like it. In the wild, nothing is more dangerous than an elephant birthing. The bulls stay close and stamp any intruder to death. On the farm, the bulls were removed to a distant compound. We dulled their hearing and senses with wine. They took to good Roman Falernum like veteran infantrymen.

After their births, the infant calves all fell to the ground and lay gasping and stunned for several minutes. Then they struggled to their feet and moved toward the females, craving mother's milk. Some calves never did find their real mothers. I was amazed at how friendly the creatures became. I took a week-old male into my quarters. The only inconvenience was waking up every two hours to hand-feed it milk from a leather flask. I allowed no one else to perform this duty, having been told by one of the old natives that the baby elephant would become dangerous unless the same person fed it every meal until it was three months old. I had to do it. And I was richly rewarded for my strenuous efforts. The beast, which I named Pyron after Hannibal's lead elephant, became as docile as a well-trained dog.

Pyron came back to Rome with me, and until he was three and had grown too big, he slept in the palace stables. He could hear for miles. When I would awaken in the morning, he would hear me stir and would trumpet until I came to pet him and feed him a sweet. Our farm produces a strain of robust, well-behaved pachyderms renowned in many provinces. The income from their sale or rental is substantial.

Tertullian traveled constantly. He went to Athens to look in on the family holdings in agriculture, olives, and marble. He cruised the Aegean islands, making a brief trip to Anatolia to investigate some precious metal mines before he sailed off to Rhodes and Cyprus, where the family iron ore mines and smelting operation were located. Everywhere he went he took a private army of forty seasoned troops. On occasion they came in handy. Once he became lax. On a short sail down the coast of Crete, Quintus, with only three companions, was waylaid by a gang of pirates. The boat was small, the winds were strong, and they were quickly overtaken. The three bodyguards fought valiantly but were chopped down. Tertullian faced the pirates alone. I read eagerly of his adventure:

When confronting brigands, especially barbarians, a courageous attitude will often serve better than a short sword. One must be commanding and arrogant. Let the criminal know at once that you consider him a piece of dung. Don't hesitate!

My linen toga was splashed with the blood and the brains of my guards, who had fought valiantly against impossible odds. I offered up a silent prayer for their salvation. One, Julius, was a Christian. Sadly I never told him that I share his faith. For him I sent a triple prayer. Then, instantly recognizing the leader of the motley group of mostly black-haired Greeks and North Africans, I pointed my finger at him and shouted, daring him to approach me. He was a bearded, slovenly, fat pig with agate eyes.

He spat at my feet.

"I don't know whether to grant you the mercy of death,"
I shouted, "or sell you as a slave."

He sauntered over and thrust his ugly face up to mine. He smelled of rotten wine and decayed fish. He sucked in his lips as if to spit in my face. Then he saw the glint of death in my eyes and faltered. I knew I had him.

"Sail at once for Larnaca and discharge me," I com-

manded. *"If you do that I shall see to it that you are all quickly hanged—without torture. If you resist, you will suffer greatly."*

The leader fell back a step. I saw he was shaken. The crew began to mutter among themselves.

"I think I know you," he yelled. "If you are the Lord Tertullian I'm going to kill you where you stand. No one will buy you, fearful of the consequences."

He began to slip from its scabbard a wicked curved blade and made a half-step toward me. I cried out to his men, "Who will dispatch this beggar and take me at once to Larnaca? Perhaps some mercy awaits there."

A swarthy Negro danced forward through the band and sliced off the head of his leader. We changed course and within hours had reached the harbor. The fools let me loose, and as promised, I had them all strung up. Without torture. That is the way a lord must act. If I had not been stern, I would have perished.

What an enigma this Tertullian! A sort of primitive of the Christian way. I was dumbfounded by this ethical and honorable man of rare courage who was too frightened to tell a man who was about to die to protect him that he, too, was a follower of Christ. How could this "Christian" be so contemptuous of the lower-class members of his faith? Which teachings of Christ did he believe and which did he deny? I raced through the rest of the scrolls. Aha! Tertullian had made his decision about Nero.

No one in my class, even those with estates to lose, believes that the madman should be allowed to live longer. Neither do I. And I cannot believe that ridding the nation of a murderer, a tyrant, an evil horror is unchristian. I am convinced that J concurs. I have not yet officially joined the plot, but I did bribe a high official in Nero's retinue to tell me when he plans to strike at me. In addition I bribed a Praetorian to brief me on the sentiments of the troops. The word is that the Guard might be willing to kill the serpent—for the sum of five hundred sesterces per man (an astounding sum). The conspirators, I found, are far too passionate. They think they have done their job in merely planning the time and means of Nero's death. Foolishness! That's the least of it. Anybody can buy killers— even for Emperors. The higher the reward, the easier it is to acquire the talent. No, the quintella [a reward in some game?] must be the selection of Nero's successor and the assurance that he will be beneficial to the state. I have made my choice. He is a deceptively clever man whose name has been greeted with puzzlement by the plotters. I told them I will join them only if they agree with my candidate and raise him to the purple. I wait. I wait with no little anxiety, however, for my informer close to Nero told me he heard the monster is heaping calumny on me and making threats that I deserve "severe censure." What to do? First, I prayed for the soul of the madman. Then . . .

Damn! The rest of the scroll was so crinkled that not a word was legible. Not even the computer had been able to make a translation.

OLIVIA

When Andrew and I returned to Naples after our week in Rome, I felt a terrible sense of dread. I didn't really want to be back there. I didn't want to go back into that strange world which made our real lives seem so temporary and small. Don Ciccio, of course, persuaded me, appealing to my scholarly curiosity. He immediately drew me into a discussion of one of Lavinius' sketches, and before I knew it, I was back in the palace, admiring the fine lines of what I think is his most delicate portrait of Phyrne.

Don Ciccio has changed and is less agitated than I have seen him in weeks. But his new calm isn't his only change. He is more secretive than ever. Andrew is suspicious, of course. "He knows something," Andrew says. "He's got to have a reason for seeming so confident. Could it possibly be that he's made a deal with the Italians?" I asked the Don directly if something had taken place in our absence. When I said he was acting as if he had no fear he laughed and said he wished it were true. I believe him. But I was puzzled on our first day back, when he told us to relax and savor rather than nagging at us to pick up the pace. That was definitely a major change.

The past weeks have moved fast anyway. The farther we go into the palace the richer and more fascinating it becomes. Although we spend ten hours a day in the place I don't recall ever feeling tired. My adrenaline keeps me going at full speed and in relatively good spirits. I'm beginning to think that I'm conquering my anxieties.

The rest of what we call the "public rooms" on the second level make everything else we have come upon so far—even the most stunning discoveries—appear paltry. Is there anything on earth more luxurious and sensual than amber? Not mere fillets or random stones or mere fragments cleverly pieced together, but unflawed sheets of it. Three small rooms near the three bathing chambers, each no larger than four by five feet, are completely veneered with amber. The grandeur of the rooms comes not only from the amber but from the unusual height of the chambers. The ceilings are at least fifteen feet high.

The sheets of amber, each shaped differently, from neat squares to trapezoids, rhombuses, and bold curvilinear forms, are illuminated by the ambient light of the surrounding rooms.

The amber panels, honey-brown, rust, a caramel crimson, and a russet pink, are set into strips of silver and bands of mirrors. Absolute perfection.

Nothing in the world is more boring than armories. When Andrew jumped up shouting *"Another!"* I cringed. But what a surprise. He had found an absolutely captivating array of instruments of carnage—round, pointed, and double-edged spears, shields, bows and arrows, maces and battle-axes. In our lights they gleamed with an almost blinding silver patina as if blood had never touched their surfaces. There are dozens and dozens of throwing knives, each a different weight. Some have hard leather grips, others have handles made from clipped fur. Why the fur? When I picked one up I knew; the fur lent the knife a delicate touch. I noticed a cork on one of the walls, and taking the slender knife I was holding, I gave it a tentative flip toward the target.

The knife seemed to jump from my grasp as if propelled. It started off a bit wobbly, then straightened itself out, spun end over end, and slapped deep into the target! I took hold of another of the fur-handled knives and concentrated on being more careful. It didn't matter. The second blade acted like the first, hitting neatly near the center of the target, close enough to the bull's-eye to make me believe I was a natural. It was not magic, just magical workmanship. The knives were so deftly balanced that you couldn't mess up.

I was balancing one of the knives in my left hand when Andrew sauntered over. He took the knife and, with an elaborate show of balancing and sighting the target, whipped it over his back, launching it like a rocket. But he had overpowered the delicate instrument and it hit hard on the handle and fell to the floor. I casually picked up another and, with a gentle wrist flip, launched it into the center of the inner target.

"Do it again!" he challenged.

I did. This time I chucked the thing underhand. It struck home. The next one I tried over my shoulder, facing away. Then Andrew did the most astonishing thing. He wheeled me around and kissed me passionately, almost desperately. He was so tender, circling my waist with his arm guiding me tenderly through the rows of sparkling weapons. Later, at home, he presented me with the beautiful throwing knife I had used for my casual over-the-shoulder toss.

"You feel better, don't you? I've been worried about you. The place seems to depress you from time to time. Now it's okay, isn't it?"

"Yes, yes," I said with a touch of impatience.

"And you're pretty much over the idea . . . of telling the authorities? I mean, we've got to hold on and play the percentages. God, to be able to get our hands on some of this. You feel differently though, don't you?"

I nodded, not wanting to start an argument. I haven't changed my mind at all and if anything am more convinced that the best course of action is to call in the authorities as soon as we have explored the last chamber. I am tempted to just do it, no matter what the Don or Andrew think, although I would warn my husband so he could take a few souvenirs. Thinking about all this, I got depressed again, and Andrew noticed. But just why the Tertullian Palace gives me such lifts and lows I couldn't explain to him—or to myself for that matter.

The next day, we explored a complex labyrinth of tiny, empty chambers ranging off each side of the armory. Only when we had gone through them did we realize how cleverly the maze had been laid out. For those who had been there before there was no mystery. But an intruder would wander for hours and never escape.

When we finally got out of there, we entered a chamber with a low ceiling and walls painted a drab gray, so nondescript that I almost sauntered through without noticing the one item it contained—a box lying on a long table. The box was large, some six feet long, covered with a skin of russet leather studded with hexagonal tacks. Two ivory handles were the only other decoration.

Cautiously, ever so gently, I raised the lid, revealing a smooth roll of glistening silk, exceptionally old and obviously Oriental.

"I'm not surprised," Andrew said offhandedly. "After all, there was trade between Rome and the Orient."

The silk roll proved to be one of the most unusual works of art we have discovered. It is an immense scroll, over fifty feet long, made of thin paper mounted on silk. It was apparently painted by an Oriental—in Roman style! But the subject matter is wholeheartedly Chinese. In fact, it couldn't be *more* Chinese. It is a lavishly detailed, anecdotal, and poignant illustrated narrative of the twelve great labors of Hercules, the "patron saint" of Herculaneum, in Chinese, if you will.

The scroll is meticulous in style, combining a frank realism with a sense of fantasy. It reminded me of the incomparable painting *Views of the City of Shanghai,* which I once saw in the Forbidden City in Beijing. But that was painted in the eighth century; *this* dates to the first century! A Latin colophon spelled out the circumstances.

Han Chuo Wen, painter to the court of Sieng Syeh, arrived in Herculaneum in the year seven of the divine Augustus [around A.D. 14] to enter the service of the Lord Quintus Maximianus Tertullian. He was given quarters, two slaves, and a horse with a groom.

Within five kalends [roughly six months], he began work on the Great Scroll. The work was completed in fourteen kalends and twenty days [a little over seventeen months]. Lord Tertullian proclaimed it a worthy history, presenting Han with 125,000 sesterces [close to a quarter of a million dollars!], four horses, a triple carriage, a guard of four foot soldiers, and a hundred swords as gifts for his lord in Cathay. Lord Tertullian had learned of the incomparable hands of the master from one of the principal traders and was pleased with the telling of the tale of Hercules, the hero of the city and the Tertullian dynasty.

I've never seen anything like it in classical antiquity. The twelve labors are all depicted, but they have all been radically altered by the Chinese artist, who was obviously reacting to what he considered the vulgarity of Roman civilization. In Han's eyes, Hercules was Rome itself, and Rome's Pax Romana was devastating to the rest of the world. When the "hero" chopped the monsters—Enchida and Typhon, the Nemean Lion, the Hydra with its plethora of ghastly heads—to bits, he also destroyed hosts of innocent bystanders. Han also condemned the Romans' hedonism and lascivious sexual attitudes. Hercules, who has an affair with Artemis, uses her as a mercenary and sleeps of a drunk while she goes off to perform one of his labors. In another of the marvelous long series, Hercules and Artemis travel to China to dispatch the dreaded Stymphalian birds. These creatures turn out to be outrageous caricatures of Roman women of rank all tarted up in wild hairdos piled a foot above their heads. Hercules, aided this time by an urbane, sophisticated Emperor, destroys the cackling birds, who perish at any sound except their own voices, with giant rattles. Celebrations take place for the victors. But instead of bloody sacrifices, orgies, and interminable drinking sessions in Roman style, there are elegant soirées, poetry readings, plays, and discussions with scholars and philosophers.

The final labor is apocalyptic. Hercules, after an incredible struggle from which he barely escapes, slaughters the dragon guarding the golden apples of the Hesperides. In a fit of madness, he lays waste the orchard and a group of people held prisoner by the dragon. After that terrible deed, Hercules stands covered with gore, holding the apples and looking around him for the opportunity of more destruction. Rome, Han was saying, had gone mad. I wonder if Quintus went mad too.

THIS evening at dinner Don Ciccio mentioned casually that he had received a visit from Giulio Cassone, who claimed to know all about our discovery. Before either of us could say anything he went on to say that Cassone had asked for half a million dollars to keep silent.

"Christ! What did you do?" Andrew asked him.

"I gave him the money, of course."

I was so shocked I couldn't think what to say.

"He'll be back for more," Andrew said.

"I suppose you're right. But I don't mind. I feel confident that for another half a million he'll keep silent forever."

"Why should he?" Andrew observed sourly. "Shit, just when I was beginning to think we had faked them all out. We've had it!"

"Nonsense," the Don exclaimed. "This is southern Italy, and I know how corrupt officials behave. Cassone is not a blackmailer."

"I don't believe you," I said. "Cassone never gave me the impression he was on the take. There is simply no way the news of this discovery will not eventually come out. Why would Cassone lay himself open to the risk of getting caught taking an enormous bribe? Something's strange. Are you sure he isn't trapping *you*?"

"I am confident that he is not."

"Well, that takes care of almost everything," Andrew said. "By God, we may have made it. Don Ciccio, may I help out on these unforeseen . . . expenses?"

"Andrew, you will not be party to this graft," I told him.

"Olivia, it's the expected thing around here—the cost of doing business. Don't be such a prig."

"I'd rather be a prig than a crook," I said, furious.

"Let's be realistic," Andrew said. "This virtually guarantees that we can do as we please with the palace and its contents. I see nothing wrong with it. For God's sake, Olivia, what's the difference between keeping this place to ourselves and buying antiquities that you know have been found recently by *tombaroli*? You've done that in the not so distant past."

"You damn well know that those are random pieces, already stripped from their archaeological contexts. *This* is unique. Part of the heritage of the whole world. It would be unforgivable and immoral *not* to share it."

"But I do want to share it," my husband protested. "Only at the right time and after we take our legitimate share for our courage, our smarts, and—dammit—our money. We are three partners—"

"What about Stearns?" I asked.

"You can't tell me you want him to learn of this! He had his chance. I say let's go through the rest of it. Then keep it to ourselves. Take a few, say five, things each as mementos. Then, after we've got a firm deal with the Italians that allows the Metropolitan to have an exhibition every two years for twenty-five years, they can have the place. Oh, another thing—I want exclusive film and video and book rights for us. That's my vote."

"Mine . . . mine is to finish the exploration," I told them. "Each takes one piece—and it has to be something that's not of major historical importance—and then we let the authorities know. Then we can negotiate an exhibition arrangement for the museum along with the book and other things."

"Don Ciccio?"

"I 'vote' we carry out the exploration fully. And then decide what to do based on what we find."

"That's not enough," I said, at which the Don shot me a cold look. "You are planning, and have been all the time, to have it completely for yourself. I suspect you have even had your fill of us. What will you do to keep us out of your precious possession? What will you do to keep me silent? Offer me a million dollars?"

"Olivia, stop it. I am quite bored with these expressions on behalf of all mankind. You two—vexatious as I find you—are as much a part of the Tertullian Palace as its treasures. You cannot be separated from it. Think rationally—the way you do when you make a decision at the museum. You have every right to take possession of this place as protectors. Who is better suited? Who would care about it more? How many people do you believe would even bother to think about the historical value of this place? Do you think the Italian government would hesitate to make a profit on it? I say let's go forward and settle this later."

I had half a mind to go to the phone, call someone from the Ministry of Culture, and bring a squad of carabinieri down on our heads. But I had no idea whom to call.

"It's settled, then," the Don stated firmly. "Let's finish our job—with as little fighting as possible."

"Good. Let's keep moving," Andrew said. "Christ, we're in the most exciting adventure that we'll ever know in our lives, and we're bickering about it. Olivia, isn't this situation better than thinking that Tertullian's dams didn't work?"

"I'm not altogether sure," I said. "All right, the vote stands. I'll continue." I realized I will have to put off forcing the issue until we have gone through the last of whatever it's going to be —his lordship's and her ladyship's bedrooms, no doubt.

Perhaps I'm more tired than I think, or perhaps I'm trying to punish myself for just going along with the Don and Andrew. I'm starting to do strange things, things I would never normally do. A few days ago I happened to bump into a table in the baths, a table stacked with dozens of those perfume bottles. Two or three fell and shattered, but I wasn't perturbed, not even in the slightest. My God, if I had done anything like that in the museum I would have been horrified at my carelessness and lack of professionalism. But before I stopped to consider it, I saw myself casually reach out, pick up another, and deliberately throw it to the floor. It was as if I had to prove to myself that it was real, that the whole experience is real. Smashing the antique didn't give me a single pause.

I can't control what's happening to me. I've gotten my fears of being trapped down there under control, for the most part, but I'm still extremely edgy. I wonder more and more whether from now on in comparison to this palace, anything, anything, especially if it's ancient, will seem boring. Who warned against looking directly into the eyes of God? I have not discussed this with Andrew. He wouldn't be sympathetic. Each new room spurs him on. He never loses the sense of excitement. But it's different for me. I am waiting for something truly amazing. Things that would once have excited me I can now easily ignore. What is happening?

DON CICCIO

Olivia is perceptive. She saw through my story right away. She knows me very well, and I have the feeling she will betray me. I concocted the ruse about Cassone because I was beginning to suspect she was on the verge of telling somebody about the palace. Who knows what to expect from her? The palace seems to have had a profound effect on her. My hope is that after tensions have waned and Olivia has the time to reflect on what the bureaucrats would do to our splendid find, she will come to agree with Andrew and me. She has always been driven. She has always been an ambitious woman, obsessed with her career. Her single-mindedness used to worry me. But now her ambition seems to have temporarily wandered. She handles the objects with longing and sadness. Perhaps she has decided to become the "savior" of this material; maybe she thinks she will become famous for giving it back to the world.

I thought it was encouraging that we had started "venturing" again, slipping away from each other to roam freely, singly, among the dark chambers. For me, confined to my wheelchair, the adventure of going off alone offers special hazards. The other day, despite the fact that I have a new chair fitted out with balloon tires, a chair twice as strong as my standard one, I plummeted down several steps. Breathless, I wondered if I had fallen into some inescapable pit.

Actually, I had tumbled onto a mezzanine a meter beneath the floor of the "public" level. I froze. I could smell the odor of ancient decay. I knew I shouldn't move forward a millimeter. With a shaking hand I locked the brakes of my chair tight. A short distance away was a hole about four feet across—a perfect circle. I had to get to it, so I slipped out of the chair very gradually and pulled myself across the polished marble floor to the bronze rim of the hole. Clutching the edge tightly, I flashed the beam of my lamp down below.

Beneath me was a huge circular room. I estimated it as fifty feet in diameter, although my lamp wasn't powerful enough to illuminate the entire chamber. The mosaic floor, gold and silver in undulating patterns, seemed to swell toward me as I trained my light on the walls of the room. The walls are unlike anything I have ever seen, sculpted in relief into a huge image of a sleeping woman. Her body, clad in a thin rippling gown, is curled up tightly.

I was so excited that I inched myself around the hole until I could see her face. I recognized her as Persephone. I could see the tears falling down her cheeks. She is exquisite and disturbing. Although the relief is no more than a half an inch deep, Persephone seems fully three-dimensional.

An arched portal stands a few meters away from the locks of her hair, which spread out on a pillow. Two large fingers are carved in low relief on one side, positioned as if they were reaching through the entrance. I knew there had to be another hole like the one I was looking through. I eased myself back into my chair and investigated, easily locating the other aperture.

Once again I had to get myself out of the chair and crawl to the rim. Reaching it, I looked down and there was Pluto, carved in the same low relief. A powerful man, he is depicted nude, squatting with his great thighs bulging and his enormous back rippling with muscles. The god of the underworld is shown trying to reach his hand through the small door to caress Persephone's head. As I edged around the rim of the second hole I had to laugh. Pluto's erect phallus is no less than six feet long! From it, gleaming like pewter, flows a stream of semen across the wide white border of the mosaic through the arch, up onto Persephone's couch, and—finally—into her womb. I roared with laughter.

With a struggle, I managed to extricate myself from the strange chamber and its singular images.

OUR exploration of the middle section of the palace ended fittingly with a court measuring about a hundred and fifty feet long. I gazed at the lofty ceiling and the host of balconies supported by a forest of columns, dozens on each level. They progress from stolid Doric on the first level to Ionic on the second, and finally to a soaring Corinthian on the third. There must be twenty different kinds of variegated marble on the balconies and revetments. The colors range from jet black to mauve. The parapets of the balconies are accented with open-work alabaster, and the wooden ceiling is adorned with a sun beaming among ideal puffy clouds. At the end of the court is a stately staircase.

"Up there. Must be the private rooms. For God's sake, let's go—I'm getting bored down here!" Andrew said. "I want the real treasures!"

And so we did. I won't describe the goodies there just now, except for two sets of books. The first, found in a chest in one of his lordship's no less than eight private libraries, is Ter-tullian's complete diary, which includes what we had already found among the laboratory scrolls and a great deal more. The other set, secreted in a false partition in the floor of Phryne's inner sanctum, consisted of her private chronicles. We read hers first.

Your first memory in life returns at the moment of death, says Agileas, the philosopher so dear to us women. My first memory is the splash of sun on my mother's breast and the warmth and fragrance of our summer estate on the northern lake near Mediolanum. Next I recall how the mouth of my first tutor fell open in awe when, at four, I spoke to him clearly in his native Greek dialect, greeting him as an equal, for I recognized at once that he would perform only as a preceptor, feeding me the things I would need to learn by rote. Clearly a prodigy, I hum-bled him and my mother sent him away within a year, which was perfect. I had drained his vacuous head, a bag full of com-monplace nostrums.

The truth is that I educated myself, with the help of my mother, Cassandra, unfortunately named, as her every utterance about the greater world proved accurate. Once I had learned how to read and write and had dispensed with the pleasures of geometry, trigonometry, and calculus, I read, in five years, every book in the libraries. I would surprise and enchant my father every time he returned from his lengthy voyages to the East, where he traded in spices and metals. The only Roman trader who never failed to accompany his ships, he was lost at sea when I was ten. We had always expected it. The same day my mother told me that I was betrothed to Quintus Maximianus Tertullian, of the illustrious house which for centuries had ruled the south of Italia. The Tertullians could easily have become the imperial family. But of course the legendary family, the most arrogant, distant, and imperious clan in the world, for-swore the purple, considering themselves loftier even than the Emperors.

When I was twelve, my mother died and I was placed in my aunt's care. By the end of my first day in her house, I had discovered that she was my—and my mother's—antithesis, fiery in all aspects of her being. I adored her for this Dionysiac passion, which manifested itself in her brilliant and aggressive attitude in discussions and in the cries of joy which pealed through the house when she made love. She told me she would teach me that special art in a year or two. That is what I longed for more impatiently than any of the other things she promised —the colt, the trips to Athens and Thebes, my portrait, and my marriage.

The moment arrived during a glorious trip to Athens. Agrippina had carefully planned everything, although she never hinted as much until later, on the day of my wedding. Agrippina had been in her youth an acolyte of the cult of Aphrodite at Locri, the curious throwback to more archaic traditions in which the followers bedded with strangers for the glory of the goddess. By the time my aunt had been introduced to the rituals, all pretense of piety had long disappeared. But she was eager to join the cult for sheer pleasure. Through the years, a thousand unblemished lovers were hers, lovers of all ages and many nationalities. She continued to entertain them until she reached an advanced age. My aunt taught me everything she learned, and, except for one man, there was not a time in all my loves when my partner did not sigh in utmost joy. My first lover in Athens was Hikon, who still brings me pleasure on my every trip to Greece. At nineteen, he was confident, quiet, civilized, and comely. He had been taught by Agrippina to kiss in a certain secret sequence, which guarantees maximum pleasure.

She had also instructed him to learn everything about the monuments of the fabled city so as to become my tutor in art as well as passion. Hikon had memorized every monument from the Parthenon to the charming funeral stelae on the Kerameikos side of the Acropolis, where the bravest heroes are commemorated. Our favorite there was the warrior striding off to battle. Above his head, the archaic Greek words read, "Only average, I go to my death."

Hikon and I lingered many hours among these glorious statues of youths, whom we felt almost akin to. We recited our favorite poems for them, including the work of Virgil, who had amazed the intelligentsia with his epic of the life of Aeneas. We also read Aeschylus. After reading the words he had written, phrases like "often the young dead speak and listen with greater

*grace than the living," Hikon and I would make leisurely love
beside the happy stones. My Hikon was a truly gorgeous lad,
lithe and sinewy. I counted, caressed, and kissed his every sinew,
wondering how many an athletic hero's body possessed. Two
hundred and seventy-five, I found, lorded over by the principal,
which was my honeycomb.*

*I made my lover mimic the stones of Athens. If he per-
formed well, I rewarded him with love. I decided that the two
things I liked best in life were lovemaking and art. I adored the
ancient sculptures of the Parthenon almost as much as I adored
Hikon. Most impressive to me were the rising and plunging
horses represented by their heads alone, heads so heavily gilded
that they seemed to glow in the light of the hundreds of torches
set up on high rods ringing the old temple. The sight of the
archaic images of the gods moved me to tears.*

*That first summer of lovemaking and art with Hikon
proved idyllic. Never again would I experience such feelings of
bliss. At the end of the summer, Agrippina had to wrest me
away, weeping, reaching out for my beloved Hikon. After Athens, that summer of my twelfth year, I traveled to the most
singular place I had ever seen, the hamlet of Herculaneum, in
the provincial and rugged land of south Italia. There lived my
betrothed, Quintus Maximianus Tertullian, and his imperious
family, the wealthiest of the entire empire. . . .*

It became an amusing puzzle to try to mesh Tertullian's
and Phryne's chronicles. What would happen when a dedicated
pagan girl, devoted to art and love, married an early Christian,
a proud, dictatorial realist who was on Nero's hit list? The most
tangled operatic scenarios were straightforward in comparison.

After reading Phryne's poignant words, I am convinced
that to hand over this material or any of the contents of the

palace to a squad of scholastic drudges, to categorize, to analyze, to pick over coldly, is anathema. I will not allow the usual battalions of curatorial gnomes to threaten this delicate world. They would destroy it. The church would eliminate what threatened its well-polished myths, relegating the documents to secret archives, never to be seen again. Then the curators would rip everything away from its proper place. Gradually the palace would be stripped or turned into a tourist attraction.

I won't allow the palace to be turned into a series of underground "period rooms" through which bored day-trippers tramp. I will not allow sacrilege. I will not even agree to Andrew's plan for the three of us to take souvenirs. The world of the palace has to remain intact. But as for what Olivia has in mind—complete surrender—I cannot allow it. What to do with her? How to handle dear Olivia, whom I have helped bring so far in life? I have to think clearly, prudently. I must find the solution. She is the only obstacle to my saving the palace.

ON my return to my villa one night I received a terrible shock. We had been caught! By the most unlikely person, old Antonio Cartageno. He was waiting for me when I arrived, and he accused me directly.

"Signor Conte, you are cheating me. I've been away for months. I return and I see you are visiting the barren site. I know you have found something down below there. Why else would *you*—not just the others, but *you*—be visiting the barren hole so many times?"

"I shall tell you everything, my friend," I managed. "I have been, I'm embarrassed to admit, forced out of any dealings in this affair by my former partners and friends, the Fosters, and the principal backer, Mr. Albert Stearns. Nothing has been found, I swear it. But the others are convinced that they must scrape away the tufa for treasure. I have been visiting the site recently because I have been trying to show them that cutting away with scalpels will be costly beyond their wildest imaginings. But they refuse to listen. I have no power over them. In a sense, they own the failed operation. It's their money that has gone down the drain and they are locked in a bitter argument over who owes whom. But because I respect you and recognize that without you there would never have been even the failed experiment, I shall give you, from my own funds, a token amount that will help you. I believe that five hundred thousand might be generous. And that will guarantee us access forever. Yes?"

Cartageno's eyes moistened as he quickly accepted the sum. He asked if I might need some assistance in seeing that the Fosters and Stearns were "dealt with," and got a good laugh from my firm response that I would take care of them in my own time.

After that, I knew it was only a matter of time before I had to confront Al Stearns, who would be, I knew, a more difficult case. He had avoided all my attempts to reach him to discuss the delicate subject of his rights and interests in the Tertullian project. But finally my repeated phone calls must have embarrassed him, for eventually he invited me to dinner in his apartment on the roof of the Teatro Marcello, one of the most appealing ruins of the early Roman Empire, much of which had been renovated in the nineteenth century to form charming private apartments. In Rome one dines late, say ten. In Rome with Al Stearns, one dines exceptionally late—for status. It didn't matter. I expected some strain.

What I had not expected—foolishly—was his contempt, his actually trying to humiliate and intimidate me. I had come to break bread, negotiate, forgive, to exchange views as a colleague. But he mocked me openly. Of course I recognized that he did it only because of his acute discomfort and, in part, to bluff. But still.

I had come prepared to tell him everything about the miracles we had wrought and allow him in—for an appropriate price of, say, two hundred million. The principal reason for wanting him back in was that I entertained the thought that, somehow, he could help deal with Olivia.

But Stearns started off the discussion by reminding me that we had "nothing in writing." He said he had "experienced some minor financial setbacks" and offered to "settle for two million." So I became aggressive.

"But Al, old friend and partner, it's not *two* million, but *ten*. But what I'm really here for," I told him, "is to tell you we have done it, really done it. You cannot imagine what has happened. I want you back with us."

Stearns turned to stone.

"Don't give me this crap, Ciccio. You conned me—you and those other con artists, the Fosters. It was a game. You *knew* there would be no 'palace' or even a fucking ancient outhouse. You goddam guineas! Every time I deal with you, it's the same. I get rooked. Why do I, a clever son of a bitch, always get conned by guineas and good-looking women? Fuck you, dwarf. You're lucky to get two million. I have half a mind to throw you out of here with nothing. Christ, to think that you expect me to listen to more of this bullshit!"

Any general in the field has a contingency plan. I put mine immediately into action. Stearns had already snatched defeat from the jaws of victory. I decided I would make that defeat a rout.

I leaned closer and gave him one of my warmest smiles. "No, no, you don't understand. Al—partner—we believe we have found the Tertullian Palace. A miracle! I must be straight with you, as always. There is a bit of a problem. Tertullian's dams were not as successful as he—or we—had hoped. In fact, they didn't work. But we know where the palace *is*. We want to scrape our way through. Drill. Laser. I do admit it will take some time. Years, yes, years. And a great deal of money. Yet we'll prevail. I know it. As our staunchest supporter I *know* I can count you in. With the ten million you owe, another twenty will suffice for, I'd say, the better part of a year."

His eyes frosted into a decade of winters. "You're crazy. Up yours, dwarf."

I allowed my benevolent mask to crumble away—it was a masterful job of acting, if I say it myself. I made as if to stammer in confusion, muttering something about not understanding, about how he must be joking, about how I had perhaps not made myself clear. I followed by imploring, pleading, and then lapsing into sullenness.

"I'll give you the two," he growled. "I'm short. Deal coming up. You understand. Otherwise count me out."

"I want the check now." I whispered the words. He looked stunned, but nodded after a moment. As he went to his desk, I threw in the clincher.

"Are you positive you don't want to join us in this new endeavor?" I asked him with just the right tone of disbelief.

"It's madness," he muttered.

"But surely you want to keep your options open."

"Open for what? More money down that drain? No."

"Well, we would certainly welcome you back to the fold anytime you want."

"No," Stearns said quickly. "You aren't going to be able to sucker me into this operation. With this payment, consider me out—forever."

"Can you jot that down in a note?"

"I'll send it to you in a letter . . . with the check."

"Oh, I don't see how I could possibly leave here without them both," I told him. "Are you sure you don't want to reconsider and stay as a member of the team?"

Stearns turned, glared at me, grabbed a piece of stationery from his desk, and furiously wrote. It was perfect! He signed away all rights, interests, responsibilities, obligations, gains, rewards, recognition. The check for two million dollars was postdated a week ahead. Of course, he'd stop payment, I thought. As it turned out, he did. But every victorious general sustains some losses.

On my return to Naples I instructed Cassone to set a plan we had agreed on earlier into motion. He informed his "superiors," the Dorsoduros, that we had come across parts of the fabled palace intact. He also warned them that he and his officials had joined in our endeavor—to prevent them from immediately moving in on us. The Dorsoduros continued their tunneling with redoubled vigor.

I told Olivia and Andrew how I had dealt with Stearns, but I didn't mention anything about Cassone. Andrew thought my ploy with Stearns was the funniest thing he had ever heard in his life, saying over and over how he admired my "mental jujitsu." Olivia listened, her face an expressionless mask. Later she confronted me alone. "I see what you're doing, my friend. By cutting Al Stearns out you're taking control even more. Very clever. But don't think I won't do what my conscience urges me to do. You can't really get rid of everybody who knows about the palace, you know. Can you? No!"

I find it terribly hard to face what I will probably have to do about her. Old memories and old loyalties are powerful forces.

With everything on track, except for Olivia, I returned to Phryne's delicious life story, sharing it, as well as Tertullian's chronicle, with the Fosters. My spirits rose when I saw that Olivia had become utterly captivated by Phryne's life story.

In the south of Italia, a mixture of diverse architectural styles is considered the highest aesthetic. I, accustomed to order and harmony—the regular placement of Doric, then Ionic, then Corinthian—was reluctant at first to accept the architectural disorder the Tertullians favored. In time, however, I learned to love the Tertullian Palace with its labyrinth of small rooms surrounding spacious halls, varied porticos, and singular colon nades. The Tertullians combined orders rarely brought together. But I grew accustomed to the family's style and the palace itself. I grew used to the precipitous stairwells, the height —five stories—and the profusion of multicolored tiles which adorned the confusing facades. World-renowned architects had been spurned. The place was filled with a sense of luxurious confusion created by energetic and demanding amateurs. The family itself seemed to have absorbed this energy.

Quintus' aging father patiently explained within minutes of meeting me and approving the match (which was already ironclad) that the dignity, wealth, and awesome power of the clan could be traced to its "fierce energy and well-chosen acts of cowardice." In time I learned how correct he had been, for virtually no one in the history of the Tertullians had ever rashly brought death upon himself. And though I have no way of knowing if it is true, my husband informed me that no one in Tertullian history had ever committed suicide. "We have contempt for waste," as Quintus put it. "We conduct our affairs with balance. We have never suffered the humiliation of defeat in battle, and have avoided serious quarrels with the so-called imperial families." These words, so truthful, entered my ears as "spirits of bitterness," as the poet wrote. I am not so given to pure reason and rationality as the Tertullians.

I might have rebelled at the match. But Quintus was so physically appealing and the house was so beautiful. The treasures have provided my salvation, even more than the children, who, after all, are only children.

My catalogue of all the works is finished. Quintus, who usually finds my activities frivolous, is pleased with it.

Eventually I found Phryne's catalogue. It consisted of twenty-five fascicles on papyrus with two or three sentences on each item—a staggering 14,254! I found many of her comments professional and sensitive.

The thirty-four Alexander tapestries were commissioned by General Seleucid (and, indeed, the story for the series was fully written and annotated by him). There were four principal draftsmen, Tantallus, Anthemius, Argo, and Nessos, and five assistants, Ekaliton, Caiphus, Ega, Soteros, and Philippos. The drawings were finished in three years. Tantallus' genius, for it is fitting to call his talent such, was in the invention of perspective. The overlapping of figures and heads is used to impart the impression of physical fullness. I admire his ability to capture the lights and darks that occur when the sun illuminates one part and casts the other parts into the shade. It is remarkable but true that the colors have remained the same for the centuries!

Phryne could become passionate about certain works, especially the jewelry, which she called "those cherished stars in the firmament of art, so lifelike that one longs to have all of mankind in the same scale." She also reserved some poetic words for the work of her lover Lavinius. "His drawings carry the breath of life," she wrote. Her more earthy assessment of the artist as lover came later.

I was interested to see that, like Olivia, she had been captivated by Han's ponderous scroll. She remarked that "his invention knows no bounds."

But she was also capable of coldly dismissing anything that did not meet her standards. In what is one of my favorite passages, she savaged a portrait of one of Nero's mistresses (who later married him) by an artist named Kiron.

Who is this wretched Kiron who has so egregiously pandered in his image of that bruised peach? He has accomplished what none of her beauticians and physicians have been able to do despite years of work and thousands of sesterces; he has liberated the pig from the mud pen, cleaned up her mottled physiognomy, recast her drooping nose, removed the water from her sagging breasts, and has, in his greatest miracle, even given her the gift of a few strands of real hair. With a genius like this, Kiron could ameliorate the whole tottering Empire!

The candor of some of her chronicle delighted me.

Quintus Maximianus was twenty-three and I sixteen at our union, a ceremony which was modest, as is usual with the Tertullian family, although the banquet was lavish. The moment of marriage came and went with a handshake, the sacrifice of a dozen white doves, and a most unusual event—a choir of young boys. They sang the ballad of Mars chasing after Venus. "Round the mountain top," they sang, "round the valley, round the tent, and into the bed."

"Oh, to play with a god, oh!" went the refrain.

The dinner consisted of twenty courses, including shellfish packed in snow sent from Sicily, and a very special wine put away on the birth of Quintus for his nuptials.

As is the custom, Quintus and I retired to the bedchamber just before the banquet was ending to consummate the union. I was joyous when I saw the muscular body of my husband, so lean and hard, with a phallus I imagined I could wind around my thigh. I acted chaste and easily convinced Quintus I was a virgin—unsuspecting men are readily fooled—though it would not have mattered if Quintus had discovered I had long ago been taken by another. Agrippina had instructed the marriage broker to reveal that I had been in the service of Aphrodite. Quintus' father might have suspected, having been acquainted with Agrippina, but I don't think my husband ever learned, not that he would have cared. Following Agrippina's counsel, I submitted to Quintus calmly and without a hint of passion. I waited patiently for him to set his seeds, which was for him a duty to be carried out as swiftly as he could. Many times since that first encounter I have wondered what he would have thought of a wife who could seduce a man like a prostitute. But, faced with this cold man, I have never been aroused. I receive and give much pleasure with my lovers, whom I do not discuss with Quintus.

I have lately turned to the delights of teaching boys. I enjoy taking them from hesitancy and nervousness to shouts of joy. To watch a sweet-smelling adolescent body experience the first eruption of love soothes me strangely. I act during each adventure, allowing the acolyte to believe I am nervous, that I am the supplicant, the unknowing pupil. Then I shock the youth by hungrily devouring the inside of his thigh with my tongue until every muscle is thickly knotted. I drain him of the juice of love, hold the briny ooze in my mouth, and then suddenly attack his wide-open, gasping mouth, tricking him into savoring his own fluid. No place can remain hidden from me. A week ago I made the youth Flavius, at thirteen still untouched by a woman, suffer fellatio for four hours. When he burst forth—in what I am convinced must have been the first ejaculation of his life—he fell into a dead faint. Lately I have tried all sorts of artisans, wondering if a talent for dance, sculpture, or painting lends itself to the arts of the couch. I have found no correlation.

I have also sought out ugly men, dwarfs, cripples, even those with the red "widow's birthmark" pocking their faces, to see if these disabled creatures have hidden reservoirs of energy in lovemaking. Most do not, but there is one, a most unexpected pleasure at my doorstep, Lavinius, the misshapen painter to my lord. He delights in drawing me in erotic poses, and I delight in his lips. I keep him performing at ever greater levels by tantalizing him with the promise that I shall let him mount me, which, of course, I will not do. Some social boundaries do exist.

I have had only one true sexual encounter with my husband. It was after the climax of the celebration of the Lupercalia, and I was shot with wine—an unusual affliction for me, since I normally abstain, disliking its sickening effects. He surprised me by entering my chambers after I had retired. Caught under the influence of the wine, I decided to surprise him by

233

running over and taking his member into my hands and then into my mouth. Quintus stood stock still in the beginning and then began to quiver all over in the most alarming manner. Then, silently, tenderly, he reached down, took my lips away from his swollen phallus, smiled wistfully, and departed without a word. He scarcely came close to me again.

His obsession with the Easterner called Christ grows every day. For the first time I fear the consequences of this passion. The Emperor, a man I happen to appreciate (for his sense of wit as well as his flamboyant lovemaking techniques), loathes the teachings of the sect and has threatened to burn them all. Yet it is not my station to discuss the subject with my lord. I worry about how I will fare if Quintus is found out. My informant in my husband's retinue told me that Quintus is dreaming of making a journey to see this so-called messiah. I worry.

Artemisia, my closest childhood friend, a dedicated writer of letters, has sent the most amusing narrative.

"Rome, it is proclaimed over and over, is the most efficient state in the history of mankind. Yet I ask you, old friend, how can this most efficient state of ours continue to dominate the world without any written laws? You would do us all a great service if you were to implore your dear Emperor friend to have his aides compile a list of existing laws. When required to decide who is right or wrong, the magistrates these days simply rule in favor of the richest or most aristocratic. This lack of codified laws is a subtle disease on the state.

"I voice another concern: the growing population of slaves. Has it occurred to you that once slaves become freedmen, they work harder and produce more? Did you know that, according to the last census, the slave population of the Empire is three times that of freedmen, and growing? You have heard the reports of the uprisings that are rapidly spreading? I find these

outbreaks ominous. Please instruct the Emperor that it makes better financial sense to free all the slaves than to keep an increasing group of humanity in bondage. If every slave had to pay for his freedom and, after that, was also responsible for taxes, then the revenues of the Empire would increase."

It was not the kind of advice I thought of giving to the Emperor, especially in the evening, when he preferred frivolity.

An evening with the Emperor is helter-skelter and invariably lasts until dawn. "I prefer to sleep most of the day," Nero says, "so my chamberlains can run the state without my interference. Ha!" The fact is that Nero's chamberlains more often complain about his absences than approve them. I have heard that with my own ears and have no reason to believe otherwise. There are always lies being spoken about anyone in power, especially Emperors, and most particularly this one, who ascended to the purple throne at such a young age and who is so different from his predecessors.

Enemies and conspiracies abound, and the chief of staff has persuaded the reluctant Emperor to be constantly attended by a guard of four. Each of these men was forced to hand over his mother or father to the Praetorians to ensure loyalty. For the first time in memory there are two tasters for the imperial food and two physicians nearby. My tryst with Nero was burdened by this entourage, but I soon learned to ignore them, and they, to avoid unduly annoying the Emperor, slipped out of sight while we made love. Nero is as charming and expansive in bed as in all aspects of life. The lovemaking, followed by one of my massages, always seems to spur him to lively talk, during which he indulges in unceasing banter.

"Do you know how I made my success?" he asked as he lay back in happy exhaustion on the couch. "I know everything."

"Yes, dear lord."

"You doubt?"

"Yes. No one, not even a god, can know everything."

"Being called a god is not being one. It is an honorific title, like being Pontifex Maximus. Pshaw! As if I traipsed around making sacrifices all day long. But I do know everything. Listen to this and you'll be convinced."

His face, which when animated resembles an adolescent's, became grave, slightly unsettling me.

"Why haven't you told me about your friend's curious ideas concerning the manumission of slaves and the written codification of laws?"

My first thought was that he was going to order my execution, despite his relaxed manner. The next instant I wondered who his spies were in our household, but then I didn't care, realizing it would take a lifetime to find them all. If Nero had taken the pains to read silly, rambling letters to me, what, I wondered, would he think of my husband's seditious thoughts and his association with the cult of the Easterner, Jesas? But my worries were soon eased. Sneering and smacking his lips, Nero raised himself off the couch, stretched like a young male cat, and delivered himself into my arms. I devoured him greedily.

Between caresses I managed to say, "I believe, young lord, you do know everything. But why spy on me?"

Grasping me roughly by the hair, he yanked my head backward. "Can you imagine me taking a lover—even if only a sometime lover—without investigating her innermost secrets? I see in your eyes that you are wondering if I've done the same with your haughty Quintus Maximianus. Yes, I have started a routine investigation. But do not worry—I am not the sort to visit on a man's family the same agony I might visit upon him. Finish your good work and we shall talk some more."

And I did. He was pleased. Why not? I was taught by the most accomplished priestesses of Aphrodite. The subsequent talk was technical—and impressive, I have to admit. Nero demolished Artemisia's untutored babblings. He told me why it is important not to codify the laws and why the slave population is allowed to grow. In both, his reasons were convincing.

"Phryne, what is the worst ill in Rome today?"

"This blind worship of the goddess Luck?"

"No! Why forbid the masses the worship of good old Roman Lady Luck? With their passion for gambling, whom else would they worship? Don't tell me you are one of those Christians who insist upon denial of every traditional belief unless they can find it preordained in one of their turgid books. I begin to suspect you."

"Lord, I am no Christian," I said. "Who would want to follow some provincial cult in which eating the body of your deity is symbolic of the thing to be attained?"

Nero smiled in satisfaction.

"Stop there!" Olivia demanded. "What does Tertullian's diary say? Did he become involved in the assassination?"

"I have it here, of course. I shall read the translation with pleasure. By the way, isn't it convenient for just the three of us to peruse these unique documents without hindrance from any official!"

She smiled as I started to read.

Four of the noblest men in Rome honored my house with their presence and explained the reasons why the madman had to be assassinated.

"Will you become one of us?" Arcadius Nessus asked.

"My lords, no," I told him. "Killing Nero is not the same as killing another man, no matter how much he deserves a wretched death."

I had ruminated for a long time. I knew that assassination might unleash a slaughter of many of my fellow believers. My decision was based on my belief that it is sinful for a noble Roman to kill the head of state. Julius Caesar's death threw Rome into disastrous civil wars. The murder of Nero—by a party of nobles, three of them senators—might bring down the world!

Disappointed, my guests nevertheless saluted the courage of my convictions.

"My decision does not mean," I told the lords, "that I have not been thinking of how your aim might be accomplished. I have sown a seed with the commander of the Praetorian Guard through a freedman in his retinue. The commander will not stand in the way of the Emperor's replacement.

"I suggest we, the highest nobility, inform Nero that we wish to raise the money to erect a monument in his honor. He will be intrigued and agree to meet with us. At the same time, I imagine, he will be conspiring to have our properties seized. We will extol his virtues and describe the monument at a banquet. But who knows what might happen at the banquet? A 'crazed' member of the Guard might go berserk. What happens to Nero will happen. If we are not directly connected, the state will be blameless. The vital thing is that there be no noble family involved and no civil war."

"It will be blamed on the lunatic Christians," exclaimed Arcadius Nessus.

Of course he was right. I was sorry for the ones who would die, but then, they would achieve martyrdom. They, like Petrus, *would probably welcome death. My noble compatriots agreed with my plan. . . .*

"What a hypocrite!" Olivia burst out. "What kind of a Christian is that?"

"Tertullian was, first and foremost, honorable to his class and his nation," Andrew said.

"So were a lot of Prussian generals," Olivia added.

"Did they do it?" Andrew asked.

I read on.

We were invited, as I predicted, to an imperial banquet at the summer palace near Stabia. Completely mad, Nero seemed to interpret the banquet as the beginning of a campaign to restore some of the territories he had recently lost to the barbarians. The guests were ordered to come in armor, each accompanied by an aide-de-camp and two slaves to carry field gear. Before the banquet, we suffered through the routine sacrifices carried out before the beginning of any military operation. Then there was the meeting with Nero, who was dressed as the god Apollo, wearing only a silver cape and golden shoes with soles made of lapis lazuli to symbolize heaven. His reading of the battle order and his description of the defensive stations was mercifully brief. "The enemy is the pig," he cried, "the crustacean, the plover, the goat, the lamb, and the smelt. We shall attack them with our knives, mouths, and stomachs, and we shall not quit the field until every enemy has been carved up into pieces and devoured. I, Apollo, shall lead you to certain victory. If encircled, we shall eat our way out! To battle! To the banquet hall!"

Phryne thought the scene amusing and made her way over

to the Emperor to tell him how brilliant she thought he was. He embraced her, all the while looking over at me. From that moment on he never stopped slavering throughout the entire display. Phryne preened in the imperial attention.

As the Emperor raised his hand, a dozen trumpeters sounded the military salute for dinner. But I could only think of our legionnaires in the field defending this imbecile with their lives. As we soldiers marched in to dinner, our divine commander approached, holding my wife, who clung to him tightly. When the Emperor beckoned me to kneel, he placed my ear close to his face and whispered, "Remember that man we tortured to death together?" I found myself unable to speak. "He was one of the Christians, one seen by my men lingering near your palace. So, you see, during the campaign this night, one of my warriors will perish—and that is to be you. You will die and your possessions will be confiscated as an offering to Apollo. The fate of your ugly wife and dim-witted children depends on the way you choose to die. Your fate will be sealed at the end of the banquet. Eat hearty!"

My blood chilled. My mind strayed from the menu. But just before the sweetmeats and the moment when I expected to hear my death announcement, I took command.

To the complete surprise of Arcadius Nessus and my wife, I rose to my feet and walked to the center of the hall. Halting the slaves bearing the multitude of gold and silver trays, I delayed the approach of my four executioners, who were following behind them. I raised my goblet to Nero, who squirmed in his seat. My only hope was to capture the speaker's role in place of Nessus and divert Nero's attention.

"Lord! Our divine and devout majesty, thou who sits amongst the blessed gods!" I cried out.

Olivia snorted in derision. "Some more true Christian piety."

Andrew laughed and continued.

"I bear the honor of representing the nation and her most ancient nobility. I have been called upon by the most high—the very gods who are your fortunate companions in heaven. They rejoice in your gifted company. They have in recent days sent a host of messengers to the mortal realm to ask why the god, the invincible Nero, has not returned to the heights of sacred Olympus for so long. Sire, your compatriot gods are sad because of your absence. . . . Lord, we are but humble mortals, subject to the will of the gods. Yet we presume to attempt to honor you for your magnificent works. We beg you to approve our way of honoring you, which includes a hundred sacrifices and daily songs to your wisdom in the schools. His estates in Baetantium are offered up by Arcadius Nessus. His lands in Spain are given to you by Caius Pontius. From this humble witness, I ask you to accept my palace in Herculaneum. And, as a most precious sign of our love, we have ordered the artisans to begin work today on your statue in bronze and gold of forty-two cubits to be erected near the Forum."

I had spoken, I hope, with as much flattery as was necessary. Some of my words must have entered the Emperor's crazed mind. Tears of joy flowed down his fat cheeks. His head collapsed onto the table. His golden crown slipped to the floor. He blubbered for a while and then rose to his feet. He came toward me, naked but for his thin cape. As he cast his wide-open eyes around the crowded chamber, he gestured toward someone in the rear, either to summon or dismiss my executioners. Then his face reddened and twisted into a demonic grin.

Flecks of white foam spread across his lips as he opened his mouth to speak. But the words never came forth. Suddenly I was thrown to the floor. A corporal of the Guard had stepped over me nimbly and in one short stroke had plunged his sword into the neck of the former god. As the tyrant fell he seized a dagger from the guardsman's belt and plunged it into his own heart. "Honorable" to the end.

The reaction from the throng of celebrants was singular. Not one cry. Not a murmur. It was as if something sacred had taken place. The only man to move was the corporal, who threw his bloodied sword upon the corpse of Nero and walked calmly away. I saw two Praetorians take him, and I never heard of him again.

His disappearance broke the spell. A frightful clamor began. The women keened as a chorus, which was soon drowned out by male laughter, and soon the women too were laughing. Only Phryne seemed distressed. Everybody remembers this banquet as one of the most pleasurable celebrations. That same night the Praetorian Guard elevated to the purple the only logical Emperor, the man I had already insisted upon to Arcadius, the man who had already acquiesced—the intelligent young Galba. In this way I was saved. Had God intervened?

"Galba? It was the good Christian Tertullian who made Galba the next Emperor?" Olivia exclaimed. "Compared to him, Nero looked like a statesman. I'd hardly call him a Christian sympathizer. Had the devil intervened?"

"Olivia, how could Tertullian know that would happen? You know how hard it is to predict how a new leader will grow into a job," Andrew said.

"Tertullian's a hypocrite and a blundering fool," Olivia

muttered. "I must say I'm kind of disappointed in Phryne. What was her reaction to this dinnertime slaughter?"

I did, I admit, shed a tear for Nero. He had been misunderstood by the nobles, or, more correctly, had been feared by them because of his brilliance and free spirit. I was not at all surprised that the nobles and the Guard had conspired to kill him, although I was overwhelmed when I saw that Quintus was the leader. These Tertullians are truly incomprehensible. What about their much-vaunted discretion? I wonder how much Quintus will make me suffer.

Nero was rash, jealous, selfish, and prone to temper tantrums. But he was neither an idiot nor a madman. Had he lived and had he been able to carry out his reforms in the civil service and the military, I am certain Rome would have become far greater than she will be under the quavering Galba. Even before Nero's assassination, his enemies had begun the campaign to vilify him, to accuse him of madness. They even claimed that he had tried to destroy the city by fire in his attempt to stamp out the Christians! Upon his death his successor accelerated the program of vilification, and within a year the name Nero had been all but obliterated.

We jumped immediately to Tertullian's diary to see what, if any, revenge he would mete out on his wife. Instead, the diary continued with his being ordered by a grateful Galba to serve in his administrative retinue at Rome. Tertullian seems to have been genuinely impressed with the elderly Galba, admiring his intellect and knowledge of ancient history. His only criticisms were directed at the lavish military programs the Emperor undertook. Tertullian suspected—correctly, as it turned out—that in his haste, Galba was in the grip of "larcenous men." When informed of this, the Emperor looked pained and launched into an account of some of Rome's most agile crooks.

When the Emperor is involved in the telling of a story, he sits upright and tells his tale in a stentorian voice. "Tell me about today's corruption," he begins, and I say that it is nothing compared to the old days! The worst times were under Agrippa, master of masters when it came to thievery. During the building of the Pantheon, that wily thief purchased enough stone, concrete, and terra-cotta with the state purse to construct two full villas for himself. Then he had the gall to invite Caesar to the commemoration dinner at the larger of the two.

Galba likes me because he learned from his spies that I insisted on him despite the opposition. He realizes instinctively that I am one of the few in the innermost circles who is not intent upon aggrandizing himself. As a reward, he has showered me with riches, and the timing proved fortuitous; the dams surrounding the palace were twice as expensive as I had estimated. But Galba was perhaps the only person who did not scoff at my precautions. His advice was to remove the entire contents to the Palatine, where he promised me a palace "twice the size of that old one." He failed to understand why I could not leave our family palace. After all, our family seat is far more ancient than any property in his family, the Julians being relative newcomers to power.

At this time my wife began to become tiresome. After Nero's death, she joined a decadent group in the imperial court, imagining I would not get wind of it. Phryne's desire to spend money also increased, yet she complained that I was spending too much money on protecting my family's palace, money I suppose she would spend on jewels, dresses, and favors for the younger members of the Guard. I have come to a painful deci-sion about her. Despite the fact that she is the mother of my two children, she will have to be gotten rid of. How and when I can manage this I don't know.

I had a most intriguing discussion with the Emperor about Christianity. The subject surfaced like one of those delicious and ferocious Campanian "fox fishes" which, when hooked, try to devour the fisherman himself. I was alone at afternoon wine with the "divine" Galba, and he casually mentioned that his spies had been following me.

"I consider it valuable to have many spies," he said, "some-thing no one would have done in Republican times. I have learned that you were suspected by Nero of being a Christian. I have also heard that he was going to have you tortured to death after the gala. I don't know why he was so hysterical about Christians. Nero was the most insane member of his family, a family which has been greatly exposed to madmen. My family was sane. And I, for one, have never felt especially threatened by Christians. I mean, they don't really eat their children, do they? No, certainly not. But Quintus, if you are a Christian, or a budding one, you must be careful. There are those who are extremely jealous of you because you are one of my inner circle."

The Emperor paused, dismissed the slaves, and ordered the guards to leave the chamber.

"Have a mind to your wife," he warned. "She is bedding every trooper who glances at her. More important, she's spread-ing stories that you are building some sort of Christian sanctu-ary down there at Herculaneum. If one of my morals police denounced her for orgiastic behavior, I could have her killed. I'll do it if you wish."

"No, lord."

"So, shall I assume that you are a Christian? If you are, I

trust you are an important one. I've heard, perhaps erroneously, that Christians want to eradicate the crown and all the nobles. True?"

"Some of them, my lord," I said with a smile. "But they are not the true ones."

"I'm not sure," he said, making himself look confused. I had come to learn that when Galba assumes his dim-witted look, it is time to flee. But I was so entranced at the dignity of the Emperor and, frankly, so taken with his kindness that I let down my defenses.

"Not many months ago, here in Rome," he told me in even tones, "there was this giant of a Christian man, crazy, too, I warrant. His name was Petrus. He told Nero's men he wanted to be killed, like this Jesas, whom, I think, one of our Palestinian courts tried and heavily fined some years ago. I hear Jesas is still alive, but doesn't preach any longer. Anyway, this Petrus asked for death and got it—quickly. Crucified. And upside down, too. Have you ever met this Jesas?"

"No, my lord. But not for want of trying. Jesas taught the Christian ethics and is now a physician. He moved with his family to lower Gaul. His preachings now are passed along by his disciples, some of whom, I'm afraid, are apt to see things in the air and hear voices in the clouds and have begun to teach his gospel in terms of mysteries. They believe he was crucified and rose from the dead."

"Gods save us from mystery cults!" Galba exclaimed, growing beet-red. "Zoroaster, Isis, Mithra, Paragon, Voddin, Baptistism, and those maddened Sicilians at Eryx! They'll bring us all down with their idiocy. Did you know Petrus?"

"I did know him, and I didn't like him at all. He stayed with me for a time at my palace just before he came to Rome. But I do happen to believe in the ethical and high moral teachings of Jesas. Jesas, it is said by some, was a king of one of the Aramaean tribes and was a powerful political leader. He believed that in time, slaves would become a burden on society. Jesas thought it would be smart to start educating them and gradually freeing them. I tend to agree, for basic economic reasons. They are growing in numbers almost faster than they themselves can work to gain sustenance. Every time I have made one a freedman, I've gotten far more work out of the fellow—for a third of the true cost."

"Quintus, you are beginning to intrigue me very much. What are some of your other beliefs?" the Emperor asked quietly.

"I also agree with Jesas that we would be better off economically if we subjugated our enemies by teaching them to be peaceful."

"Didn't this Jesas claim he was actually the son of some unique Eastern god—wasn't it someone called Jevhah or something? Does that sound practical?"

"No, sire, Jesas never made the claim, but since he never denied it, some of his disciples—those I referred to, they call themselves 'zealots'—preached this."

"Doesn't much matter," the Emperor muttered. "These days everybody seems to be a god or related to some god. I ought to know. You can go to the speakers' platforms in the old Forum and listen to god, any given day. One of these Christians does interest me, the writer—Johannis, is that his name? He writes about the end of the world, I hear. I'm rather interested in that subject myself. I happen to think we may be close."

I told the Emperor about J and said that he was staying at my palace.

"I would dearly like to meet him. But both of us need to be very careful about our meetings with the Christians."

When Andrew stopped reading, none of us could utter a word.

"Can you imagine how the Vatican will react to all this?" Andrew said.

"Do you believe any of it?" Olivia asked. "That's more to the point."

"There have been no end of books trying to prove that Christ was a teacher of ethics and was never crucified," I answered. "The theories range all over the place. He was saved from crucifixion and fled with Mary Magdalene and his son— yes, *son*—to France to establish the Merovingian bloodline. Or he escaped to India and became a guru."

"But none of these silly theories had any kind of backing or proof!"

"Well, here's the proof!" Andrew remarked. "Tertullian says without the slightest trace of doubt that Jesus was never crucified and that he went peaceably to France to be a doctor. Imagine! Olivia dear, think of this. Don't get me wrong, but what do you suppose will happen when the church learns about this? When we give up the palace to the authorities for the benefit of mankind, won't this material be jeopardized? Face it —the chronicles of Phryne and Tertullian will be destroyed, along with a great deal more, I figure. Come on, Olivia, you've got to agree with that."

I could not have done better myself.

"Dear Andrew, I am not you—yet, anyway," she said.

Despite her retort, I'm sure Andrew's point struck home. If it helped change her mind, it will save me considerable anguish.

OLIVIA

Damn Andrew sometimes! No matter. My position is firm. When we've had our fun, we must reveal everything to the authorities, without making any deals. If I can't confide in Giulio Cassone or somebody else highly placed in the Ministry of Culture, if the Don has bribed them all, then I'll go to the press. I have stopped talking to Andrew about this. When I last brought the subject up, he simply smiled patronizingly at me. Damn Andrew!

DISCOVERY

I had somehow gotten it into my mind that the private quarters would be small in scale. But they are huge and include several salons easily equaling those at Buckingham Palace in size, for lord and lady. Phryne had six spacious rooms, Tertullian had no fewer than eight. Adjacent to each suite are half a dozen servants' cubbyholes, separated from the master and mistress by draperies. It reminded me of the eighteenth century when personal servants lived in the same rooms as their masters, separated only by screens.

The apartments contain thousands of things, all rather casually placed. There is something eerie about these rooms. There is no sign of panic. What was on their minds when the tremors hit and mud began to engulf the dwellings nearby? Why was Tertullian so confident that he would return to the palace when the disturbance was over? We assume that like the rest of the city's residents, he couldn't really imagine the extent of the destruction. Perhaps he took his family to some place he thought was safe. What if they were trapped somewhere? Why didn't he try to dig back down after the mud had cooled somewhat, before it solidified?

My, his lordship must have been vain! His cabinets contain a staggering quantity of cosmetics from shops in Alexandria, Athens, and Crete, and there are cubbyholes for his hairdresser and a pair of valets. When I saw his clothes collection, I knew why Quintus needed two aides to dress him. There must be a hundred togas, many trimmed in purple velvet and ermine. Others of purest silk are decorated with round patches with various initials embroidered in silver and gold thread. He also had a whole wardrobe just for cotton shorts and jerseys—obviously for athletics.

I opened a closet and discovered a welter of Chinese robes of the most exquisite silk embroidery. I found Mongolian felt trousers and vests. One of the uniforms is a smashing leather suit of armor, sweat-stained and dented by hundreds of blows.

Phryne's six closets are jammed with some of the most beautiful garments I have ever seen, all perfectly made and none showing any wear. If she could be said to have favored any one couturier, it was the one who designed her many-layered diaphanous gowns, which resemble the revealing low-cut dresses of the Third Empire and include several petticoats, each thin enough to see through, and a lace bodice.

Did the lady like jewels? Very likely, but Phryne's jewelry, filling thirty-five chests lined in chamois tinted rose, is located in the master's quarters! He had, no doubt, chosen it all, and, for all I know, told her when to wear what. The prize pieces were made in the family factory and although of higher quality are much like the beautiful things we found earlier. Phryne had some of the largest and most colorful pearls I ever remember seeing. Suspended on a special mount for viewing (nothing if not ostentatious, Lord Tertullian) is a necklace, or actually more a stomacher, with nine strands of pearls ranging from those the size of grapes in the center to seedlings on the outside. Each strand is a different color—white, cream, tawny yellow, flame red, black, purple, silvery, golden, and cerulean. There are also fifty or more pairs of earrings, each pair a matched set of "baroque" or irregular pearls. Some are mounted in amusing shapes—two deer, a pair of cranes, and two cavorting putti. Along with the pearls are hundreds of pieces fashioned in miniature mosaic from variegated bits of mother-of-pearl, including two brooches six inches across inlaid with spectacular hippocamps. In one of the chests are filigree pieces, in another a set of Hellenistic enamels which portray the gods of Olympus. But the knockout is nestled in a huge leather trunk which opens like a triptych to reveal three sets of drawers. There are two hundred and twelve individual pieces of golden jewelry—all Greek, early fifth century B.C., made for a Scythian chief-of-chieftains whose name was Aryx the Invincible. I was incredulous. A thin gold table recounts Aryx's exploits, the conquest of "a thousand lands," the seizure of "tens of thousands of slaves," in the conventional way. But the jewels are different. They are rapturous and poetic, illustrating the life of Aryx and his two horses. I snitched a ring incised with beautiful images of Aryx and his steeds, Hero and Starfire.

There is simply no doubt we've missed whole sections of the palace. Andrew believes there are other nooks and crannies between the floors. He wants to find them all. I don't feel at all adventurous and annoy him by refusing to help. So he plunges off into the gloom by himself, leaving me there gritting my teeth. Yesterday he came back laughing happily. I forgave him, especially after he guided me to what he called "my *finest* discovery."

Imagine a snaking tunnel, some fifteen feet in height, frescoed from floor to ceiling, equipped with beds and couches at convenient intervals. Guests were apparently expected to wander through, gazing at the startling paintings and occasionally stopping for refreshment on one of the beds.

Andrew was quite pleased with himself for finding this tunnel, but he needed me to tell him what the paintings are all about. I explained to him that they represent the Metamorphoses of Ovid. They are splendid, executed in a style full of a sense of celebration! We walked slowly, hand in hand, through the lovely scenes of the flight of Icarus and the story of Apollo and Daphne.

We laughed as Apollo attempted to seduce the gorgeous, athletic nymph. Far from being a frightened, unwilling prey, she taunted and enticed him. When she relented, he would gently reach for her and they would fall into slow, tender love-making. By their third coupling, I was weak in the knees, and when Andrew abruptly picked me up and put me down on a Roman bed piled high with ancient cushions, I was virtually ready to scream. But I decided to forgive my dear husband for all his sins.

DON CICCIO

It was, at last, time to deal with the Dorsoduros. Their tunnel was getting close. I had a nightmare in which their crew burst through the wall into Tertullian's bedroom and started plundering the palace.

Reality was, predictably, more interesting. Enrico Dorsoduro and his band had been remarkably tenacious and skillful. I was wrong to think that they would grind their way through the tufa using high-speed drills and a small bulldozer to cart away the crumbled tufa. Instead, they had sought and found a series of underground passages formerly used for drainage and utility pipes of various kinds. These tunnels simply link up with some of the ancient tunnels, and my men informed me that the Dorsoduros were within days of reaching us. I alerted Giulio Cassone and told him about a little surgical operation I had been planning. He told me that there would be no official objection to the scheme, and I gave the necessary instructions.

I had always known that the batches of nitroglycerine Al Stearns had ordered up would come in handy. My Arturo planted the necessary number of charges impeccably, slipping them down five aluminum tubes into a municipal tunnel from the nineteenth century, a tunnel which intersected with one used by the Dorsoduros. The ensuing blast, triggered by the Dorsoduros, caused no loss of life except theirs. The property damage was modest. The media covered the "gas explosion" routinely; it was a chronic problem. Nothing has been heard since of either Enrico or his sons. In Naples the abrupt disappearance of the family was greeted for the most part with shrugs and whispered comments.

After the incident I increased the security at my villa. But my informants assure me that the remaining Dorsoduros are too dispirited to retaliate. The family, after centuries of effort, has tired of the quest for treasure. At last, the Dorsoduro stranglehold on antiquities has been broken. My only lingering concern is a problem Arturo brought up. "Was the explosion too close to our tunnels?" he asked. "Might it cause problems underground?" I have asked myself the same question. But life has risks.

Finally, I am free. No one can keep me from my palace.

All the peculiarities of the architecture of the palace—if this haphazard stitching together of odd spaces can be called architecture—mesh together in a singular fashion in the private apartments. Just when we were sure we'd found the last cubicle, the final nook, we discovered another lair filled with new delights. There always seems to be another partition or well-disguised door hidden in the back of a closet or storage space. Rummaging around in a pantry, I spotted, almost by accident, a thin vertical crack in one of the walls. Close examination revealed a sliding door. When Andrew and I opened it and shined our lights inside, we had a pleasant surprise. The chamber contains hundreds of Greek vases—black-figured, red-figured, Attic, proto-Corinthian, Apulian—all signed. Arranged in chronological order, they begin with works from the seventh century B.C.—with old Nestor, I'll be damned—and end with a series of giant terra-cotta and soft-paste fourth-century tureens from Centuripe, all painted in garish yellows, violets, and golds. The collection rivals the British Museum's. Each vase is pristine, coated with lacquer shined to a mirrorlike gloss. What a stunning impression.

Most of the private apartments are decorated with stucco in the thinnest possible relief, delicately painted. Of special excellence are the landscapes, offering glimpses into every exotic land where Rome's explorers and adventurers sailed. One scene —sere, barren, windswept—looks a lot like what I imagine Newfoundland, Greenland, or some area of Hudson's Bay might have looked like at that time. Did the Romans—or Tertullian—discover America? It would no longer surprise me to discover they did.

I may have detected a chink in Olivia's armor. She hinted to me that although she had not changed her mind, she would make her ultimate decision on how to handle the news of the palace *after* we have gone through all the rooms. Then she went on and on praising the Scythian gold jewelry. It is remarkable, even I have to admit. I teased her, asking her whether the bureaucrats would give her permission to have a long loving look at the jewels after they took over the palace. Then I teased her a little bit more. I said that it seemed to me that the set of Scythian gold was incomplete. It appeared to me, I said, that something was missing. She blushed furiously. Aha! She fled. "You see, you're really one of *us* after all!" I called after her.

If you see the palace as a living thing, and I do, then it's appropriate for the brains of the entity to be on this top floor. I mean the books, thousands of them. They represent the intellect of the entire Roman world, up to 79 A.D. anyway. After a cursory inventory, we calculated that there are about eleven thousand codices and scrolls—mostly scrolls, which are easier for the computer to record and translate. What a literary treasure house. Here, in incomparable condition, are all the classics and a myriad of writings which the world knows nothing of: poems, plays, comedies, histories, philosophies, rhetorics (almost too many!), architectural tracts, geographics, spiritual treatises, even twenty-two cookbooks, medical theses, mathematical analyses, and agricultural treatises. Every exalted name is represented, from Homer to Herodotus, Socrates, Plato, Aristotle, and Thucydides. All the playwrights are on the shelves, from Aeschylus, to Sophocles to Menander. Every volume contains a host of "lost" or unknown works. I tallied up fifteen new plays by Euripides, eight by Aeschylus, seven by Sophocles, and thirty-one by Terence! Socrates' "Secret Journal" is there. And so are the complete works of Virgil! I came across a group of *odes* composed by Julius Caesar! And I also pulled out an unspoiled copy of the histories of Herodotus!

The religious library contains more material than I can begin to assess. Each sect, mystery cult, and philosophy is neatly catalogued. Perusing the section on the cults of the northlands,

I was amused to find the legends of Wodin, Thor, and Freya. They sound remarkably like the musings of Nietzsche and the librettos of Richard Wagner. An entire alcove is set aside for the soul. I found that highly entertaining, especially considering Tertullian's apparent lack of interest in anything so tenuous. I pulled out a scroll marked "Orphics" and fed it quickly into a small computerized laser scanner I had installed. The writing is Tertullian's typical style.

> *Orphics maintain that there is a soul of divine creation imprisoned in our bodies, which are unworthy of it. These bemused Orphics claim that the primary struggle in life is keeping the soul pure in this world so as to inherit blessedness in the next. The pure souls, according to the Orphics, gain eternal bliss after death. The incurably evil go to a state of eternal suffering. The rest agonize in purgatorial pains, atoning for each sin ten times over until the time comes to be reincarnated. What prattle these Orphics preach!*

Tertullian haunted religious ceremonies of every denomination. I was fascinated by his account, filed under "Egyptian Frivolities," of a séance conducted by an itinerant group of Osiris worshipers.

> *The temple's Stygian darkness was illuminated by three curved black candles. There was a great deal of wheezing and belching by the "priest," whose utterances in the language of the great Pharaohs seemed as devoid of spiritual content as the mutterings of any*

old drunken night watchman in the city. What chi-
canery! And to think I had been told by a devout seer
that the religion of Osiris was more serious than the
simpleminded cult of Christianity.

Rummaging around in his chambers has strengthened my
conviction that the real treasures of this place are not the works
of art or jewelry, but the diaries of Quintus Maximianus Tertullian. I read them hour after hour, finding surprise after
surprise. Andrew and Olivia agree. I'm beginning to think
there is hope for her after all. I must say her views on Galba
changed after she'd heard Tertullian's account of their final
meeting.

I had the opportunity to meet with the divine Galba once more
before departing for the provincial delights of Herculaneum.
The Emperor expressed his profound sorrow at my leaving and
honored me by appointing me hereditary Master of Imperial
Works. In a jovial mood, he spoke of events of hundreds of
years ago as if he were reading from a journal filled with copi-
ous detail. His attempts at prognostication were entertaining
and insightful. He said Rome would, of course, extend its dom-
ination of the known world by conquering "some familiar trou-
blesome lands and subjugating a few that we haven't yet
discovered." Then, without warning, he turned the conversation
to Christianity.
    "I have read into it quite extensively since we last talked,
and I have become even more concerned about your getting
mixed up with this lot. Though I respect the set of ethics of the
Christians, the followers of this sect of yours are trying to make
the good teacher, Jesas, into a god, or at least the son of one.

What's next? Will they claim he can raise the dead—like the messiahs of Palestine? Then what? Where are these false witnesses, these mystical confessors, taking this philosophy? You must be wary, and if you persist in these quaint nostrums, try to spread the word that hocus-pocus is not the way to build a solid religion. I would be sorry if this sect became an enemy of the state. I say it as a friend." Then he bade me farewell.

Too late I realized that I had revealed a dangerous amount about the faith. I was worried when I thought about what could come of this. But I had no fears of the Emperor's rancor. What a clever mind! How prescient! And how practical! I left Rome on the morrow. I worry that the appearance of my family home will be ruined by the massive dams, which are finally complete. Have I destroyed my home, my most prized possession, because of unwarranted fears?

Afterward, when he had carried out a rigorous inspection, Tertullian was "as satisfied as I have ever been over a construction project." But he stayed in Herculaneum barely a month before embarking on a business trip to Egypt, accompanied by Marcus, a trusted assistant. Before departing he threw a two-day banquet for every member of the house and all his friends in Herculaneum.

This, I recognized to my delight, was the musical fiesta depicted so magically by the silversmith in the massive table fountain we'd discovered in the silver factory. Tertullian describes the affair with gusto. In one passage he muses about his wife's "seeming to have cast aside her licentious attitudes." He applauds her efforts to act "not only civil, but affectionate."

For hours, I devoured QMT's journals. I was drawn in by his accounts of his business affairs. The backbone of the Tertullian fortune was not the massive holdings in agriculture or textiles (the elephant-breeding operation had apparently fallen upon hard times and had been scrubbed), but slave trading through Tertullian's subcontractors in what are today Iran, Syria, and Yemen. In a document comparable to a modern company's annual report, he points out how his personal design of the interiors of his slave vessels enabled "hundreds more of the savages to be shipped on each vessel with only a slight increase in the number killed." And Tertullian had managed to cut down on disease and deaths among the slaves after "breeding" them. The secret to his success was typically "Tertullian."

> *My personal study of the breeding pens showed me at once why the mortality rate was so high. They were filthy. My father's Egyptian physician insisted that if human beings kept their homes and bodies scrupulously clean, sickness would virtually disappear. So I had the compounds scrubbed until the wood shone like blades. Eventually the numbers of those who survived the first month rose to about an eighth of those born—about the same as human beings. Families should not be split up. Their babies live longer. I also allowed mothers to keep their children for a year. The babes flourished. I now have the most productive slave-breeding farm in the Empire.*

Slaves were an important part of the Tertullian profits, but so were other industries, like grain and wheat, wool and flax. Shipping was an especially productive business, as was a giant fleet of oxcarts that slogged throughout the Roman territories and beyond, into India and China. From what I could decipher, the Tertullian shipping operation had subsidiaries in what are

today Thailand and Vietnam. A surprising breadth of enterprise! But more amazing by far is what I think *must* have been
an expedition to the threshold of America itself.

*Two out of five long boats I dispatched to the western end of
the earth returned. The men were reasonably hale, and the
senior captain, one Titan the Strong, came before me to give an
account of the singular voyage and exploration of the far-off
lands. According to Titan, these western lands, sighted in the
past by others, could be seized and developed for a variety of
agricultural purposes.*

*What a symbol of indomitable Roman seafarer this Titan
is. True to his name, which he admits he invented, he is as huge
and hard as one of those iron stanchions that dot our piers. To
him nothing is sacred. Not the Emperor ("that accursed, shivering weakling"). Not the gods ("those accursed, puny, imaginary, never-to-be-seen 'wonders' "). And not even me. He must
have consumed a gallon of my choicest Falernum as he related
the saga.*

*"Master and lord," he began, "we sailed on the upper
trajectory route, along the path charted by the great star. We
traveled nearly two hundred and fifty days without seeing land-
fall. Then, two hundred days out, we began to sail through the
first of the frozen mountains. Yes, mountains. What else would
you call slabs of green and blue ice five times the size of the
vessel?*

*"Another forty days went by. It was cold, but those fresh
furs of yours easily kept us warm and dry."*

*The uncured bear pelts, still thick with grease and flesh,
had been my idea. I knew that the north sea would become
brutally cold, so I had a host of bearskins laid on board. When
the ship set sail, they were still dripping blood.*

"We began to sense that the climate was warming," Titan continued. "We began to smell land, grasses, swamp odors. It was just in time! We were down to the last of our dry food. Water was almost gone. Two seamen drank seawater for a week or so. They went mad, screeching like cats all day and night. They'd try to crawl and scratch their way to what was left of the fresh water. Of course, I didn't let 'em. They'd made their choice, and they began to eat their bearskins—imagine that! So I strangled them and threw them over the side.

"The day after we got that first whiff of land, the fog was as thick as the bearskins. We lashed the boats together, bow to stern, so as not to get separated. When the fog finally lifted— oh, so slowly—we saw shining green low land not more than a quarter of a league away.

"The land was quiet, beautiful beyond thinking after all those terrible months at sea. It looked peaceful, too, although it wouldn't've mattered if the low white cliffs had been lined with Gauls or Persians—we'd have gone ashore anyway.

"On shore, we found no one. This was a strangely flat land, a plateau, nothing like anything in the Empire, except, perhaps, for the northern isles of Britannia. Yet this place was far flatter. There were no hills at all, only rolling grasslands with hardly a tree except for a few which appeared in clusters, as if they were holding themselves together against the wind. That wind! Like the tramontano but plenty colder. But there were animals, plenty of them feeding from the thick grass— thicker than anything I've ever seen here. Sheep and goats. By the hundreds. And not frightened by us at all. So, we had this splendid feast. I produced some wine I'd hidden away for the last minutes of my life.

"So we were having our feast, and although it was late into the night, it was light. All of a sudden we found ourselves

surrounded by men garbed in sheepskins, all holding spears—
fifty of them, maybe more. Their hair was deep black and their
skin was the color of copper. These men drew close and
watched silently. They could easily have killed us all because—
and I blame myself for this—I hadn't set up any guards.

"I slowly got to my feet and gave the chief the biggest
smile I have ever given anybody in my life. I held out a slice of
roasted lamb. This man, named Tark (we called him Tarquin-
ius, and he didn't mind), took the food, ate it, and let out a cry,
a cry of pleasure. Neither Tark nor any of his men had ever
eaten a piece of meat that had been cooked, the custom among
these barbarians being to eat everything raw. The tribe—there
were only about two hundred of them living on the island—
became our friends, especially after we gave 'em a load of short
swords and daggers. We never did learn a word of their lan-
guage, nor they ours. We communicated by drawing pictures in
the ground. The one thing these people could do well was to
draw. They had dozens of sheepskins with maps of their island
and the surrounding waters and lands. They also made carvings
out of bone and drawings on bone."

He gave me a sack full of bone carvings and some small
sculptures in soft stone. Remarkable! Animals of fanciful shapes
—huge bears, bulbous creatures with no legs and tusks, men so
swaddled in skins that only a small round part of the faces could
be seen—men with strange, slitlike eyes. Realistic images? Unlikely, I thought. Yet the small, well-rubbed pieces were appealing. So I kept them in the special sacks that Titan had
brought along with them, sacks made of the softest, whitest fur
I have ever seen.

"This is mind-boggling," Andrew cried out. "He must be
talking about Eskimo carvings—and Newfoundland."

"I think I know where these carvings are," I told him. In Tertullians's map room my eye had settled for an instant on the oddest set of objects, several round cases made out of what then had seemed to be the most unlikely substance—the fur of baby seals. As quickly as we could we made our way to the alcove reserved for charts and maps.

"There they are!" Andrew said. "Three of them, with sinews for laces."

Somewhat feverishly I opened them. And there they were, a seal about a foot long, carved out of one piece of walrus ivory, a tiny Eskimo in a green-gray stone, and a whalebone polar bear.

Olivia reached over and gingerly took the Eskimo into her hands. "How thrilling. Think of holding something that Tertullian was so fond of. You can almost feel the man's presence."

The Eskimo fisherman is depicted kneeling on the ice with his spear raised just before striking an unseen quarry. The statuette is filled with a remarkable sense of expectancy.

"I can't believe this," Andrew said with a laugh. "Who ever expected to discover the earliest works of Eskimo sculpture in the history of mankind—in the house of an ancient Roman? Add to that that it was not Leif Ericson or Columbus but a character named Titan who discovered North America. Who the hell will believe this?"

"They're going to think we planted all this," Olivia said with a little sigh.

"My darling, imagine what the world reaction is going to be when we announce the following: one, there's a Roman palace the size of Versailles intact down here; two, its owner was a secret Christian who hated Saint Peter and had John the Evangelist as a houseguest; three, he killed Nero; and, four, he discovered America. We've got to keep this our secret!"

Olivia looked at us quickly and turned away.

Before we had completed the exploration of the family quarters, we found, among other things, three more libraries, a massage room, a theater seating twenty, a chamber with some rather stimulating pornography, a luxurious suite of guest rooms, and another complex of eight rooms for the children and their tutors.

OLIVIA

Never in my life have I been as moved as I was by the children's bedrooms and playrooms. None of the magnificent treasures we had found could compare to the poignant objects which filled these rooms with overpoweringly human memories. I almost wept at the sight of some of the children's things. Everything seemed so innocent. I wondered what had happened to the chilren once the eruptions started and the mud began to spill and the lava surged down toward them. Did they die in agony? She in the arms of her father? He trying to protect his mother?

The boy lived in a delightful state of male chaos. His clothes, toys, writing tablets, and a collection of models of weapons were strewn about his rooms. He was the perfect reflection of his mother. The girl's room, however, was meticulous, prissy, you might say. Her dresses hung neatly in two lockers, and a group of stuffed animals and dolls were arranged in precise order. Daddy's girl.

I shuddered to think of these tender belongings being packed up and moved into some cold and austere museum. Such protection might be—dare I say it?—wicked.

After leaving the children's wing, I encountered Andrew and the Don, engrossed in QMT's chronicle and a story none of us were prepared for: Tertullian's account of his journey to Gaul to meet Jesas.

Just before my departure John came to pray for me and tell me about Jesas. He looked ruddy, and I wondered if he was ill. Soon, however, I put the thought from my mind. There were many things to consider before the journey. "May God's grace grant you and your servant complete safety and spare you particularly from all danger," John prayed for me. I asked him if I should bring Jesas a gift as dictated by custom. He insisted that I should not.

"Bring your naked soul, alone, and your affection," he commanded. "You will find Jesas difficult to understand and unlike any man you have ever encountered. Believe and question what he tells you. He will try to appear simple, modest, not the messiah, not the son of God who will embrace sacrifice to save mankind. But, surely, he is the messiah."

I told my dear friend that he seemed to be espousing

*Peter's irrational mysticism. At this, a most unusual expression
came over John's face. He drew very close to me. Suddenly I
was moved and troubled. There was the odor of death around
him. "I have been composing for weeks," he said. "The first
part of my chronicle of Jesas is almost finished. My predictions
of the end of the world have been set down. When you return
I shall read them both to you. Jesas is a complicated subject,
you'll see."*

Being so damned "practical," Tertullian made certain that
he conducted some business along the perilous journey to Gaul,
which he undertook alone except for his trusted house assistant,
Marcus. After the calm overview of his nine enormous estates
in the north of Italy, Tertullian and his servant headed across
the Alps through the chain of valleys that border today's Bren-
ner Pass. They emerged eventually in the south of France.
Tertullian described the hazardous passage.

*The forbidding mountain passes rejuvenated me. My sole regret
was not having an artisan like Lavinius with me to record the
wondrous sights of nature. I did have Hannibal's account of his
crossing, and each evening after Marcus pitched camp, I read
another chapter. The silence of the mountains had impressed
Hannibal more than anything, even more than the snow squalls
in summer. He described how he would sit in solitude at the
entrance to his tent, as I did, reveling in the sunset, awed by the
quiet of all the birds and creatures. Taking up our journey
again, Marcus and I, like Hannibal and his men, would pause
to observe the sudden arrival of a misty snowstorm. Even in
July the snow surged down like the foam of the great waves
plunging into Baia in early spring.*

On our fifth day in the mountainous valleys, Marcus fell from his horse into a ravine. I could not save him. He passed his last breath in my arms without a word. For weeks I trudged on alone. Finally, on my forty-third day in the mountains, I reached a village, where an elder, whom I thought a native, surprised me by speaking flawless Latin. He was a retired legionary. Even more astonishing, he had not only heard of the man Jesas, but knew where he lived, a town half a day's journey away. He offered to guide me for a modest amount. I accepted, less for want of a guide than for desire to hear what the old soldier thought of Jesas.

"He is a kind and great man. A healer. He came from the East, and he came to cure the sick. There are many here. What's that? Has this Jesas ever said he was the son of God? Ah, I see you do know him. He is, of course. Although he also says that every man is the son of God. He is beloved around here, not because of his mystical sayings, but for his healings. I am old. I have traveled the earth for the Empire—India, Levant, Egypt, to the north of the land of the Picts. But I have never met anyone like him. He truly loves every man. Soon after his coming here, an epileptic man of the village tried to kill him. With his bare hands he took the man's pike away and then . . . embraced him. The epileptic collapsed and then awoke. He was smiling, can you imagine! An epileptic actually talking and smiling. He never raised his hand against anyone again, and never fainted again. That is the measure of the healer Jesas. Of all the other healing men I have met through the years, none is like Jesas. He will heal you, too."

The town where the soldier took me was larger than I had imagined, having high wooden walls with imposing stone towers at the four corners. The principal gate was tall and decorated with tiles, another indication of the wealth of the town. My companion took me directly to a hospice attached to "his hospital," despite my objections that I was not ill. I was tired from the ardors of the journey and decided to take rooms there. I was surprised when the innkeeper greeted me deferentially as "lord." My supper was robust. I fell into my bed—the first one I had seen in over a month—and slept for half a day and a night.

The legionairy came to fetch me in the midmorning and took me to a courtyard covered by freshly swept sand. A tall man came out of the door of a long whitewashed building and walked slowly across the courtyard toward me. The soldier said, "It's Jesas," and left me.

Jesas was remarkably thin, looking as if strings were stretched tightly underneath his skin, which was very fair. His eyes were soft brown, and his auburn hair was thinning and had graying ends. This man would stand out among all others, simply for his imposing looks and uncommon height. But it was the aura of assurance surrounding him that struck me. I had encountered men who possessed calmness and self-assurance, but no one like this man. Jesas, in a word, was regal. I was struck by his hands and long, slender fingers. You know how it is with certain leaders—their hands seems to have a voice. Jesas' hands had the same quality. And he held them delicately.

I did not know what to say first, so I kneeled in submission. He responded with a solemn and penetrating gaze, then a smile broader than I would have expected from an ascetic. His voice, though soft, had the authority of a sword's edge.

"What an imperial greeting!" He laughed. "I have in a sense been expecting you. You came from Rome? You are, I see, from a noble class. Why have you come?"

"I am an admirer, lord, of your ethical teachings. I am a believer, a bishop from far-off Herculaneum. I believe your faith will change mankind for the better. Yet I come with some anxiety about the future of your teachings."

Jesas turned his eyes to mine. They burned into my heart. Gesturing me to draw near and sit down, he sat next to me and came closer. His eyes still locked onto mine. Then he reached over and placed both of his large hands on my chest.

I felt much as if I were entering warm water. I felt pressure and a sensation of intense, yet not painful, heat. At the same time my body grew lighter. It was almost as if I were being lifted into the air. My chest expanded half a palm beyond what I was capable of breathing before! My head felt clean. A rush of perspiration came suddenly, and then I felt strangely pure. It was a physical catharsis!

When his hands left my chest I leaped involuntarily to my feet. I felt years younger. The hot, scratchy rasp in my chest that had overcome me in the mountain was—gone. A persistent ringing in my ears—I had had this minor affliction for years— had disappeared. The ache in my left shoulder had ceased.

Jesas smiled at my reaction and remarked in a crystal-clear voice, "You are truly a believer!"

I fell to my knees and embraced him. In an instant he placed his hands on my head. How to describe the feeling? What to say about what happened? The feeling was, again, one of lightness and healing. Jesas kept his hands on my head as he talked.

"You do believe, but as you say, you are worried."

I spoke bluntly, my usual direct self. I told him that his teachings were in danger of being lost in the masses' desire for magic and mysticism. False disciples were increasing, fabricating lies about him and his teachings. They said that Jesas had been killed; that he had risen from the dead; that he had ascended into heaven to rule at the right hand of the one God.

The myth—the "lie"—was gaining in intensity after much repetition. It was even being written down as the gospel. Why? Why didn't he, a sensible teacher of ethics and a wise physician, come out with the truth?

"Reality does not interest me as such, only parable."

"Is it true that you were arrested and brought to trial before Pilate!"

"Not true."

"What about your claim to be the son of God? What about your opposition to the Senate?"

Jesas smiled. "Come," he said, motioning me to enter a building. "You must eat. Then I shall explain what has happened and what seems to have happened. The facts are not as important as the allegory. There are but three things you need to know."

The meal was simple, yet I have seldom partaken of anything so satisfying in my life. The mundane elements of life had gained luster. Jesas talked quietly.

"The ethical rules are these. No one should kill another human being. You should always act toward another as you would want him to act toward you. You should not hate your enemy. Only by following these principles will mankind flourish. If mankind follows these rules, the abundance of the world will be shared by all people, not only the powerful. My wish is for the weak and the gentle—even the ones with little or no intelligence—to share a place in the world. I seek sharing—"

"But that is why," I interrupted, "many have accused you of trying to overthrow the state."

He smiled in resignation. "So many fanciful things have been said about my philosophies! No, I have nothing against the state. The Caesar has his work, and we who seek to change the primitive ethical procedures have ours. Despite Rome's cruelty, I shudder to think of what the world would be without the mortar of Rome's influence and power! Augustus tried to ameliorate some of the crueler human practices, although Nero, I am told, halted the progress."

I told Jesas that Nero had been killed by a member of the Praetorian Guard in a conspiracy that I had been involved in. His gentle eyes burst into flame.

"Contemptible! You nobles kill with impunity, masking your sin behind a false righteousness!" Jesas rose from the bench and walked over, looked down threateningly. For an instant I thought he might actually strike me. I was amazed at the fury beneath the surface of the man and remembered what John had told me: that Jesas could fly into rages, sometimes joyfully, predicting the destruction of all the ungodly. For the rest of my stay, despite his pretense of acceptance, I suspected he held me in contempt. I felt as censured as if the Senate itself had voted officially against me.

That first day, I begged his forgiveness. He told me that he could not forgive, that only his father could pardon my sin. But if, for the rest of my life, I followed the trinity of ethical rules, I might receive salvation. I assured him I would. And I meant it. Jesas clearly recognized that I was speaking the truth.

It was then I told him that Petrus had stayed at my palace briefly, but I decided not to remark on my feelings about the man. He gazed at me impassively and said, "Petrus is the most honest and courageous of men. He will become more renowned in the history of Rome than Caesar himself."

I told him about John. And he said, "John is the most important of all the witnesses. He will write three works. One will be a history of my life, another will be a poem of my life, and the third will foretell the end of the earth. John is a man of contradictions, and those contradictions will assail him."

I persisted in asking him about his feelings toward the state.

"Tertullian, although I am not opposed to the state, I am doubtful that the powerful and wealthy will ever be redeemed. As one of my earliest followers, Matteus, said in good humor once, 'It will be easier for the hawser of a boat to pass through a hole in a saddlemaker's needle than for a rich Roman to enter the gates of enlightenment.' Rome hails only the material profits. A worthy adoration of all of one's fellows would be more beneficial than all the wealth in Rome!

"You ask about these stories of my arrest, torture, execution, death, resurrection, and ascent to the side of the one God? Parables. Physically, all this did not happen. Metaphorically, it all did. I was tried. The Sanhedrin had accused me of preaching blasphemy. I had. I was censured. Then some of my bitterest enemies claimed I had sought the overthrow of Roman rule. Untrue. I was brought to trial and interrogated in the Roman way. I was judged by Pilate himself, who proclaimed me innocent of the charges. My enemies tried to have me executed. Though Pilate told them he would have nothing to do with such an act, he complied with their wishes in symbolic form. At the weekly execution Pilate ordered a third gibbet to be erected with a placard for Jesas of Nazareth, King of the Jews and the Confessors. At once, the stories began that I had perished on the gibbet and had disappeared into the skies. I was seen several times, and that gave rise to other fanciful tales. Then, for the sake of my followers, I fled. I am dead in my former land, yet I live on. I have been 'resurrected' here, for I continue my work of healing.

"You should speak out and convince others of the value of the new ethics. You must be clear and rational. Tell the story any way you want, but proclaim the trinity. I know that much

about me and my life will be written and rewritten. A myriad of mysteries and fanciful stories will be born over the centuries. Yet the only thing that will prevail will be the three great rules. Live, henceforth, by them. Preach them. Come."

Jesas commanded me to kneel before him and once again placed his hands upon my head. This time he cleansed from my mind those thoughts I might have harbored against him. He left, and I soon departed for home. I tried to live by the three great rules—sometimes with greater success than others. I also tried to convert members of my social caste. Jesas was right. Incredible stories about him flourished. And, as he told me, the most active poet of fancy was John.

"Could this be true?" I asked sharply.

"I have no doubt at all," Don Ciccio said. "If it is not true, then the entire palace and all its contents are a fabrication."

"If *this* gets out," Andrew continued, "this chronicle will be attacked and destroyed as quickly as possible."

Amazing. But I believed it, too. I believed it because this brief exchange in casual words contained the embryo of what, much later, would become the basic beliefs and the Trinity. Christ *was,* after all, a healer. It sounded like the gospels, in which he almost always speaks in a confusing manner. His parables are riddles—deliberate ones. Later, the incredible tales would have come, the proliferation of miraculous events. I did believe it the more I reflected on it.

Even before I began to read the next portion of Tertullian's diary, I had a premonition that we would be confronted with something cataclysmic. And we were. Tertullian returned to Herculaneum, discovered that John had died, and jumped to terrible conclusions. The diary entry was short and chilling. "I am convinced Phryne poisoned John—for what reason I cannot guess—and so I instructed my physician to do away with her. She died stoically. At the end I felt a pang of the old affection. And then she was out of my memory forever."

"What the hell is this?" I cried out. "He killed her? Why? That rotten bastard murdered her? Just for having seduced John? Didn't he even ask her?"

"Listen to her side of it," Don Ciccio said.

I had been mistaken about Quintus' plans to surround the palace by a wall of stones and mud. The builders, following his design, have completed a series of earthworks which in no way do aesthetic harm to the buildings. I have become a believer, but despite my praise, he stares at me with a coldness that grows each day.

He has even been silent about his journey to Gaul. Quintus spurns my every attempt to discover why. I have fallen into a state of confusion and helplessness. My attempts to apologize to my husband are spurned. My hands reach out toward him and he moves away from my touch. My confused state had enfeebled my body, I fear. For the past two weeks I have felt a certain heat grow within me. As my body slowly grows warmer, I become weaker and weaker. On occasion, I stumble and fall. I see double, and in the middle of the night, I become dry-mouthed and dizzy with nausea. The only surcease comes with fasting. When I do, the heat diminishes and once again life surges through me.

No one else in the household is sick. Only me. I know the reason and recognize that there will never be a cure. Quintus is having me poisoned. And I am submitting.

I suppose I have wronged my husband. I have by no means wronged others or my class and surely not my heritage. But I suppose I have wronged Tertullian. I dared to ask him about his displeasure, not mentioning that I had found out he was poisoning me. But he turned to stone.

What is left for me to do, cast aside, hated by my husband? He refuses to divorce me, something he could do by simply telling me that divorce is his wish. I have tried to approach the subject, and as soon as he suspects it, he retreats.

There is virtually no pain, only a growing numbness and gradual shortness of breath. I am thankful to Quintus for that, for he could have used a cruel potion. What to do? Commit suicide? No. That would remove the burden of guilt from my husband. Instead, I lie in my deathbed, making my farewells to the children. Tonight I summoned my husband to me for what I know will be the last time. I was pleased to see the anger in his eyes as he saw me, indifferent to my fate, only mildly distracted by my illness. I'll show him how to die, I thought to myself. I allowed myself one moment of anger. I said to him, "I feel unwell, and believing I am about to perish, I urge you to quit my chamber lest you are afflicted by the disease." For the first time in months Quintus lost his equanimity. Then I voiced my last words to him, "Do not fear, Quintus, I shall continue to take my medicine." With that I turned away from him. This night, I know, will be my last.

"That's terrible," I cried. "That foolish woman allowed that swine to kill her, simply because he wanted to?"

"And apparently in Roman times no one could stop him," the Don remarked.

Idiot woman! What a nice Christian our Quintus Maximianus Tertullian was. Suddenly I hated them both. I hated the weird, twisted palace. I regretted having come to Naples, having gotten involved in this search, having discovered the place, having read the diaries.

"I hope that bastard got it real good and slow," I shouted to Andrew and the Don. "I wish Nero had set his torturers on him."

"Knowing him," Andrew muttered, "he'll become the first Pope."

I intended to go on reading. But when I scanned the next few pages I couldn't, I was so flabbergasted. I just handed the pages over to Don Ciccio.

DON CICCIO

For a moment I thought Olivia was going to faint, and within seconds after reading the next entries in the chronicle of Tertullian, I questioned my own equilibrium. Suddenly all the wondrous things in the palace were eclipsed.

I had John's body embalmed by one of my Egyptian slaves, who has knowledge of the ancient techniques. Then we transported his body deep underground to the sanctuary constructed for the faith. There he will lie forever along with the cherished scriptures, his "Apocalypse," as he called the work, and his witness and confession of the deeds and preachings of Jesas. The witness is admirable and offers a truthful account of Jesas' life so far, from his baptism to his teachings in the Temple, his trials before Herod and Pilate, his release, his further teachings, and his departure from Palestine. There is also a description of the basic schisms and false beliefs and untruths. The truth concerning the symbolic crucifixion is clearly spelled out in rhetorical stanzas.

I have also placed in this sanctuary the life of Jesas compiled by the zealot Lucas. He wrote a fanciful and mystical version of his life, a story filled with miracles and ending with the literal crucifixion of Jesas. The Lucas account presents Jesas' resurrection and ascension into heaven as fact. What future generations will think of these peculiar stories I do not know. But I feel obliged to preserve a record of them, if only to show that there were two different and opposing ways of looking at Jesas and his life—the factual and the purely mystical.

Another reason why I want to preserve Lucas' book is that in its frontispiece he drew a splendid portrait from life of Jesas in ink.

There was a hush. I was bewildered, incapable of thinking rationally. It took a while to realize what Tertullian was saying. Olivia broke the silence.

"A burial chamber ... in the palace? With John's mummy and his 'true' gospel? And a 'mystical' one by Luke? And a drawing by Luke ... of Christ ... a life portrait? Plus the Apocalypse?"

"Where the hell is it?" Andrew asked. "I knew we must have missed some chambers."

"It must be down," Olivia said. "Remember—in the fragmentary scroll—Tertullian's account of the earthquake mentioned some place deep underground."

"But where? The place is so huge. And what will it look like? Any hints?"

THERE were, unfortunately, few clues to guide our search. But the lack of information didn't daunt me. I had my computers. They were capable of solving the most carefully constructed puzzles in the contemporary world. But could they, I wondered, crack Tertullian's last secret? I have Andrew to thank for showing me how to start the search.

"Knowing now about this underground sanctuary," he said, "I think I might have the key to solving what I've always found a persistent mystery about why Tertullian went to all that trouble to build the dams. It's occurred to me, and I'm sure you've both had the same thought, that Tertullian didn't go to the expense and difficulty of erecting all those bulwarks merely to save the family treasures, at least the old, pagan treasures. His diaries show him only moderately interested in the works of art. They were Phryne's pleasure. Oh, he dotes on *some* of the pieces—the silver and gold booty, for example—but at times he almost denigrates the art. Perhaps because she loved it. I'll bet if we analyze his description of the dams and his account of the earthquake in which he first mentions the sanctuary, we'll get an idea where to start looking for this place."

I labored alone through that night, the next, the next. I ran thousands of statistics through the machine—lava depths, the dimensions of each room we had discovered, and countless other measurements. It took longer than I thought it would but finally the computer revealed the most likely area for the entrance to the subterranean sanctuary. I slept for twenty-two straight hours, then, as calmly as I could, told my friends the likely whereabouts of the entrance. The computer had pointed to the end of the corridor way down in the first level where we had, so long ago, found the tack room and the stables and chariot room.

Armed with our set of powerful headlamps, we searched along the walls and on the floors, hour after hour, looking for traces of a disguised entry. In vain.

A second day and a third went by. Then we found a suspicious series of cracks in the plaster of a wall in a storage area near the chariot room. Feverishly, Andrew chiseled away the plaster. Nothing. We chiseled at half a dozen more cracks and found nothing.

We were sitting silent and defeated when, suddenly, Olivia raised her head and said, "We're looking in the wrong place."

"But the computer . . ."

"No. We're in the correct *area*. It's simply that we are looking for the wrong clue. Cracks aren't what we should be looking for. We should search in places where the plaster is smooth, or perhaps behind a wall painting or behind where there's something already hanging."

"Do you mean we have to hack away all the plaster from every wall in this whole section?"

"I don't believe so. I may have figured it out," Olivia whispered.

She motioned us to follow her. We wended our way behind her past the laundry and the jewelry factory, through the great mosaic-floored courtyard. We were so intent that we barely gave the marvelous ceiling a glance as Olivia led us farther and farther, past the cubicles of the freedmen and finally to the shooting gallery for the crossbows.

"My God, the target!" Andrew exclaimed.

"It's a thought, anyway," Olivia said. "Try to remove it."

Andrew pried loose and removed the target with the crude image of a man. Behind was plaster. Again nothing.

"Hold it," Andrew said. "There. The outline of an arch, there in the stucco."

Within minutes Andrew had removed the plaster with his crowbar. Before us was a stout wooden door sheathed in bronze plates. A heavy lock lay at the center of the portal. Andrew pushed the door as hard as he could. It didn't budge.

"What now? Blast through?" Andrew asked. "Let's get the rest of the nitro."

"No need to," I remarked with some degree of pride. "I think I know where the key has to be. Do you remember in the early days how fascinated I became with the locksmith's shop?"

" 'Addicted' is a better word," Olivia said. "You're right. The key must be there! Oh, God!"

THE key *was* there, on a great bronze ring with a number of smaller keys. The doorway opened onto a circular staircase—about ten feet wide—made of marble revetment that, within twenty feet, became a forbidding black lava. Like a corkscrew, the staircase plunged straight down, so precipitously that it gave me, perched on Andrew's shoulder, an annoying case of vertigo.

I shrugged the unpleasant feeling away. No doubt where we were headed! On every tight, steep curve of the stairs someone had carved a Christian symbol—the dolphin, an ax, the anchor, or a female "orant" figure.

Traveling farther and farther down, we confronted a succession of wooden doors. At each we suffered nerve-shattering anxieties, convinced that *this* would be the portal for which we had no key. Each time we found one, thank God. The deeper we penetrated—we must have been at least one hundred and fifty feet beneath the surface of the first level, and it was very, very cold—the thicker the doors became. The sixth was no less than a foot thick. We knew it would be impossible to open if we didn't find a key. Blasting would have required so much nitroglycerine that the place would have been buried. The key ring had twelve more keys. Andrew had marked each one we had used. This journey was going to take us to hell and Cerberus himself! We did find the key to the sixth door, but at the seventh portal, none of the keys fit.

"Damn, damn, damn," Andrew said quietly.

He delicately twisted every key there was left on the ring in the lock. He was about to dash the key ring to the stone floor when he froze and said, "Hey, wait a second! Look here! Some of these keys have numbers . . . and some of them have *two* numbers. This has II and VII!"

The door opened effortlessly.

As it did, our earthquake sensors began to click, then rattle. As soon as she heard them, Olivia bolted up the narrow stairs with Andrew after her. There I was, alone, abandoned, while the tremors began to build. I was going to die. I felt no fear—only profound sadness that I was going to perish before looking into the holy of holies. The quakes surged around me like waves, closing in. Then, abruptly, they receded far away, to levels way above me. In less than half a minute, the tremors had subsided.

Andrew, a bit shamefaced, came to retrieve me. I said nothing. Olivia's reaction to the incident was to disappear to the Cartageno villa, where she remained incommunicado for three days.

"Andrew what *is* wrong?"

"It's not fear," he told me. "I think she's mulling everything over."

"I don't understand."

"I'm not sure I do, either."

When at last she emerged, it was as if nothing had occurred. Unflinchingly she went back down into the staircase. I admired her immensely. We got to the eighth door. It needed a new key. Then there was the ninth door, which opened with key number one. Down we went. By now we must have been two hundred feet down. I felt the pressure in my ears, and it wasn't reassuring. The air itself seemed to be getting thicker.

At last we were standing in front of the eleventh portal. It was painted crimson and had a simple cross whitewashed in the center. It had to be the entrance to the sanctuary. Beneath the cross was a rectangular lock.

Methodically Andrew tried every key. None fit. He took a deep breath and tried every one of the keys on the ring again.

Nothing.

We must have sat there for a greater part of an hour—at least it seemed that way—without saying a word. Olivia's face was an impassive mask. Andrew sat huddled, shivering slightly in the dank chill, his face hidden behind his hands. All the incomparable treasures we had come across, all the triumphs we had experienced, seemed to dissolve into bitterness.

"Are you sure you took every single key from the lock-smith?" Andrew, practical to the core, suddenly asked me.

"Good thought! Do go and find out," I urged. He dashed off, and while we were waiting Olivia walked over to the portal and studied it intently.

"Ironic, isn't it," she said. "The closing of the circle. Another door, more mysterious than the first. I wonder if this one, too, has its own trick."

Andrew returned with a handful of keys. Every one was obviously too small to work. "Let's use some of that nitro," he suggested.

"No. I fear the effects of another nitro explosion," I said.

"Another? What do you mean?"

Without thinking I told them about my use of the nitro a few weeks before.

"You mean that wasn't a gas explosion? And the Dorsoduros died in it?" Olivia asked in horror.

"I had good reason to see them finish themselves off."

"Jesus, kind of rough, isn't it?" Andrew said tightly.

"My friend, this is southern Italy," I observed.

"Let's get out of here. I'm freezing," Olivia said in a strangled voice. She avoided my glance. How quickly human relationships can change.

All the way up the stairs, Andrew kept complaining. "I refuse to accept this. We are inches away from the summit, from the most stupendous discovery of all time—inches!—and we are going to let it beat us? There's *got* to be something to do. Can't we hire a locksmith? Why not take a chance with the nitro? We can't let this defeat us! It's like Hillary giving up ten yards from the summit of Everest."

Olivia had been silent. It was only after we had returned to the villa that she spoke.

"I have the solution to the last door."

"You do?"

"I'm confident I do, yes."

"Well?"

"I'm not going to tell unless . . ."

"Unless we bow to your wishes, eh?" I said as calmly as I could.

"I do not practice blackmail. That would put me in your league. All I want is a straight story from you, Don Ciccio," she said. "What do you propose to do with this palace, and what have you arranged to ensure your getting away with it?"

I tried to be charming. They both looked at me coldly. So I spelled it all out bluntly and quickly—how I had manipulated their sabbatical, how Enrico Dorsoduro had fooled me into buying the scrolls and deciphering them, how he had taunted me. I revealed every detail of the agreement I had made with Giulio Cassone, even to the point of telling them about his true vocation as a member of military intelligence.

"My dears, I am, I suppose you now realize, somewhat more powerful than you might have thought. And wealthier, too, although I am not going to let you in on those details. Basically, in exchange for my help in obtaining vital evidence on the corrupt Prime Minister and the illegal activities of the Dorsoduros—"

"You killed them in cold blood . . . for 'illegal activities'?" Olivia asked.

"Yes, with the acquiescence and support of Cassone's entire intelligence section. You must understand that Enrico and his sons have been responsible for a number of assassinations."

"Mafia justice."

"This is *not* America," I snapped. I was not willing to

listen to any more of her idle chatter, so I continued my story. "In exchange for that information and for my commitment to help Cassone become Prime Minister, I am in possession of a new contract that assures us total control of the palace, virtually in perpetuity."

"Then why do you need us?" Andrew asked.

"I don't . . . now."

"Dammit, don't forget that I've got some cash invested in this deal!"

"A pittance. I'll be delighted to reimburse you—even to double the sum. But I *did* need you in the beginning. I could never have started things without you. Besides, I love you both and I want to share this—everything—equally. Andrew, you are on my side, I'll bet. Olivia, you, dear, are the last remaining obstacle in the way of my obsession."

She started pacing slowly back and forth across the room in long smooth strides like a restless athlete before the start of a race, her blue eyes shining.

"I firmly believe that the palace and all its contents—all, even the Tertullian diaries—must be shared by mankind through responsible and ongoing scholarship. If I had my way, right now I'd be on the telephone to the press. After what you have told us, you can see why I wouldn't dare tell anybody. God knows what deals you've made, with whom. I'd have the place closed down to everybody but a prize crew of Italian, and only Italian, scholars to spend as many years as they wished to carry out a legitimate examination of these thousands of things. I'd give them all our notes and videotapes. I'd give them everything that we've taken. Starting with this ring from the Aryx jewelry I took. Then I'd leave. Expecting nothing."

"And unless I agree," I began, "you'll also reveal to the press how the Dorsoduros—"

"I told you I'm *not* a blackmailer!" she said sharply. "There will be no unless."

She came over to me and leaned over until her beautiful face was inches away from mine.

"I don't ever want to see you again. I don't care if Cassone's agency approved those killings. No, I'm not going to tell on you. As a matter of fact, I'm not going to hold you up' in any way about your obsession."

For one of the rare moments in my life I stammered. "I don't understand. I was sure you were going to insist that we had to give it up. I—what has made you change your mind?"

"Irrational reasons. For one thing, I still felt some affection for you, at least a few days ago when I made up my mind. And Andrew helped. He convinced me that there are people who would do anything to destroy these things. I agree the church will definitely get rid of the diaries. But the principal reason I changed my mind is the children."

I was transfixed.

"Maybe because I don't have children, seeing those children's rooms and their toys—his room in disarray, hers so lovingly arranged—had a devastating impact on me. I admitted to myself that we scholars and curators *do* take a toll when we protect and preserve things. We can deaden things. I won't prolong this. You get the point. Here are my terms. We keep it a secret for the rest of our lives. The one of us who survives the other two will reveal it an orderly manner in his or her will. There will be no museum loans and positively *no* souvenirs. Simple. Do I hear a dissent?"

"Yes." It was Andrew. "It's such a pity that you had to suffer so much about this. Yet I'm happy. I agree. But I have one objection. It's about souvenirs. Denying ourselves completely is unfair. Each of us should take one thing—a modest something—permanently, and then make a list of, say, ten pieces that we should have on personal loan for a year at a time, renewable after the decade's up. We deserve this for the struggle, the money, and the danger. After all, we are professionals who know how to keep works of art in good condition. Olivia, I insist on this. Don't be a prig."

"I'll think it over."

"That's a yes?"

"Andrew, I said I'll think it over."

I didn't know how to react, although I knew enough not to heap thanks on her. Could I ever win her back? With what? I had an intense pang of self-pity. She steadfastly avoided my eyes. I had lost my Olivia.

"The door. Its secret?" Andrew said.

"Do I have an agreement?" Olivia demanded. Andrew and I nodded. "Good. Now put it in writing."

I swallowed my pride and did so. "The existence of the palace, its location, its description, will be noted in the will of the last of us to die. I shall get together our notes, our diaries, and the videotapes and put them in a safe deposit box to be opened only when all three of us are dead. Does that do it? Yes? Fine. Until then, the palace shall be *ours!*"

"I approve," she said coolly.

"Olivia, now, the secret of the last door!" Andrew pleaded.

"You can enter anytime you want," she said. "There is, to my complete surprise, no key. The final portal was constructed for believers. There cannot be a locked door to a true Christian sanctuary. While you were rushing around frantically looking for keys, I studied the door. It's open."

Damn.

We were so eager to penetrate the ultimate mystery that for the first time we violated our cardinal rule of never entering the palace until darkness. Early the next morning we sneaked in and made our way down the precipitous stairs. This time I had insisted that Olivia take my small, portable wheelchair. At length, we stood in front of the eleventh door.

Gingerly Olivia placed the tips of her fingers on its surface, and gently she pushed. The door swung inward without a sound.

I motioned her forward. She had every right to be the first to enter one of the most sacred shrines in Christendom.

She bowed her head. Tears came to her eyes. "No."

Andrew slowly sat down. He gazed at her in deep affection. He took her hand tenderly in his. "I think I know what you're going to say, darling."

"I'm not going in. What I might see will ruin everything else in life for me. After what I have experienced already in this palace, I've been damaged . . . yes, I'm serious. Damaged in the real sense that I can never look at another antique sculpture, fragment of a painting, vase, bit of jewelry, the Parthenon, or any of the grandest ancient treasures in all the museums on earth—without thinking how sad everything is! How broken! How imperfect! The palace has devoured my aesthetic curiosity. It has almost totally jaded me. If I don't walk through that door, if I don't look into the face of God, I can still preserve some shred of expectancy, some hope that I haven't seen everything. You do what you like. Don Ciccio, Andrew, go in. But you must swear to me that you will never, never utter a word to me about what you have seen. Or to anyone. Let the word come out after I'm dead."

"Go ahead, Don Ciccio," Andrew whispered. "I'm staying outside with Olivia. Give us your word."

I made my pledge and wheeled in alone, the light from my wheelchair assaulting the darkness of the solitary chamber, where an alabaster bier held a corpse, dried-out but perfectly preserved. It was John, slight, ascetic, negroid. The leathery mummy was dressed in simple white linen chasubles, and adorned with a cross in pale red embroidery. The arms were crossed.

A low wooden chest against the stucco wall next to the bier was the only other object in the room. I wheeled my chair over to it and opened it. There were three books. One was the Apocalypse written in John's own hand. The second was his gospel, in Greek which the later computer translation told me did not begin with the familiar words of the New Testament, but with, "The word of God was in the heart of my friend, Jesas, from the day he was born and throughout his life of healing. . . ." I decided I had to take it along with me and stuffed it into my bag.

I smiled when I saw what the third book was. The gospel of Luke, with what we all know—miracles, mystery, crucifixion, resurrection.

Opposite the title page was the portrait of Christ. It was signed by Luke. The artist-evangelist had imbued the face of his friend and master with a combination of strength and tenderness. Looking at the image of Christ, obviously drawn from life, I realized sadly that Olivia had been right. In that instant I knew I was destroyed.

AT our final dinner the atmosphere was strained. Then Olivia gradually warmed, mostly because Andrew was at his jovial best, talking directly about the problem between us.

"I'm going to make a toast and play a game," he surprised us by saying. Olivia and I looked warmly at each other—virtually for the first time since I had blurted out what I had done to our competitors—and a smile came to her lips. She sighed and took my hand in hers. "The toast. To the enchanted and ever mysterious palace of the Tertullians. It has changed us forever. Someday it will change all of history, too."

"Bravo!"

"And now for the game," Andrew went on. "For pure fun, everybody—you too, Olivia—make a list, a list of the one piece we'd all like to have as a souvenir, and then the top ten. Just for amusement. Here's mine. The souvenir, a crossbow. On my list of ten I'd—"

"That's enough!" Olivia said. "You win. I agree. One souvenir and the ten . . . loans."

"What are you going to take? Come on, Olivia. A piece of the Aryx hoard—perhaps that gold ring?"

"Not at all," she said softly, her face breaking into a grin. Suddenly she had shed all the anxieties that had threatened to consume her in the past weeks. "For my souvenir I want the Aryx ring *and* the fur-handled throwing knife. And my first ten will include the Han scroll, a perfume bottle, Phryne's diaries, one of her portraits in ivory—"

"I insist on an Alexander tapestry for one of my ten," Andrew cut in.

The evening was one of the most memorable and pleasant I have experienced in years. And why not? I have won everything I wanted, and Olivia has come to her senses. I shuddered to think what I had been thinking, oh, it seemed so long ago. Nothing would have kept me from holding on to my prize.

I THINK we were all amazed when we realized it was nearly time for Andrew and Olivia to return to New York. But the months before they had to leave were like an enchanted summer as each of us returned again and again to our own favorite parts of the palace. I haunted the libraries, beginning a proper inventory of the thousands of scrolls and codices, sorting them into categories and priorities.

Using a half dozen computers for translating, I raced through the texts, making notes on what I had to read at once. To my annoyance I found that a third of the writings were worthless and boring. Tertullian had preserved every notation about his business dealings. There were acres of religious documents—sermons, descriptions of ritual. Still, I couldn't complain. There was also a lifetime of literature and history to savor.

Olivia, relieved by our decision about the palace, was quiet and nostalgic. She returned to the children's rooms day after day. I would hear her talking quietly to the Tertullian children as I passed in the hall.

Andrew wandered everywhere, always underfoot, talking constantly, getting ready for his return to the city and the museum, with its prima donnas and power wars. Andrew could have New York. Soon I would have Herculaneum and all its treasures to myself. I would be blissfully alone in my perfect world.

Then, as my anticipation became almost unbearable, my reveries were shattered. At dinner one evening, Olivia turned to Andrew and said, "I think it's time to tell Don Ciccio what's on our minds, darling."

"Don Ciccio, we've made a decision," Andrew said. "These last weeks have changed us. I, even more than Olivia. For the first time in years I feel free. I have no overbearing curators to please, no arrogant artists to flatter and baby. I remember now how I used to feel about art before I got drawn into all the museum games. I am content just looking at these pieces, letting them draw me in. It's been a long time since I could look at a piece of art without worrying that some other museum would get it before I could. Do you know how long it's been since I've enjoyed life? I want to stay here."

I gazed at him.

"We've decided to live here, in the world of Quintus Tertullian. We've decided to stay. We're going to resign from the Met. With the palace, we don't need any museum. We've a world of unending discoveries right here."

"Andrew, I, pardon my surprise," I stammered. "Olivia, my dear, the museum is your life. How can you give it up? And what about your nerves? Aren't you worried about an earthquake?"

"Even with my fears about a quake," Olivia said, "I feel less anxious here than in New York and, you see, there's something else. I want . . . a child, children. I'll bet you never thought you'd hear me say that but . . ."

"You're not . . ."

"No, not yet," she said, laughing.

"Can you believe it, Don Ciccio?" Andrew said. "Three or four little Fosters following you around these halls for the rest of your life?"

I struggled to recover. What a mistake I'd made, what a terrible misjudgment! "But are you sure?"

"We've made up our minds," Olivia said. "You know what happens when I make a firm decision."

I laughed. "I suppose this calls for a celebration," I said as I ordered the chef to begin a different, more festive dinner. I instructed Arturo to bring up wines that had been laid away for half a century, and we ended the evening on a note of celebration. That night was like meeting a new Andrew and Olivia. They positively glowed.

When they finally stumbled off to bed, I descended into my subterranean chambers. I bathed, washed away the effects of the libations, cleared my mind. Then, I proceeded to my computers and set them up for the most delicate calculations. But before I began to calculate, I chose from among the hundreds of chambers the perfect place for a surprise party.

It was the armory, of course, a section of the palace far removed from the libraries and the staircase leading to Tertullian's sanctuary.

I started to plan. Over and over. There could be no mistakes; there was no margin for error. Though I was exhausted, I forced myself to run the figures through the computers twice more, analyzing the physical and geographical characteristics of the area. The nitroglycerine charges had to be carefully placed.

At dawn, I left my underground laboratory with my plan.

Did I regret what I had to do? Did I experience remorse? Of course, but I steeled myself against my heart. Nonetheless, in the few hours I slept I dreamt. I heard Olivia's soft voice that first time I met her, the night she saved my life. "It's all right," I heard her say. "It's all right."

The explosion took place two days later—at 3:14 in the afternoon. The shock was over in seconds. Not a single reverberation appeared on my computer screen. The explosion was confined, just as I had planned. Excellent.

I agonized as I waited in my laboratory, the computers humming softly, their screens glowing pleasantly in the muted light of the great hall. I didn't wait long. A signal announced that Arturo had returned from the Palace and was waiting outside the laboratory.

He saluted me. His clothing was covered with a light coating of tufa dust. I raised my eyes, asking the question.

"Crushed, master. They are gone."

"Quickly?"

"Instantly."

I gazed at him, raising my chin. I was totally calm. "The rest of the palace?" I asked.

He brushed some dust from his jacket.

"Master, all of your palace remains intact."

I smiled. My perfect world.

THOMAS HOVING, former director of the Metropolitan Museum of Art in New York, is currently the
Editor-in-Chief of *Connoisseur* magazine. He is the
author of two novels, *Discovery* and *Masterpiece,* and
three works of of nonfiction, *Tutankhamun: The Untold Story; King of the Confessors* and *The Chase, the
Capture*. He lives in New York City.